Rafe leaned forward, ruthlessly ignoring the scent of her, the nearness of her, and his physical reaction to both.
"You think I am a madman?"

"Of—of course I do," Olivia whispered.

The catch in her voice, the little hesitation that revealed her fear, undid him. How dare she fear him, when he was the good guy? It didn't occur to him how ludicrous it was to be so indignant that his cover was working well enough to fool even this brilliant, beautiful scientist.

He advanced on her, deliberately brushing his lean body against hers. She retreated, step for step, until she was backed against the door. He pressed mercilessly into her and reveled in the trembling of her body. He was undeniably aroused.

"Maybe I *am* a madman," he muttered darkly, just as he caught her mouth with his.

Dear Reader,

This is officially "Get Caught Reading" month, so why not get caught reading one—or all!—of this month's Intimate Moments books? We've got six you won't be able to resist.

In *Whitelaw's Wedding,* Beverly Barton continues her popular miniseries THE PROTECTORS. Where does the Dundee Security Agency come up with such great guys—and where can I find one in real life? A YEAR OF LOVING DANGEROUSLY is almost over, but not before you read about *Cinderella's Secret Agent,* from Ingrid Weaver. Then come back next month, when Sharon Sala wraps things up in her signature compelling style.

Carla Cassidy offers a *Man on a Mission,* part of THE DELANEY HEIRS, her newest miniseries. Candace Irvin once again demonstrates her deft way with a military romance with *In Close Quarters,* while Claire King returns with a *Renegade with a Badge* who you won't be able to pass up. Finally, join Nina Bruhns for *Warrior's Bride,* a romance with a distinctly Native American feel.

And, of course, come back next month as the excitement continues in Intimate Moments, home of your favorite authors and the best in romantic reading.

Leslie J. Wainger
Executive Senior Editor

Please address questions and book requests to:
Silhouette Reader Service
U.S.: 3010 Walden Ave., P.O. Box 1325, Buffalo, NY 14269
Canadian: P.O. Box 609, Fort Erie, Ont. L2A 5X3

Renegade with a Badge
CLAIRE KING

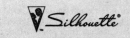

INTIMATE MOMENTS™

Published by Silhouette Books

America's Publisher of Contemporary Romance

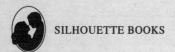 SILHOUETTE BOOKS

ISBN 0-373-27149-2

RENEGADE WITH A BADGE

Visit Silhouette at www.eHarlequin.com

Printed in U.S.A.

Books by Claire King

Silhouette Intimate Moments

Knight in a White Stetson #930
The Virgin Beauty #1038
Renegade with a Badge #1079

CLAIRE KING

lives with her husband, her son, a dozen goats and too many cows on her family's cattle ranch in Idaho. An award-winning agricultural columnist and seasoned cow-puncher, she lives for the spare minutes she can dedicate to reading and writing about people who fall helplessly in love, because, she says, "The romantic lives of my cattle just aren't as interesting as people might think."

To Terrell,
computing for me in my darkest hour.

Prologue

The little boy wore his hand-me-down shoes only on the days his mother made him go to school. Those, too, were the only days he spoke English, and then only to please his teachers. His family, his friends, everyone he'd ever known, in fact, spoke the quick, energetic Spanish of the *barrio*.

He was barefoot, then, when the police came, and had to run to the room he shared with his brothers for his shoes. When he saw the two officers—dressed as his older brother dressed when he came to the *barrio* on Friday nights to visit the family and see his *compadres*—he knew he needed his shoes. It was a special occasion.

His mother began to scream before he had time to tie the frayed laces, and the boy raced down the hall to her, his shoes flapping on his bare feet. She clutched at him, at the other brothers and sisters who'd also run to her at the sound of her wailing.

"He's dead," she shrieked in Spanish. "Our Jorge, my first-born son, my baby, is dead."

Rafael wrenched himself from her snatching fingers and stood staring at the *policia* who were standing near the door, looking solemn and nervous and sad.

"My brother?" he asked in English, though both men were Hispanic. English was the language of the uniform, if not of the men. "My brother George is dead?"

The men glanced at each other, looked down at Rafael.

"*Sí,* little brother. He was killed in the line of duty."

Rafael swallowed unmanly tears. "Was he brave?"

"He was very brave, little brother."

"Do you know who killed him?"

"*Sí.* We know."

"Then you must make him pay."

"We will make him pay, little brother. We will bring him back to the United States and take him to a judge."

Rafael nodded. George had told him many times how important it was to bring the bad men before the judge. It was the only honorable way to keep the peace in America. He peered up at the men, who stood very tall, very somber and straight, while his mother sobbed her grief behind him.

"If you do not," he said, making the first of many vows, "I will bring him to America and make him face the judge myself."

Chapter 1

Olivia Galpas hated parties.

She frowned into the dimly lit motel bathroom mirror and tucked a disobedient strand of dark hair back into the tidy, wide braid at her back. Her thick hair was objecting to the first freshwater washing it had had in three weeks. It was better accustomed to saltwater and dish soap.

The frown lines between her flashing eyes deepened further. *Stupid parties. Stupid hair.* She considered hacking off the offending piece with the scissors in her Swiss Army knife, but decided that would be shortsighted, and worked it more carefully into the braid. Where it stayed. For ten seconds. She finally routed a hairpin from her backpack and shoved it in, capturing the wayward strand.

It wasn't that she was unsociable, she thought, turning her attention to inspecting her teeth for remains of the tacos she'd just finished. She sucked a bit of cilantro from between her perfect front incisors and reached for her toothbrush.

No, she wasn't unsociable at all. She loved people, considered herself adept with them, despite a certain natural reserve she'd inherited from her proud Latino father. She'd just finished a three-week assignment in this little village in Baja California—or, more accurately, on the village's nearby beach—cheek by jowl most days with her team of three fellow oceanographers and one marine biologist on loan from Sea World who were studying the effects of current on winter whale migration. And she hadn't suffered at all from it. And marine biologists were *notoriously* difficult to get along with. Obsessive, whale-loving creatures.

But *parties.*

She spit toothpaste into the sink and rinsed her mouth. "Eeh," she said to the mirror.

Olivia studied the paltry array of cosmetics on the bathroom counter, delaying the inevitable. She'd happily come to Baja three weeks ago without so much as a lipstick. Who knew she'd become the object of the town bigwig's affection and be required to tart herself up for a going-away party?

But she had, inexplicably—and so had had to go shopping this afternoon, another chore of which she was insufficiently fond. And not just shopping for the makeup, but for the pretty Mexican peasant skirt and blouse she wore, and the impractical, adorable sandals that even now were beginning to make her feet ache.

Olivia sighed. Three weeks in a bathing suit, a pair of quick-dry shorts and rubber sandals spoiled a girl.

"Eeh," she said again, this time sticking out her tongue.

She'd been trotted out to a hundred parties since she'd joined the senior staff at Scripps Institute of Oceanography in San Diego two years earlier. As one of the few female oceanographers at the university—and the youngest— she'd endured more Cajun shrimp and mini-quiches and cocktail chatter than one person should have to in a lifetime. But this party was different.

The host was Ernesto Cervantes.

Very interesting person, this handsome Mexican man.

Rich beyond what seemed reasonable in the small Baja village, smartly dressed in a sharply pressed khaki uniform that marked him as the chief of the local law enforcement agency; courtly, attentive, well-spoken.

And decidedly captivated by Olivia Galpas.

The chief, everyone in Aldea Viejo called him. *Hefe.* The sheriff and the wealthiest man between the border and La Paz. Ernesto wore the title with all the importance it implied, used his family's money to do good in his poor community, and had enough free time left over to spend almost every day for three weeks at the beach camp set up by the institute, courting the lovely Dr. Galpas.

She was flattered—but Olivia, practical to a fault, suspected Ernesto would have fallen madly in love with any woman who'd met his criteria. He seemed rather more enamored with the courtship than he actually was with her.

He'd been at camp the first day she'd arrived, along with a phalanx of similarly uniformed men, to welcome them. As team leader, Olivia had accepted the formal welcome with all the equanimity of a woman well-accustomed to the stately and ceremonious rituals of the Mexican aristocracy.

He'd come to camp the next day, too. And the next. Each time on some pretext of duty. But the pretext fell away soon enough, and he began taking Olivia, alone, on walks along the beach. Well, not quite alone, Olivia recalled. Every step had been monitored, oddly enough, by at least one or two of his deputies. Nevertheless, Olivia got the gist.

Ernesto Cervantes was fast approaching fifty and had not yet found a wife. Olivia, with her education and genteel manners and impeccable Mexican heritage—Ernesto would kindly overlook that her family had been in San Diego for a hundred years—fit the bill exactly, it seemed.

Olivia had to admit she was more than a little interested in his oblique suggestions of a future together. She may have been preoccupied with her job, but she wasn't immune to perfect breeding and a handsome face. And given time and Ernesto's proper introduction to her family and an assurance that she could continue her work, she'd probably agree to marry. That little biological clock she'd been ignoring wouldn't tick forever.

But Olivia was a woman of science by education and of prudence by nature, and three weeks' worth of walks on the beach were not enough to convince her of anything.

So tonight, wearing makeup and a decent outfit and with her hair forced into place, dammit, she'd attend the going-away party Ernesto had planned and eat shrimp and make cocktail-party conversation. Tomorrow, she'd follow her colleagues back home.

And after that? Well, prudently, she'd just wait and see what happened.

She left the motel and walked through the quaint, quiet streets of Aldea Viejo. She knew where the *hacienda* was, of course. One could catch a glimpse of it from almost any vantage point in town.

The house was all that Ernesto had said it was, Olivia thought as she walked through the open iron front gates several minutes later and strolled across the manicured front lawn, which looked bizarrely green in its desert surroundings. It was grand, ancient and graceful, as every old Mexican mansion should be. Olivia was terribly impressed.

She smoothed her hair, grateful the wind hadn't whipped it from its pins on the short walk up the hill from the village, and pressed her lips together to make certain she'd remembered to put on that hastily purchased lipstick.

She was glad she'd bought the long skirt and matching blouse. It was made of inexpensive cotton, but it was of a traditional style that suited the house, and it was certainly better than her other ''best'' outfit—chinos and a camp shirt.

Olivia took a last, deep breath before she entered the wide-open doors of the front entrance to the *hacienda*. The double doors were made of solid oak, she noticed, and reinforced with beautiful flat iron scrollwork.

If she was going to have to attend a stupid party, this was certainly a nice place to do it. She doubted she'd find a single mini-quiche in this gorgeous house.

"Olivia," Ernesto said, as she entered the foyer. He disengaged himself from a small, attentive group of people to come to her. Candles glowed everywhere, giving off the scent of Mexican jasmine and the aura of old-world elegance. Ernesto was dressed impeccably and he, too, smelled slightly of jasmine. Olivia had to struggle not to fuss with her dress.

"Ernesto," Olivia said, and let him kiss her on the mouth. He had to bend slightly to do so; his elegant, lean frame towered by several inches over her smaller one. "Your home is more beautiful than you described it."

He smiled graciously. "It seems, Olivia, that my father built it just so that beautiful women would be impressed by it." His deep brown eyes glowed with sincerity and the reflection of a hundred candles. Olivia flushed at the compliment.

"I'm sure they are, then," she said.

"Your team?" He made a show of looking around. "They have not come with you?"

The invitation had been for all of Olivia's team, but their work had been finished the day before, and as none of them were being courted by the local *hefe* they'd decided to pack up camp and leave this morning.

"No, and you should be grateful. They'd have eaten you out of house and home," Olivia said.

Ernesto smiled indulgently. "That, as you can see, would be difficult to do." He led her into the main salon, where people appeared to be waiting for her arrival. "I have some people here I would like to introduce you to."

Every eye turned to her as Ernesto introduced her to the room at large. He made careful mention of her position at Scripps in the introduction, Olivia observed.

"I'm only an assistant department head, Ernesto," she whispered to him after the introduction was complete and she had been greeted like a queen. "There are four of those in my department alone. You made it sound as though I was running the whole place."

He handed her a flute of champagne. "I am proud of you," he said gently. "That is not such a bad thing, is it?"

"No," Olivia admitted, taking a sip of champagne. "Oh! Dom Pérignon."

Ernesto laughed. "I knew you were a woman of breeding, Olivia. But a wine connoisseur, as well? You will be a blessing at my table." He kissed the hand he'd been holding. "Most of my friends, though I love them like family, don't know a Dom Pérignon from a cheap Chablis."

"Oh," she said into her glass. "Well, thank you for inviting me."

"No, Olivia," Ernesto said, gazing meaningfully into her eyes. "Thank you for being here. It means so much to me."

Olivia smiled and took another quick sip of champagne.

She had no idea what the intent, mysterious gleam in his eye was all about, but she would have bet that it didn't have anything to do with identifying wine.

"I'd like you to meet some of my friends," Ernesto said, taking her arm.

"*Some* of your friends?" Olivia said, looking around the crowded room.

Ernesto laughed again, and Olivia couldn't help but smile. Oh, the man was in his element.

Olivia allowed him to guide her through the crowd. They made it just one or two steps forward at a time, as everyone wanted some attention from the *hefe*. Ernesto skillfully worked the crowd, while Olivia smiled and spoke easily with his guests, slipping automatically into Spanish, the language of her childhood home. But she had the oddest itch at the back of her neck, and it wasn't until nearly an hour after she arrived that she figured out why. Everywhere she looked, there were uniformed men standing guard. Armed with unsmiling, intimidating faces and big, scary guns.

"Uh, Ernesto?"

Ernesto turned at once at the small tug on his sleeve. He covered Olivia's rough, sea-weathered hand with his own smooth, manicured one and smiled deferentially down at her. *Oh, yes,* Olivia thought, distracted for a moment. This man could run Mexico from this *hacienda.* He had all the charm and old-world refinement of a *Don.*

"Yes, Olivia?"

She blinked up at him. "Pardon?"

Ernesto brought her hand to his lips. Olivia wanted to snatch it back; it looked like a sea hag's gnarled fist against his full, beautiful mouth.

"You are tired of all this inane conversation, my dear?"

"What? No, of course not," she protested, though, in truth, she would have given her right arm for a cold Mexican beer, her laptop and her narrow cot in her beach camp tent right about now. "I was just wondering about all the men here."

Ernesto lifted one graceful brow. "The men here?" he said.

Olivia felt a little chill slide right past the itch at the back of her neck, but decided she must have imagined the slight menace in Ernesto's perfectly modulated tone.

"I mean the men you have in uniform. Your deputies. Why are they here, at a party?"

"Ah, that. To protect my guests, of course," he said, relaxing visibly. He swept his arm in an unmistakably urbane gesture. He smiled again, that charming flash of teeth. "They are unobtrusive, though, are they not? I believe it's your American sensibilities that made you notice them at all."

"Why do your guests need protection?"

Ernesto sighed, then turned away for a moment to greet yet another supplicant. Olivia did a quick count of Ernesto's not-so-unobtrusive pack of gun-toters. Fifteen!

"I'm sorry, Olivia," Ernesto said when he returned his attention to her. "You were saying?"

"Why do you have so many men posted here at the *hacienda?* Have you had trouble? Are you expecting trouble?"

Ernesto's lips compressed ever so briefly, then he took Olivia's arm again and led her to a relatively quiet corner. "Olivia," he began patiently. "I am the sheriff of Aldea Viejo, as well as a very wealthy man."

"Yes, I know, Ernesto."

"And as such, I face many dangers, every day. We have criminals here in this small village, just as you have in your large American cities."

"But at a party?"

Ernesto shrugged, his broad shoulders enhanced by the fine cut of his suit.

"Have you been robbed here at the *hacienda?*"

Ernesto's eyes darkened. "Certainly not."

"Are your guests in the habit of walking off with the family silver?"

"Olivia," Ernesto admonished, offended.

Olivia smiled, but rubbed at the back of her neck all the same. "I'm teasing, Ernesto."

He watched her carefully for a moment, then leaned to kiss her lightly on her mouth. "I should hope so. Do not concern yourself with these questions, Olivia. I have my men here to protect my guests." He smiled gently. "Most especially my guest of honor. It is my duty to protect you, Olivia. And it is my pleasure."

"I don't need protection, Ernesto," Olivia said meaningfully. *Best to begin as you mean to go on,* she thought. "I have been taking excellent care of myself for several years now."

Ernesto wrapped her hand around his forearm, scanning

the crowd of guests absently. "Another thing I admire about you, Olivia." He brought her hand to his mouth again and kissed it. "But in all your travels, I cannot imagine you have come across the kind of men I am dealing with now."

"The smugglers?" He'd mentioned it before, on one of their walks. Drug shipments had been coming through Aldea Viejo, out of range of the Mexican Federal Police, the *federales,* in La Paz. Ernesto was determined to bring the smugglers to justice, but they'd been as slippery as reef eels so far.

"They are very dangerous, these men," Ernesto said.

"But not stupid. I doubt very much they'd crash this party."

Ernesto's eyes narrowed fractionally. "One never knows what the criminal mind will think of doing." Ernesto smiled, nabbed another glass of champagne from a passing tray and toasted Olivia cordially before taking a sip. "Does one?"

Rafael Camayo crept through the house, using the clamor of the party on the floor below to cover what little noise he made. Though his mother would be shocked to know it, this was hardly the first time he'd broken into someone's home and searched through every room like a bandit.

It was, however, the first time it had ever been so important to him.

Rafe skirted a lighted doorway. A fussy little powder room, he noted with disdain, wondering how many of the ladies and gentlemen using the elaborate, gold-plated facilities knew how Cervantes had paid for them.

He smiled grimly. Probably more than a few. Rafe knew from years of tracking Cervantes that many of the man's friends were actually more like associates; partners in crime, so to speak. Not that Rafe's employers—the United States Drug Enforcement Agency—or their associates in the Mexican government had ever been able to get the goods on any of them. Lesser men fell, swept up in routine drug raids, while Cervantes and his swanky pals held lavish dinner parties and toasted each other's cleverness.

He and his partner, Bobby, had been in Baja California for months now, trying to change all that. They'd been methodically stealing drug shipments from Cervantes's men and slipping them surreptitiously into the hands of DEA agents across the border in Mexico. They made no arrests, busted neither the men at the drop site nor the runners who brought the stuff over from mainland Mexico. They simply swept in—or snuck in, depending upon the situation and the likelihood one of them would be shot through the head—and stole what Ernesto Cervantes firmly believed was his.

It was a last-ditch effort, a plan devised by Rafe and Bobby alone, and one that neither the *federales* nor Rafe's superior officers at the DEA thought likely to succeed. But Rafe and Bobby were determined.

They knew Cervantes—knew him inside and out— though neither of them had ever been within fifty feet of the man. They knew he could outwait the authorities and their traditional methods forever, keeping his minions on the front line while he led his respectable, lawful life.

But he would never tolerate being ripped off by a couple of filthy, low-class *bandidos*.

It was driving the big man crazy, Rafe thought with an unprofessional smirk, just as they'd hoped it would. Cervantes was a canny kingpin, but a kingpin nonetheless, and with the ego to go along with the title. It wouldn't be long—*couldn't* be long, according to Rafe's superiors back in San Diego—before he showed up at one of the shipment sites himself. Rafe could almost smell Cervantes's frustration, could almost touch it.

It was certainly evident by all the thugs he had posted at this little soiree.

Rafe had easily slipped past them all, of course. Another

thing that would have shocked his mother. Ten years as an undercover DEA agent was excellent training, but it was nothing to the years in the San Diego *barrio* of his youth. A boy who spoke no English learned how to fade into any background in the border towns of San Diego, or he risked being picked up by cruising immigration officers looking for his illegally "immigrated" parents.

Rafe searched the next room he came to, wincing slightly as the heavy carved door creaked atmospherically on its iron hinges. The four men the Mexican *federales* had inside Cervantes's organization had already been through every scrap of paper in Cervantes's office, but had yet to find anything incriminating. The party tonight had given Rafe the first opportunity since he'd come to Baja to get inside the rest of the house and do a little snooping of his own.

Nothing in this room; not that he'd expected much. Cervantes was unlikely to keep records of his illegal activities in an upstairs guest room. Still, procedure dictated a thorough search. He closed the door behind him and stood absolutely still in the gloomy hallway, listening, waiting.

Rafe cocked his head at a small sound, separate from the cacophony coming from downstairs.

Well, hell. Someone was coming up the second stairway.

He looked quickly around and decided the best he could do on such short notice was try to melt into the wide, darkened doorway behind him. If he tried to get back into the room he'd just left, the damn door would give him away. He cursed old houses and all their charm. Give him a nice, quiet apartment with brand-new vinyl doors any day.

He stood perfectly still and let the person walk past him. *A woman.* Before he could make out her face or shape, he could hear the seductive swish of a skirt, smell the faint scent of perfume. She had a beautiful scent, this woman. She smelled like the sea.

Lord, it had been a long time since he'd been so close to a woman.

Against his better judgment, Rafe lifted his eyes. He knew that people seemed to sense when they were being watched, and the last thing he needed right now was for one of Cervantes's snotty dinner guests to start screaming about bandits in the upstairs hallways.

But he couldn't resist. He was partially aroused from the scent of her alone. *Oh, yeah,* he thought ruefully, shifting his weight slightly. Way too many months on the job.

The woman passed by him on her way to the bathroom.

Rafe nearly snarled out loud as he recognized her.

The princess. Cervantes's princess. The woman, he knew from his informants on the inside, that Cervantes planned to marry. Dr. Olivia Galpas. He'd made it a point to find out her name the day Cervantes first visited her on the beach. He'd had her investigated, of course. Anyone Cervantes spent that much time with, American or not, female or male, had to be checked out.

She'd been clean, as far as the DEA was concerned, but that didn't make her any more likable in Rafe's mind.

She was a *princesa,* from one of the oldest and finest Latino families in San Diego. Her mother was some famous artist, her father was a physician. She was a doctor herself, born with a silver spoon in her mouth, and handed every opportunity. While he'd been picking avocados to get through junior college, the *princesa* had been whiling away her time at Stanford and then MIT.

Apparently, all the expensive education hadn't made her any smarter, Rafe thought sourly as he watched her flick on the light in the small room and close the door behind her. She was keeping very dangerous company, and seemed to be enjoying herself doing it. Rafe's eyes narrowed in the darkness. Money and power were vigorous aphrodisiacs to a woman who was accustomed to having both in her life.

Like was always attracted to like.

Olivia Galpas was here in Cervantes's house, upstairs even, where guests did not usually go. So, there was more to this relationship than he'd thought, was there? He'd have to keep that in mind. Maybe the pretty little doctor knew exactly what kind of dirty drug money paid for the gold-plated fixtures in the bathroom she was using.

Rafe shook his head slightly. *Settle down, there, Rafael.* A rather intense reaction to one glimpse of a woman in a hallway, he had to admit. And jumping to conclusions was not his style, either. He was a very deliberate sort of cop.

But Olivia Galpas was everything in a woman Rafael Camayo naturally resented, everything he instinctively despised. He liked women with heart, with passion, with guts. He didn't like pampered, overeducated, rich girls who slept with any drug runner with a woman's soft hands and a big house. Especially one they'd known just three weeks.

Only, God, she smelled good. It was indefinable, that scent of the beach and woman she left in her wake. He'd never smelled anything like it. Not perfume, but…essence. If he could have dragged enough of it into his lungs, he thought, he could live on it alone for a week. No food, no water—just that smell.

He knew he needed to move on through the house, use every opportunity the party was giving him to find what he could and then get the hell out. But something about the woman behind that powder room door—aside from her scent, he told himself firmly—kept him rooted to the spot. Maybe she'd come back out and he'd give her a little talking-to, American to American. Let her in on the secrets behind Ernesto Cervantes's "family" wealth. Haul her gorgeous little rear end right out of this house and get her on the next plane Stateside. As any good American law enforcement agent would do.

Only, he couldn't. And wouldn't.

Ernesto Cervantes had killed his brother almost twenty years ago. He and Bobby—who in addition to being his partner was his *carnal,* his blood brother from childhood, his cousin, and the godson of Rafe's dead brother—had spent those twenty years plotting, planning the kind of revenge that would have made George proud. They'd joined the local police force, then the DEA; had worked their way up the ladder in all the ways that mattered—for this one bust. He wasn't about to give up those years, those plans, for one amazing-smelling woman, American or not.

Besides, he mused, she may not even want to be saved. His informants had told him how cozy the couple had become. How long the walks, how intense the talks, how delicate and intimate and revolting the whole relationship had become. Maybe Olivia Galpas was in exactly the hot spot she wanted to be in. Maybe she knew everything.

Olivia stepped out into the darkened hallway, flicking off the light behind her. She'd used the facilities, washed her hands, put lotion on, checked her hair, washed her hands again, straightened all the lovely linen guest towels then sat on the edge of the vanity for five minutes, considering the merits of a hot wax treatment to smooth out her sea-coarsened hands. No woman should have rougher hands than her boyfriend, she thought.

But there was no getting around the fact that she had to go back downstairs. Eventually. Even now, Ernesto was probably wondering if she'd eaten some bad shrimp.

She smiled slightly to herself, rolled her eyes. She couldn't imagine Ernesto Cervantes ever wondering about her digestive health. He was so polished and dignified, she didn't think he'd be able to bring himself to admit women *had* digestive systems, much less to talk about them.

She started down the hall, grateful that for the first time since she'd entered the house she wasn't being stared at by some glowering, khaki-covered baboon. This hallway was obviously in a private portion of the house, where guests were not expected to wander. Well, she'd wandered, and she could hardly see the harm in it. She personally thought Ernesto was carrying the whole protection thing to the limits of high drama. What kind of criminal would break into a man's house while two hundred people were drinking and dancing downstairs?

She stopped before she reached the stairs. That itch on the back of her neck was really driving her crazy. If she didn't know herself any better, she'd think she was having some sort of woman's intuition. But that was ridiculous. She didn't have woman's intuition. She was a scientist.

She turned very slowly and looked right into the face of the man watching her.

Olivia felt as though every ounce of blood drained from her head and leaked out her toes. She had never been so unnerved in all her life. The itch at the back of her neck slithered around her throat and clutched at her jugular. Adrenaline pumped through her like a drug. She didn't know this man, didn't know why he watched her with such intensity, such malice, but she knew she should be afraid of him. And by God, she was.

They stared at each other for what seemed to Olivia like hours, though, of course, it couldn't have been more than a few seconds. He was partially shadowed, but Olivia glimpsed a rough, unshaved Latino face, all planes and angles, with cheekbones that looked sharp enough to cut glass. He had a starved look to him, as though he'd never quite had enough to eat. She sucked in a reflexive breath, unaware she'd stopped breathing.

Rafe's heart thundered in his chest at the sound of that deep breath. He was ready to bolt if she screamed. He'd be no good to this operation—or to George's memory— with a bullet through his heart.

But she didn't scream. She just watched him, calm except for the breathlessness. He respected that even as it occurred to him that perhaps she didn't scream because she was a *princesa* and thought herself impervious to strange men in dark hallways. He ought to disabuse her of that notion, Rafe thought. He worked up a sneer but could manage nothing more menacing than that. Olivia Galpas was the most beautiful woman he'd ever seen. And frankly, he'd never had much stomach for threatening women, pretty or not.

She was small, no more than five foot four. Rafe was taller than most of the men in his family by several inches, and this woman's head would hit below his chin. Her hair was plaited down her straight spine in a heavy braid that reached the curve of her bottom. He wondered about the texture of all that braided hair, wondered what it would feel like if he ran his thumb down the length of it.

Her breasts were discreetly camouflaged by the peasant blouse she wore, but they looked small enough for each to fit whole into his mouth. Rafe swallowed hard at that ridiculous idea. This was Cervantes's woman. He no more wanted to touch her than he wanted to put his hand in a basket of rattlesnakes.

Her face was flushed from fear or the sun—he could see the color high on her classic cheekbones even in the dim light of the hallway. She had a small, full mouth that she'd set into a brave and stubborn line he had to admire.

And her eyes. *Her eyes.*

They were dark, those eyes, with whites like snow and thick lashes Rafe thought she probably used to hide the truth. Her pupils dilated, until he imagined every spark of light in the hallway had been swallowed up by them.

Her eyes flashed at him, and Rafe found his knees weak. An absurd reaction for a man such as Rafael Camayo, he thought. But what could he do? Like a green boy, he was weak-kneed after one look from Ernesto Cervantes's American lover.

Olivia was experiencing the very same sensation in her knees, but for an entirely different reason.

"Who are you?" she said. She'd meant to sound authoritative, barking out a question to be answered at once. But her voice sounded much more like a mewl than a bark, and she could have kicked herself for it. Of course, the man didn't answer such a pathetic little question. Olivia cleared her throat and tried again. "*Señor* Cervantes has men all over this house, whoever you are,'' she said, sounding stronger. "If you're not a guest here, I suggest you leave.''

Oh, did she? Rafe almost smiled. "I don't take orders from you, *princesa*,'' he said, speaking in Spanish, as she had.

"Who are you?'' she snapped. Though, of course, she already knew. The drug smuggler, or at least one of them. A man this frightening could only be a pirate, a smuggler, a thief.

She took a step forward, in exactly the opposite direction her prudent, cautious brain was telling her to go. Typical. First her hair and now her feet. Her body was being very disobedient tonight, and if she got out of this little confrontation alive, she intended to have a stern chat with all her various parts.

"Answer me,'' she said.

Answer me? Rafe's mouth moved back into a sneer. Good grief. Every word out of her mouth was a command. She certainly spoke like a *princesa.*

The man clearly was not going to answer, even though she'd finally worked up a decent bark. Olivia pulled her lips through her teeth, swallowed the lump of fear in her throat, clamped down on the trembling that was beginning to make her hands shake and her mouth quiver. Demanding answers wasn't going to work, and she clearly was incapable of doing anything as judicious as hiking up her skirt and fleeing down the stairs, screaming bloody murder. Still, this man was invading Ernesto's beautiful home. What kind of friend would she be if she did nothing about that?

"If you don't leave right now,'' she said calmly, firmly, "I will alert the guards.''

Rafe smiled, a flash of white teeth in the shadows. "You won't alert the guards,'' he said.

Olivia blinked, unnerved by that fierce, confident smile.

Weren't smugglers supposed to be furtive? This one was cool as a cucumber. "I won't?"

"No."

"Why won't I?"

"Because you're a woman, Dr. Galpas, and women are more practical than men."

He knew who she was. Olivia felt the impact of her name on his smirking lips shiver all the way down to the backs of her thighs, raising the fine hairs there.

"How do you know me?" she whispered.

Rafe shrugged. "It's a small village. You're a beautiful woman. And a smart one," he reminded her pointedly.

Obviously not, Olivia thought wildly. Smart women did not converse with *bandidos* in dark upstairs hallways while their almost-fiancés waited downstairs with fifteen armed men. Smart women screamed in situations like these, or at least fainted so they wouldn't be held responsible afterward. Olivia considered both options.

Rafe watched her carefully, saw her eyes dart toward the stairs, measuring for the first time the distance between herself and safety. About time, he thought. Stupid woman, to be standing here talking to him.

"Too late, *señorita*," he whispered, stepping from the deep doorway and taking her arm.

He moved so quickly that Olivia had no time to choose between screaming or fainting. One instant he was a shadowy figure several safe feet away, the next his hand was wrapped hard over her biceps and she was deftly turned and pressed back against his body. Her breath left her again.

Rafe slid his free hand to her throat. Stomach for it or not, he had to keep this woman from exposing him, at least until he got out of the house. After that, let her scream until she turned purple. It would only serve to further pique Cervantes's pride and temper, having had the bandit who had been stealing from him invade his very own *hacienda*.

The operation was what mattered, and damn his weak knees. And whatever else was reacting to Olivia Galpas.

"Stop struggling," he hissed in her ear, "and listen." He ran his thumb along the base of her throat and let it rest in the hollow there, for his own pleasure. He felt the woman shudder in his arms and wondered briefly what it would be like to make her shudder from something other than fear. He shifted again, hoping she didn't feel his arousal at her backside. "You can scream, you can run, you can alert every man in the building, and I will not leave this house tonight alive. That's true."

Olivia felt him shift behind her once more, prayed he'd moved far enough away that she wouldn't have to feel his lower body against her again. She'd been shocked by his obvious excitement, terrified that he intended more harm to her than she'd assumed.

But he was clearly trying to spare...one of them, anyway, from whatever that arousal implied.

"But I won't die alone," he continued softly at her ear. "Do you really want to take the chance with the lives of your lover and his friends?"

Olivia thought to correct him on that count; Ernesto was not her lover. But then, she thought as his hand reached up to clamp gently around her throat, she had more important things than semantics to worry about right now.

"Do you?" he repeated harshly.

"No," Olivia whispered.

"I thought not. I will leave when I'm finished, and no one will be hurt. Unless you make a mistake, *señorita*. The fate of these people are now in your hands. I urge you to make the right decision. Do you understand?"

Olivia caught a whiff of something as he breathed on her. Peppermint? Had this desperado brushed his teeth before breaking into the local sheriff's house and crashing her going-away party? What the hell kind of bandit was this?

"When you're finished?" she blurted with uncharacteristic indiscretion. "Finished with what? Are you robbing Ernesto? Are you the smuggler?"

Nosy, reckless woman. Rafe shook her slightly. "Do you understand?" he repeated, sounding dangerously provoked.

"Well, can you tell me how long you'll be?"

Rafe nearly burst out laughing. "Doctor."

Olivia nodded briskly. "Yes, yes, I understand."

"And Doctor?"

"Yes."

"I will kill him first. I want you to remember that."

Olivia nodded again, swallowed hard. "Yes, I will," she said in a strangled voice.

Rafael let her go, almost reluctantly. His head was buzzing from the contact of her body against his, his blood was running hot through his lower body, his fingers itched to touch the smooth skin of her neck a second time.

"One thing more," he said through gritted teeth, suddenly as furious with himself as he was with her. For lingering, for getting caught, for finding Cervantes's lover more arousing, more attractive, than any woman he'd met in years. For caring what happened to her.

Olivia's chest was heaving, her body beginning to shake in reaction. She'd been in grave danger there for the briefest moment, but she was unsure exactly what the threat had been.

"What?" she breathed, her eyes locked on his.

"Get out of here as soon as you can. Get back to the States on the next plane or bus or vegetable wagon." He reached out, gave a gentle tug on the long braid that had come to rest on her shoulder, running his thumb along the broad length of it. "I don't know how much you know," he said, almost to himself, "and I don't care. Just get out."

And while Olivia stood, trembling, wondering, the man disappeared without a sound down the dark hallway.

Chapter 2

Olivia endured. That was the most she could say about the remainder of Ernesto's lavish party, his expansive hospitality, his determined and public attentions.

It had been a terrible mistake coming back downstairs. She should have taken the advice of the smuggler and fled the house, Aldea Viejo, the country. Let Ernesto think his shrimp had actually killed her. *Oh, God.* She clamped a hand over her mouth to keep from bursting into hysterical laughter.

She'd still been shaking when she'd stumbled down the stairs, even after spending another five minutes back in the powder room, splashing water on her face and muttering recriminations to herself in the mirror. But she knew what she had to do if she wanted to keep Ernesto and his friends from being splattered across the beautiful old plaster walls of the *hacienda,* so she pasted a smile on her face like a prudent little scientist would when faced with empirical data.

The lanky man with the smirk on his mouth and the

hunger in his eyes was very probably taking a bead on Ernesto right this minute, waiting for Olivia to come to her senses and fall into a crying, squalling heap on the floor. Something she very much felt like doing, as a matter of fact.

It was midnight now, and Ernesto was calling for a toast. Thank heavens. After that was finished, she'd go straight back to the motel, wait sleepless until morning, when she would take a taxi—or a bus or a vegetable wagon—to La Paz, and then the first plane home.

A flute of champagne was pressed into one hand, while Ernesto pulled her gently to his side by taking the other. Olivia went willingly. No point fighting the inevitable. She would smile at the sure-to-be elaborate toast—then get the hell out of Dodge. She'd had enough Mexican hospitality to last her a lifetime.

Ernesto launched into his toast with full vigor. She listened with half attention and smiled politely at the beaming crowd. Where was the criminal, while these people quaffed expensive champagne? Slitting throats? Stealing silver? Pressing up against some other unsuspecting female with that steely body and that shocking arousal? She took a gulp of champagne and choked on it.

"And if she will do me the very great—" Ernesto paused for effect here, and Olivia smiled gamely up at him, her face beet red from suppressed coughing, trying desperately hard not to spew Dom Pérignon onto his silk suit, "*very* great honor of becoming my wife, and the mistress of this house and the mother of this humble village, I will be the happiest man on God's earth."

The crowd erupted. Olivia let go with a spasm of coughing that had Ernesto patting her on the back. When she was finished gagging on her hundred-dollar champagne, she looked blankly around at the people crushing in on her, then, stupefied, up at Ernesto.

"What?" she whispered.

Ernesto bent his head to kiss her. "Say yes, my darling," he said rather fervidly into her ear.

"To what?" she asked, spilling champagne on her clothes as someone jostled her from behind. She barely noticed. She had no idea what he was talking about. Had he just proposed? To whom? To *her?* In front of hundreds of people? With a sexually excited smuggler loose in his house?

Impossible.

Ernesto's smile went a little stiff. "You are shocked." He laughed heartily, though it sounded forced to Olivia's ears. "I am shocked myself. I have been a bachelor for almost fifty years."

"Ernesto, you can't possibly—"

He cut her off sharply. "But I had never met a woman who could share my house and my life before now, Olivia Magdalena Rosanna deRuiz Galpas."

Olivia almost groaned aloud. Not the whole name. He must be pretty damn serious if he was using her full name.

"You are a prize," Ernesto continued in his beautiful voice. "A woman of education and family. The great-granddaughter of Don Ricardo Galpas of Chiapas," he said loudly, though Olivia was sure he'd already mentioned that at least three times during the toast. "You will be the perfect wife for Ernesto Cervantes."

At this show of bravado, the crowd erupted into cheers again. Olivia looked around, nearly bursting once more into hysterical laughter. The entire evening had been thoroughly surreal.

"Ernesto, we have to talk."

He kissed her lavishly, his tongue breaching for the first time the seam of her lips. The man had just proposed marriage, Olivia thought, dazed, and he'd never even kissed her properly. She'd had a bandit pressed against her more intimately just an hour ago than this man had ever been. She'd never so much as tasted Ernesto Cervantes, who now fully intended to become her husband.

Olivia touched Ernesto's shoulder to break the kiss.

He smiled down into her face, glowing with triumph.
"I must attend to my guests, now, love."

"We need to talk, Ernesto," Olivia insisted. She needed
far more time than three weeks to decide on a husband for
the rest of her life, no matter how perfect the man appeared
to be. And there remained the small matter of how she was
going to explain to him that she'd had a friendly little
conversation in his upstairs hallway with a drug smuggler
but had neglected to tell him.

"We will." He kissed the hand he'd been clutching.
"We will."

But they didn't. Olivia wandered around in a daze for
half an hour more, caught up in a bizarre frenzy of con-
gratulation and speculation, while Ernesto seemed to carefully avoid her.

Fine, she thought. Their discussion of this bizarre public
proposal would be better conducted when they were alone,
anyway. Two hundred complete strangers and one smuggler whom she practically knew in the biblical sense were
not conducive to a quiet chat about the future.

She looked at her watch. Almost one. Surely the smuggler or thief or whatever he was would be gone by now.
Surely. Unless he'd been caught and was even now being
beaten to a pulp by an enthusiastic deputy. Olivia shud-
dered slightly. The man had terrified her, but she didn't
want anyone beaten. Jailed would be fine. Where he could
face punishment for his crimes and still get three meals a
day to fill out those hollows under his cheekbones.

She slipped back upstairs while the *mariachis* played
and the wine and tequila flowed. No one, she knew, would
miss her. Ernesto was very busy being the host, the bride-
groom-to-be, and the rest of the guests were having far too
good a time to notice that the bride-to-be had absconded.
She'd wait upstairs until the melee died down, and then
have that little talk with Ernesto. Might as well, she
thought. There was no way she'd sleep a wink tonight. No

boring party she'd been to in the past two years had offered both an intimate moment with a criminal and a marriage proposal.

Just as she reached the second floor, she heard a heavy tread on the stairs behind her. She froze for a moment, panicked, expectant. Then it occurred to her that the bandit she'd met had not moved with such plodding thumps of feet and weight. Olivia doubted he made any sound at all, unless he wanted to.

A guest, then. *Eeh.* She looked around for a hiding place. She did not want to be caught in this dim hallway with one of Ernesto's rowdy revelers. There was far too much clear thinking to be done to waltz through the niceties with a stranger. She opened the closest door and slipped inside.

The room was dark. Even the moon was shut out by gloomy, thick draperies. Olivia leaned against the door for a moment to catch her breath, then peeked carefully out into the hallway again. Wonderful. There was not one man, but three, all waiting for the bathroom. She closed the door again quietly.

"That was a very touching proposal."

Olivia spun around. She could see nothing, not even shadows, but she knew the voice. Would recognize it until the day she died, she realized.

"Ay, Dios," she whispered.

Rafe did not turn on any lights. He knew he couldn't be seen from outside—he'd closed the drapes himself—but he'd neglected to eye the distance between the bottom of the door and the threshold and didn't want to take any chances. He was sure he couldn't stand to look into her eyes, anyway.

"Have you come up to his bedroom, then, as a small treat before the wedding?"

"You said you were leaving!" she whispered furiously.

"I said, when I was finished."

"My God, how long does it take?"

"How long does *what* take?" Rafe asked, almost as amused with her as he was infuriated. Engaged, was she? To that murdering scum?

"I don't know! Whatever you were doing. Stealing. Smuggling."

"Smuggling?" Now she'd surprised him. What the hell *did* this woman know?

Olivia could have kicked herself. "Or killing people, whatever you do. Where are you?" she whispered hoarsely. "I can't see you."

"It's better, I think, if you meet him in the dark, *princesa.*"

He heard her small gasp, relished it. It made him mad, knowing she had come up here to meet Cervantes, after that nauseating public proposal. Unreasonable that Rafe should suffer over something that did not concern him in the least. But he did. And he wanted her to suffer a little, as well.

Olivia felt the whirling in her head subside to a manageable spin, felt her stomach settle from the shock of his voice. She'd been certain he'd be gone from the *hacienda* by now. It had been hours. "Why are you still here? If Ernesto catches you in his house—"

"Don't worry, I'm leaving. You came up the stairs just as I was about to go down them."

"Down them? Are you insane? Anyone could have seen you."

"It's past midnight, Doctor. By my estimation, most of the people downstairs were too drunk an hour ago to notice if an elephant walked through the room."

"You promised me. You said no one would be hurt. Ernesto—"

His hand shot out from the darkness, startling her. She'd never even heard him move. His strong fingers clamped around her wrist.

"Stop calling him that," he said. "Do not call him Ernesto, as though you know him. You know nothing about him.''

''No. You're right. It doesn't matter.'' She was frantic. If anyone caught them together, all hell would break loose. She knew this man would do what he'd threatened, and innocent people would be hurt. Maybe even Ernesto. Most likely Ernesto.

Olivia squared her shoulders. ''Okay, now you listen to me. You have to go before he finds you here.''

''And you will stay,'' he said flatly, coldly.

''What? Yes.'' Olivia shook her head to try to clear it. ''What is the matter with you?''

''Why didn't you leave today with your people?'' She was so close. So close. He bowed his head a fraction of an inch, breathed in the smell of her hair. He loved the faint scent of the sea on her, as though she never really left the water, as though it ran through her veins. ''Why did you come here tonight for this farce of a proposal?''

''My people? How do you know about my people? And what do you mean, this farce of a—? Are you nuts?'' she whispered fiercely, coming up on her toes to hiss at him. ''Mentally deficient in some manner? You're a *drug runner*. He's the sheriff of Aldea Viejo. And you have the nerve to call my perfectly good marriage proposal a farce?''

''I told you, *princesa*, that he's not what he seems, and you'd be better off back in your little office at Scripps than down here, playing with men you know nothing about.''

Olivia's eyes widened. ''How do you know where I work?''

''I know everything about you. Including your obvious proclivity for madmen.''

Olivia blinked into the blackness. She could feel his breath hot on her face, and looked up. Her eyes had become just enough accustomed to the stygian darkness that she was able to see the sharp outline of his uncompromising jawline, the white around his shadowy pupils. "*He* is not the madman," she said.

Rafe leaned forward again, ruthlessly ignoring the scent of her, the nearness. His physical reaction to both. "You think I am?"

No. She instinctively knew that whatever else dishonorable and desperate this man was, he was not mad. Not in any sense of the word. "Of course I do," she whispered.

The catch in her voice undid him. How dare she fear him, when it was Cervantes, with his elegant manners and his elegant mansion, who lived so well off the suffering of drug-hungry Americans? Rafe was the good guy. It didn't occur to him how ludicrous it was to be so indignant that his cover was working well enough to fool even this brilliant, beautiful scientist.

He advanced on her, deliberately brushing his lean body against hers. She retreated step for step, until she was backed against the door. He pressed mercilessly into her and reveled in the small trembling her body made against him. He was undeniably aroused. "Maybe I am a madman," he muttered darkly.

He caught her mouth with his, was elated when it parted for him, even though he knew her lips had fallen open in shock and not arousal. He swept his tongue seductively inside. It didn't matter. Didn't matter.

Olivia thought her head had been spinning before. Good heavens. She was being kissed—and quite skillfully—by a criminal! She knew what a prudent woman would do in this kind of absurd situation. A prudent woman would ignore whatever excitement insane danger evidently stirred in her blood, knowing it for the temporary, stress-induced mania it was. A prudent woman would not give in to weak knees and shocking, reckless, sudden arousal. A prudent woman would fight.

Olivia opened her teeth as wide as she could and clamped down.

Rafe lifted his mouth the instant before her teeth

snapped painfully together. He rubbed his thumb across her mouth once, twice, watching the movement with his eyes.

"Don't bite me," he admonished gently, and kissed her again.

Olivia was stunned, not just by the soft admonition, but by the tenderness of the kiss. Did criminals kiss like this, with such soft intent? With such sweet breath, and small sounds of pleasure? Surely not. Criminals had foul breath that tasted of tequila, and they groped at innocent women, violently. They didn't seduce with soft, sucking little kisses and careful, stroking hands and eyes closed so tightly.

Olivia's eyes closed, too. So she could think, she told herself. So she could use her excellent, well-educated and analytical brain to get herself out of this preposterous situation. Out of this preposterous town, where men proposed marriage in front of hundreds of other people and bandits kissed like angels.

Oh, pull yourself together, she told herself, keeping her lips vised together despite the fact that the smuggler was now licking at them. *Licking!*

She felt her body flood in arousal, and was mortified. Such a physical reaction from such a cerebral woman. It was a bizarre case of chemical response, she knew. People in peril often reacted against character. She'd read studies in which women in very dangerous situations had formed relationships they wouldn't normally consider…wow, was he nibbling her lower lip? Oh. Oh, *dear.*

Okay, okay, she didn't have to be governed by a simple chemical reaction. So he knew how to kiss. He knew how to kiss…her. And so no one had ever kissed…her quite like this before. She was a scientist, for God's sake. She could overcome plain old ordinary knee-jerk response, couldn't she?

The smallest moan escaped her when the smuggler gave up on her mouth and moved to her neck.

Couldn't she?

The doorknob turned at her back, and only then did she realize she was jammed against it. Her hands went flat against the bandit's chest, and she shoved as hard as she could.

Rafe staggered back, staring at her. Her mouth glistened from his kiss, and her eyes, in the darkness, glittered wildly. She was as turned on as he was, he realized, stunned. He'd meant to teach her a little lesson—and this was how she reacted? Crazy woman. He was reaching for her again, desperately, when he heard the small sound.

She swiped at her mouth, as Rafe stood, paralyzed, in front of her. For the first time in his life, he had no idea where to turn. His first instinct was to grab the woman and make a run for it. He knew the instant the thought came into his head, it was insane. He had to get out, and fast. But he could not leave her. Not with Cervantes.

"Olivia?"

It was Ernesto. Olivia put her hand over the doorknob at her back, and realized she had inadvertently pressed the button on the knob with her hip, locking him out of his own room.

"Yes?" she said, her voice ringing hollow and terrified in her own ears. Why was the bandit just standing there, watching her? She wanted to scream at him to go, but she knew Ernesto would hear.

"Olivia, open the door," Ernesto said sharply.

"Yes, all right, Ernesto," she said, but did not move. Her eyes were locked on those of the man who had just kissed her, whom she'd very nearly kissed right back. A drug smuggler, the worst kind of man. Mortification tightened her chest, and she struggled to breathe.

"It's dark in here," she called through the door, stalling for time. "I'm sorry, I can't find the light."

"It's next to the door," Ernesto said impatiently. He banged on the heavy door with his fist, making Olivia jump. "Why have you locked the door?"

''Go,'' she breathed. And in an instant, the dim outline of the man faded from her sight.

Olivia squeezed her eyes shut, popped them open again. She'd not even heard him move, had no idea where he was.

She fumbled with the door as long as she plausibly could, and finally got it open, allowing the light from the hallway to spill into the room. She resisted looking over her shoulder to make sure the smuggler was not standing behind her.

Ernesto frowned at her. ''Why are you in my room?'' he asked. ''And in the dark, with the door locked?'' He surveyed the large room carefully from the doorway, then moved past Olivia and stalked across the tile to the thick Aubusson carpet that lay beneath the huge, dark canopy bed. ''Olivia?''

Olivia snapped her attention back to him. She, too, had been scanning the room. The bandit couldn't have simply disappeared; he had to be in the room somewhere.

''I'm sorry, Ernesto,'' Olivia said. ''I came up to use the powder room and I stepped in here by mistake. I didn't even know where I was until I turned on the light. What a beautiful room.''

Her breathing was steadier now, and she folded her hands in front of her demurely, hoping Ernesto would not notice that her breasts were full, her nipples peaked against the peasant blouse, her cheeks flushed. It shamed her, her irrational reaction to the smuggler, who represented everything in the world she condemned—but she would deal with that later. In the convent she fully intended to join the instant she got home.

''It is a beautiful room,'' Ernesto conceded, his eyes narrowing. He walked over to her. ''Your hair is mussed. And your cheeks are pink.''

''I…I was dancing earlier,'' Olivia replied with a laugh. ''And I have had too much of your excellent champagne, I'm afraid.''

He scrutinized her for a minute, then, seemingly satisfied with her excuse, smiled. "Have you been enjoying yourself?" he asked softly, taking a strand of her loosened hair between his smooth fingers.

"Very much," Olivia said brightly.

"And you like my house?"

"It's everything a house should be, Ernesto," she said sincerely. "You have exquisite taste."

His face relaxed even further at the compliment. "I'm flattered, though I must admit I have decorators. I have never had a wife to advise me in matters of the home," he said easily.

Olivia felt that prickly sensation at the back of her neck again. For heaven's sake, now what?

Oh, Lord. How could she have forgotten? Not an hour ago, this handsome, intelligent, well-mannered and propertied man had stood in front of two hundred of his closest friends and announced he wanted to marry her.

Funny how the kiss of a bandit could make you forget the important things in life.

"Ernesto, let's go back downstairs," Olivia said, tugging on the sleeve of his beautiful suit. This one might just be Armani, she thought as her fingers slid over the fine fabric.

Ernesto stood his ground. "No, Olivia, not just yet," he said, his voice husky. "I like your hair after dancing. After we are married, we will dance every night before bed. It makes you look like a wanton," he finished with a small smile.

Which is just what I am, Olivia thought grimly. *Only not with Mr. Right, here. With Mr. Utterly Wrong.*

"Ernesto, we must talk about your proposal," Olivia began.

"We will, *querida.*" Ernesto took her hand from his arm and drew her gently toward him. He took her chin in his hand. "I know there are many questions in your head, about your work and your duties here. But these questions will have to wait. Now, we have time only for this.'' He dipped his head, grazed her jawline with his lips.

He smelled of expensive cologne and expensive champagne. Olivia fought back a repulsed shudder, and wondered why the perfect man made her want to run in the opposite direction, while the last man on earth she should want could seduce her with nothing more than his voice in the darkness.

''You look so beautiful tonight, in your Mexican peasant clothes,'' Ernesto murmured. ''Have I told you that?''

''Ernesto, your guests—'' she protested weakly.

''We will attend to them in a moment, Olivia.'' He banded one strong arm across her back and drew her against him.

He was partially aroused, and Olivia again had to bite back the urge to flee.

''Do you realize, this is the first time we have ever been truly alone together?'' he breathed, nipping at her earlobe.

Olivia squirmed slightly, but when Ernesto seemed to take the small movement as encouragement, she went stiff in his arms.

''We are not alone,'' she said as reasonably as she could. ''There are two hundred people here.''

He laughed softly. ''Outside then, where our guests will not interrupt us.''

''Not our guests, Ernesto,'' Olivia said firmly. ''*Your* guests.''

His hand drifted to her breast, squeezed. ''Our guests soon enough, my love,'' he whispered, then took her mouth with some fervor, pushing his tongue past her lips.

Olivia was too shocked for a moment to respond one way or the other. But soon enough her instincts kicked in. She protested the kiss against Ernesto's mouth, but the sound was muffled, and even to her it sounded like a whimper of passion. Ernesto gripped her breast, pinching at the nipple, and ground himself against her.

And then, so suddenly she couldn't comprehend it, he

was gone. She rocked on her feet, holding out a hand for
balance.

The other man stood before her now, breathing fire. His
chest was heaving and his dark eyes were slitted until she
could see nothing but black pupils. For a moment, he simply glowered at her, wordlessly accusing her. She felt an
absurd contrition, as though he'd caught her cheating on
him.

He turned to look at the man sprawled on the floor.

"Sorry to interrupt," Rafe sneered at his mortal enemy.
At the man who had killed his brother.

Chapter 3

Ernesto stared up at him, his flushed face a mask of angry confusion. "Who the hell are you?" He raked Rafe's simple clothes with an experienced eye. "You were not invited to this party."

"No." Ernesto began to rise, but Rafe put a foot on his chest.

Olivia noted he was wearing black running shoes—of distinctly American origin.

He slid his foot toward Ernesto's throat. "An oversight, I'm sure," he added casually. "My partner and I attend most of your parties, after all."

Ernesto's eyes went blank in bafflement, then slowly narrowed as he caught Rafe's meaning. "So you are the infamous Rafael," he said between his teeth.

"You know my name," Rafe said mockingly. "Very good for three months' work, *hefe*."

Ernesto spared Olivia a quick glance. "You will pay for what you have done, *cabrón*."

"What I have done tonight? Or what I have been doing

for months, without you having the slightest idea how to stop me?'' Rafael laughed acidly. "I best you at every turn, *señor*.'' Rafe removed his foot, stepped back and readied himself for the attack he was eager to meet. "It seems to me that you pay, Cervantes. Not I.''

Predictably, Ernesto launched himself at him, and Rafe caught Ernesto's head full in his gut.

Olivia heard the air rush from Rafael, heard Ernesto grunt at the impact, but other than that, they made little noise.

It was instantly, horribly ferocious.

Olivia could scarcely comprehend the violence that erupted, as if by some mad sorcery, from both of them. It seemed unfathomable that Ernesto would so hate the man before him. Wasn't he just another criminal, just another smuggler?

And the man Ernesto had called Rafael? What possible motivation could he have for the enmity flashing like deadly daggers in his dark eyes?

Whatever the explanation, Olivia knew instinctively that this was no ordinary fistfight between a lawman and a law-breaker. This was something much uglier—and one of them would die at the end of it if she didn't do something to stop them.

Rafael was younger, faster, tougher, but Ernesto out-weighed him by fifty pounds and used his weight merci-lessly, keeping his head lowered and battering at Rafael like a bull. Rafael efficiently countered by raining swift, brutal blows to Ernesto's handsome face whenever the op-portunity arose. It was a nearly silent, intentionally deadly bloodbath, and Olivia had never before seen anything like it. Had never imagined there could be anything like it.

Ernesto thumped heavily to the ground, catching Rafael around the knees as he fell. Rafael's black shirt came un-tucked from his black jeans, and Olivia gasped when she saw the small, shiny gun Rafael had shoved into his waist-band. She prayed, for Ernesto's sake, for the sake of everyone in the *hacienda,* that the man would not remember it was there.

She watched in horror as Rafael brought his arm back and slugged Ernesto square in the face. Blood spurted gruesomely over his fist as he drew back for another blow.

No, he wouldn't remember the gun, Olivia thought. He seemed determined to kill Ernesto with his bare hands. She bit back a scream. Rousing assistance at this point would be fatal to at least one person in the room. Olivia calculated the odds that it would be her or Ernesto, and decided not to take the chance.

Cervantes ducked the fist coming at his face, used the momentum of Rafael's body to slide himself out from under the younger man's straddle. In a blur, they both whipped to their feet—Ernesto's nose gushing blood; Rafael's jaw clenched, his breath coming in short puffs from the body blows he'd received.

Each holding a gun in his hand.

Olivia did scream then, in shock and dread, the short sound rising unexpectedly from her throat. Neither man looked in her direction.

Rafael grinned at Cervantes, though the pain in his chest was excruciating. "I've wanted your blood on my hands for a while now, Cervantes," he said hoarsely.

"I will soon have yours on mine," Ernesto retorted thickly, his voice sounding as though he had the worst kind of cold. "No man steals from me."

Rafael smiled. "I'm surprised. It's very easy to do."

Ernesto swiped at the blood on his chin, smearing it grotesquely across his swelling jawline.

Olivia heard footsteps pounding down the hall. Two hundred people, law-abiding friends of the local sheriff, would be upon them at any moment. They would kill Rafael where he stood—and all three of them knew it. Ernesto began to smile, blood showing in the spaces between his perfect, white teeth.

Olivia would excuse her rash behavior later by telling

herself she acted without thinking. But she did think. As
clearly as she ever had in her long and thoughtful life. In
the split second she knew she had before Ernesto's men
came through the door and put at least fifteen bullet holes
in the man who'd kissed her, she decided to save his life.

Not because she understood what he did to make his
way in the world, not because she liked him, excused him,
had hope for him. But simply because she could not allow
another human being to die in front of her eyes if she had
any way of stopping it. She hadn't known that about herself, exactly, but in that instant she saw it with perfect
clarity.

Olivia knew Ernesto no longer remembered she was in
the room, and suspected the smuggler had forgotten her
presence, as well. She threw herself in front of Rafael just
as the door burst open, grabbing his free hand and bringing
it to rest at her throat. She heard his loud grunt of pain as
she gripped his hand there and began, imprudently, shrieking like a lunatic.

The men barreling through the doorway stopped dead,
staring first at Ernesto, then at her and Rafael, then back
again. But the momentum of two hundred curious dinner
guests propelled them into the room, along with the dozen
people behind them. A minute later, there were more than
twenty citizens of Aldea Viejo in Ernesto's lavish bedroom, gaping at the bloody, dramatic, noisy tableau the
three of them made. Olivia closed her eyes, still wailing
theatrically, and thanked God.

Rafe saw stars. When the woman had wrenched his arm
up, he was sure a rib had gone straight through his lung.
But he was still breathing, still standing, and though he
could barely do either, it was enough to convince him he
was still alive.

It took him just a moment to divine the doctor's fool-
hardy plan, and he tightened his hold on her fractionally.
"Stop screaming," he hissed in her ear. "They get it."

She quieted instantly, nearly sighed with relief. So, he

understood the plan. Excellent. Maybe everyone, then, would get out of this charming *hacienda* alive. Including her.

"Stop where you are," Rafe said to the crowd, so menacingly that even Olivia shivered slightly. He carefully shifted his free hand until the gun was pressed against Olivia's temple. He glanced down briefly, saw her pulse beat under the barrel of his gun. He cocked his weapon, for effect, in the sudden silence of the room. "I will kill her," he said, his voice flat.

Several of Ernesto's well-dressed female dinner guests gasped at that threatening statement, but the men in front, now just a few feet away thanks to the press of the inquisitive crowd behind them, were silent. Olivia, for her part, was beginning to wonder if she'd had some sort of brain-debilitating stroke. When the man named Rafe had cocked the gun, she'd realized just how disastrous one moment's impetuousness could be.

No choice now but to go on, though. If she turned back now, he'd shoot her through her malfunctioning brain.

She whimpered noisily and snapped her head up, as though Rafael had tightened his grip at the sound. *"Ay, Dios,"* she breathed dramatically. She watched one man swallow hard and look to Ernesto for instruction.

Rafe almost laughed. He was barely holding her. Even if he hadn't been suffering from what he was certain was at least one cracked rib, she could easily have escaped him by simply stepping out of his reach and into the waiting arms of Cervantes's thugs. Instead, she was hamming it up for their audience, and saving his hide by doing so. If he hadn't wanted to throttle her for letting Cervantes grope her earlier, he would have kissed the top of her head.

He glanced over at Cervantes, who was standing, albeit unsteadily, with his gun still leveled at Rafe's head. Cervantes glared at Rafe for a moment, taking his measure, then jerked his head at his henchmen.

"Get out," he snarled.

"I don't think so," Rafe said quietly. "I think we're leaving, instead, if it's all the same to you."

Ernesto was visibly seething. Olivia could practically see his blood simmering behind his swollen eyes, could clearly see the struggle he was having to keep himself in check. She half expected smoke to come out of his nostrils at any moment.

On the one hand, he very probably wanted Rafael dead more than he wanted another sun to rise in the morning. On the other, he had announced in front of his entire town, his family and dozens of honored guests that the noted Doctor Olivia Magdalena Rosanna deRuiz Galpas of the famed Scripps Institute of Oceanography was to be his wife. Any risk he took with her safety would be noted, reported and discussed, on both sides of the border, for years to come.

Please, Olivia prayed silently. *Please, Ernesto.*

Finally, Ernesto's trembling hand lowered, the gun coming to rest at his side. He did not take his eyes off Rafe.

"Let her go," he said hoarsely. "I will guarantee you no one will touch you if you let her go."

Rafe smirked. "Forgive me, *señor,* if I do not trust you." He pressed the gun more tightly to Olivia's temple. Her head tilted to the side, and she whimpered again. *Good girl,* he thought. "Drop your weapon."

Again, Olivia waited, breathless, while Ernesto decided how much of his pride he was willing to sacrifice for her. Enough, she noted in relief as the gun clattered to the floor. Ernesto nodded at his men, who grudgingly laid down their guns, as well.

"Now," Rafe said calmly, "since I assume the rest of your boys here are armed, I'll just ask *Señorita* Galpas to escort me out of here." He looked down at Olivia, saw her face had gone another shade of pale. *"Señorita?"*

Olivia shot a last look at Ernesto. The blood coming from his nose was slowing to a grisly trickle that skirted his full upper lip to drip to his jaw. Olivia willed him not to do anything. Though she had put herself in this position of her own free will, she had no desire to get shot over one moment's deranged impulse. And Rafael would shoot her, she was pretty sure. He might have the mouth of an angel, but he was still a drug smuggler, and Olivia was certain "ruthless" was part of the job description.

Besides, she thought dizzily as he pulled her none-too-gently backward through the parting crowd of party-goers and household staff and grim-faced deputies, if he didn't shoot her, someone else would in the riot that would surely follow.

Heaven help her, what had she done?

Rafe's hand had tightened on her throat, and she realized she'd stopped moving.

"No cold feet now," he said in her ear. "This was your idea, *princesa,* so move it."

She stumbled against him again and allowed him to half drag her to the stairwell. He backed himself against the thick plaster wall and began stepping sideways down the stairs, Olivia trying to match her tread to his. He grunted softly at every step, and Olivia could feel the short breaths he expelled against the skin of her neck.

Like automatons, the people on the stairs, who had not been able to squeeze into a space in the crowded hall, parted silently in front of them. Those who had been in the hall and in the bedroom followed their slow progress down the stairs with their eyes. No one spoke, no one moved. Only Ernesto came through the crush of people to follow them.

Rafe watched him carefully, his eyes scanning the rest of the dinner guests briefly every few seconds. Olivia was starting to balk, giving him another thing to worry about.

Tough luck for the princess, Rafe thought. She'd put herself in the middle of this drama. And if she changed her mind now, they were screwed six ways from Sunday. She'd be hurt in the cross fire, possibly killed. And as furious as he was over that disgusting scene in Cervantes's bedroom, he wasn't about to let a bullet meant for him hit her. She'd just have to go through with the charade. He'd figure out what to do with her once he got her away from the *hacienda.*

"Only a little farther, *princesa,*" he whispered.

"Don't call me that, you psycho," she hissed back. It was the worst epithet she could think of, though she'd spit it out in English so he probably wouldn't understand it, anyway. *Dammit.*

"Olivia!" Ernesto shouted to her as they reached the wide, welcoming front doors of the house.

Olivia stopped, forcing Rafe to stand behind her. She knew from the way he was breathing in her ear that he probably didn't have the strength to drag her out if she didn't want to go. She looked up at Ernesto, felt a horrible pang of regret. He looked anguished, enraged.

"Ernesto," she said quietly, and for the first time felt Rafael tighten his grip on her. "I will be all right."

"I will come for you, Olivia," he said dramatically, and Olivia had the strangest sensation he was speaking not to her, but to his enthralled guests. *Come for her?* Surely he did not think this drug runner would keep her. The bandit would be suitably grateful for her saving his life and he'd let her go. He had to. She had a plane to catch in the morning. She had a job to go back to.

"I will kill you for this, Rafael," Ernesto shouted, as Rafe passed through the front entrance.

Rafe didn't bother to answer. He pulled Olivia out the door after him, and after a quick scan of the compound from right to left he grabbed her hand and started a painful, shuffling jog down the front steps.

"Let me go, now," Olivia said, pulling at the hand that gripped her. She was grateful to have the barrel of his gun pointing at the ground now instead of at her temple, but she wasn't grateful enough to let this go on any longer. "Listen, you, let go of my hand."

"Not yet, sweetheart," he said grimly. "Look around. We've got company. Now come on."

Olivia glanced quickly around the pretty yard. There were people everywhere. In the darkness, she couldn't tell who was pursuing them and who was simply observing their bizarre exit from Ernesto Cervantes's party, but Rafe gave her no time to figure it out. He ruthlessly dragged her in his wake as he left the wide driveway in front of the house and melted into the scrub around the manicured yard.

And *melted* was the only word for it, Olivia thought. If she hadn't been attached to him, she'd never have believed he could move so quietly and efficiently. Wouldn't have believed anyone could.

"Where are you going?" she whispered. It did not occur to her to scream out their whereabouts to potential rescuers.

"Where are *we* going, *princesa,*" he corrected breathlessly.

"I said, don't call me that," she snapped furiously.

"Be quiet. You make as much noise as five regular women, I swear," he muttered. He could hear thrashing behind him, knew Cervantes's men were just hitting the brush. At least, with Olivia tagging along, they wouldn't shoot at him. Or let dogs loose on him. He'd been chased more than once by dogs in the *barrio,* usually after he'd performed some moderately illegal act. He hated being chased by dogs. It made the hair on his neck stand on end.

"How many 'regular' women have you kidnapped?" she demanded. Personally, she thought she was holding up pretty well.

He didn't bother to answer, just dodged hard left, dragging Olivia along pitilessly. Both of them hunched over to make themselves invisible in the low, thick brush. He tucked the gun into the waistband of his jeans and wrapped his free arm around his chest. It didn't help much, but at least he didn't feel as though he was going to pass out.

They made their way in that odd, shuffling, walk-jog for what seemed to Olivia like an hour, though when she looked back at the lights of the house she knew they hadn't gone nearly far enough for Ernesto's men to have given up the chase. She wondered, as she caught her sandal on another prickly clump of sagebrush, if any place on earth would be far enough.

They reached a road, or what passed for a road in this part of Baja California. Rafe paused, still keeping his death grip on Olivia, and studied the terrain. He cursed quietly.

"Yes," Olivia said encouragingly. "This looks very bad. We'll never make it at this pace. You must go on without me."

"Shut up, will you?"

"I'm slowing you down. Leave me here. You'll make better progress without me."

"If you don't stop yanking your arm around, Doctor, I'm going to pull it out of the socket and drag you through this brush on your butt," Rafe said sharply.

Olivia peered through the darkness at his face. He looked ghostly pale despite the run, and she realized he'd been holding his chest as though to keep his internal organs from spilling onto the desert floor.

"What's wrong with you?"

"Nothing. Be quiet," he growled.

She glared at him. "Very nice," she said, her breath coming out in gusts after their flight. She waved wildly in the direction of the *hacienda*. "I just saved your ass back there, if you weren't paying attention."

His head whipped around, and Olivia was instantly sorry she'd poked at the wounded beast.

"I was paying attention to everything you were doing back there," he said through his teeth. "I was certainly paying attention when you let that son of a bitch put his tongue down your throat and his hand on your—"

"He's practically my fiancé," Olivia said rashly.

"The hell he is," Rafe muttered, and started walking

again. He pulled her roughly along when she slowed. They crossed the road and dove back into the low, sand-swept cover. This time, they headed west, toward the foothills.

Olivia stumbled along as best she could, every few minutes or so experimentally tugging at her hand, which was still clamped firmly in Rafael's. "Are you going to tell me where we're going?" she asked again after a while.

"No."

"Ow," she said loudly as her sandal snagged on a rock, peeling a strip of skin from the side of her big toe.

Rafe didn't so much as glance back at her exclamation or slow his pace. "Quiet."

"I think you just ripped off my toe."

"You wear stupid shoes," he muttered, though the first glimpse of her small, slim feet in those strappy sandals back in that dim hallway had made his mouth water. "I'm surprised you have any toes left."

"I didn't know I was going to be kidnapped tonight or I would have worn something more sensible."

He stopped, turned very deliberately to her. "I didn't kidnap you, *princesa*," he said, and watched the light of fire come into her eyes. Good, it would help propel her the rest of the way up this mountain tonight. When Bobby discovered Rafe had never made it back to the beach camp, he'd meet them there. Rafe and Bobby had worked out a contingency plan weeks ago, before Dr. Galpas had ever come along to ruin his mission and his destiny and possibly his life. "You tossed yourself into this whole mess headfirst."

"What was I supposed to do—let Ernesto kill you?"

He snorted. "You think he could have killed me?"

Olivia gaped at him. "He had a gun, you moron."

"So did I."

Olivia threw her free hand in the air. "Are you stupid? What makes you think he wouldn't have shot you first?"

Rafe shrugged. "I'm faster."

Olivia hoped a derisive snort would let him know her

opinion of that bit of lunacy. When he appeared unfazed by it, she decided to make her point more forcefully. "You're not the sharpest tack in the box, are you."

Rafe glanced over her shoulder. He could see men fanning out into the scrub around the *hacienda*. "Keep your voice down."

"You may have been faster, but you were in his house," she continued in a furious whisper. "Without me, you never would have gotten out alive."

He looked down at her. Her mouth was swollen—from the bastard's kisses, he thought sourly. Still, he could think of nothing he wanted more than to pull her into his arms. She *had* saved him. She was far braver than he ever would have given her credit for. Far braver than any woman he'd ever known. Not that he'd tell her that.

"Now is not the time to congratulate yourself, *princesa*," he said into her ear. He bit down on her lobe, making her gasp. "If you don't start moving your butt up this mountain, your efforts will have been for nothing."

"Why are you holding onto your chest like that?"

"I think your boyfriend broke me," he said shortly. "Let's get moving."

"He broke you? He broke your ribs?"

"Yes."

"Oh, my God. How many?"

"I don't know," he said. "My X-ray vision is on the blink."

"Let go of my hand. Let me feel."

He eyed her suspiciously. "I don't think so."

She hissed at him like a snake.

"You're not that kind of doctor, anyway," he said. The truth was, he didn't want to let go of her hand. He couldn't have explained it, but he felt that if he did, she'd disappear into the desert and he'd never see her again.

"No, I'm not that kind of doctor, but I can help you if you let me, you dufus."

The American slang sounded incongruous, preceded as

it was by a long stream of furious Spanish, and Rafe had to bite back a smile. *Dufus?* He couldn't think of a Spanish equivalent. Now, *psycho*—

He let go of her hand, then realized his was sweaty and wiped it down his pant leg.

"Lift your shirt."

He gingerly lifted his black shirt, and heard her gasp.

"You look like you've been hit by a truck," she said in English.

He watched her curiously as she bent over and ripped the bottom half of her long skirt along the slim strip of embroidery that attached it to the top half. She straightened.

"What are you doing?"

"Applying first aid," she said.

"With your dress?"

"Well, I could take off my bra and snap it to your chest, but then you'd have a lot to explain to your cell-mates once Ernesto throws you in jail."

She clamped the bottom of her skirt to his chest with one hand and began wrapping the material tightly around him.

"If you don't hurry, he will throw me in jail," Rafe said, sucking in his breath as she touched a sore spot.

"I'm hurrying, I'm hurrying, you ungrateful pain in the neck."

He heard her mutter in English, and he smiled over the top of her silky hair.

"Good thing I was wearing a skirt like a proper damsel. Good thing I'm not a respected scientist or anything. Then this would be absolutely absurd. Oh, if my parents ever find out about this…Oh God, and Dr. Eames—at least he won't make me do any more press conferences—" She tucked the end of the fabric into the wrapping and stood back. "There," she said, switching to Spanish again, proud of herself.

"Thank you."

"I don't have to go with you."

He put his chin on his chest to check her bandage. Good field dressing. "Yes," he said. "You do." He moved experimentally. His ribs did feel slightly better. They'd be able to move much faster now. Before she could think to run, he clasped his hand over her wrist.

"No, you'll be safe now," she insisted. "I'll go back down the mountain, divert their attention, tell them you went in the opposite direction."

It made perfect sense, Rafe knew. And he wouldn't have let her do it in a million years. She was not going back to Cervantes. Not only did the thought of the bastard touching her again make Rafe nuts—for some ungodly, Neanderthal reason that he'd need a psychiatrist and an anthropologist to explain to him—but Cervantes was one slip-up away from being taken down by the United States Drug Enforcement Agency and a half-dozen cooperating Mexican law enforcement organizations. No way was Rafe letting any woman, willing accomplice or not, rush back into a situation as volatile as that. His mother would murder him.

Olivia Galpas had saved his life tonight. And she *was* an American. A spoiled and wealthy American who had an obvious knack for getting herself into trouble, but an American nonetheless. She deserved some consideration from a DEA agent such as him.

"You're coming with me, Doctor," he said.

Olivia put her foot down, such as it was. "No," she said quite firmly—even barked the word, she might have said. "I am not."

Rafe leaned forward. "Once again, *princesa,* you're wrong."

Suddenly, his head whipped up like that of a wolf scenting prey, and she heard the sound of men coming through the desert.

"Come on," he said, and began to run.

Olivia had no idea when the bottoms of her feet began to bleed, or when the blisters on her heels popped. Or when the moon came up. Or when the wind died down and left the desert quiet enough to hear the small animals scurrying home at their approach. Her world had winnowed down to the hand in hers and the mountain in front of her.

He let her stop for a while once during the night. But just for a few minutes, and even then he did not let her take off her sandals.

"I'm beginning to be very sorry I didn't let them kill you," she muttered at him in English, while he stared off into the distance, obviously trying to pinpoint any men who might be following them up this godforsaken hill.

She thought she saw him smile, but decided that was impossible. He had never spoken a word of English. His clothes, his speech, his Spanish dialect all told her he was a peasant; she was sure he did not speak English. Which was good, because she'd been muttering at him in English for most of the hellish trip up the mountain, and she fully intended to mutter at him until he let her go or until one of them died of heat exhaustion or pursuing lawmen or bloody feet.

He made her get up after a short rest and follow him again up some indistinct trail to some obscure place only he knew about and only he could imagine. All Olivia could see was rock formations and low brush, the silhouettes of barrel cactus and dusty, endless sand. And behind her, far in the distance now, the Sea of Cortéz shining in the moonlight.

She cursed at him in English all the way up the mountainside. If his chest hadn't been so sore and his mood worse, Rafe would have laughed at her. The esteemed doctor knew some good, dirty American swear words. His mother would be shocked. He imagined *her* mother would faint dead away.

They reached the predetermined meeting place just as the sky lightened. They'd left any pursuers far behind, but Rafe knew it was only a matter of time before Cervantes

and his goons picked up their trail in the bright light of a
Baja California day. He turned just as the sun seemed to
break the surface of the gulf. In spite of everything, the
sight took his breath away.

Olivia sat on a rock and watched him. She hated to
admit it, but he was sort of…beautiful, actually. His eyes
were tired, and seemed to her to be tinged with some
vague…regret. His gorgeous mouth was relaxed as he
breathed in the morning air, his edgy face showed shadows, softening the angles into something almost artistic.
Her mother would kill to paint that face, Olivia knew.

"Why do you do it, Rafael?" she asked.

He turned to her. "What?"

"What you do." She saw his eyes narrow, but kept hers
steady on him. "Run drugs."

His face went expressionless. "Is this what your lover
told you?"

"He told me there were two men in the area, bringing
drugs from the mainland through Aldea Viejo. From his
reaction to you in that bedroom back there, I'm just assuming you're one of them."

"I'm one of them," Rafe said.

"Why?"

Rafe ran a hand down his face. Working undercover
meant lying. Lying to everyone. Telling the good doctor
he was a common bandit. He could not take a chance that
this extraordinary lovely woman would reveal his secret.
She could easily return to the arms of Cervantes, tell him
the DEA, not common thieves, were trying to catch him
red-handed in his own crimes. Cervantes would surely pull
back then, lay low, become impossible to prosecute.

Rafe watched the sun rise another minute, trying to
come up with a convincing reply. With thoughts of her
lifetime of privileged status, he asked, "Have you ever
been poor, Doctor?"

Olivia shook her head.

"Then don't question why my people do what they do

to put food in their mouths." He turned back toward the gulf, scanning the hillside for any sign of Bobby.

"What your people do hurt my people," she said.

"Americans?" he scoffed. "Americans can't get enough of what Mexico has to sell them."

"It doesn't make it right. It doesn't make it legal."

He ground his teeth together. He wanted to end the lie, to tell her of his obsession to stop the real drug runner. To agree with her in every way. To make her see him as a man of honor.

Choking back the truth, he shrugged, knowing his cover had to remain top priority. "A man like me," he said slowly, carefully, "is nothing but the smallest fish. A small fish does little harm." He gazed across the morning haze to the spot where he knew Cervantes's house sat. He couldn't see it, but every sumptuous carpet and ornate piece of furniture and thin crystal glass stood out in sharp relief in his mind's eye. "You should worry about the sharks, Olivia. Sharks prey on the poor and the addicted, and they grow wealthier and wealthier with each passing year. They are not struggling to feed their families. They are killing your high school kids to make themselves rich. You, of all people, should know how much damage a shark can do."

"You try to excuse your actions by telling me you're only a small dealer, insignificant in the wave of drugs that comes across the border." It made her angry that he would dig for any excuse at all. "But you are a part of it—you and whoever your partner is. You are still in the wrong."

Her tone infuriated him. She was right, of course. He'd spent his entire adult life dedicating himself to stopping the flow of drugs between the two countries—but to hear her condemn him made him crazy.

"What do you know about right and wrong, *princesa?*" he said, putting every ounce of disdain he could manage into his words. "I don't imagine you have had to make

any real decisions about right and wrong since the day you
were born.''

"Are you kidding me?" Olivia jumped up, her aching,
oozing feet forgotten. "Do you think because you were
born poor and I wasn't that you have had all the moral
decisions to make?"

He nodded slowly, enraging her further. She poked him
in the chest, ignored his wince of pain. "Well, I have news
for you, *amigo,*" she said. "I make moral decisions at
every turn. Do I marry to please my parents and give them
the grandchildren my culture and my hormones demand,
or do I make my own way in a man's world? Do I work
myself to death, or let my father's money help me slide
through? Do I hold onto my cultural heritage with both
hands, or bleed into the Anglo life to make things easier
on myself? At every turn I have chosen the right path.
How dare you accuse me of not knowing the difference
between right and wrong simply because *you* have chosen
poorly.''

Her chest was heaving, her wild, messy hair was tossed
back by the freshening wind. She looked every inch the
princess he accused her of being.

Rafe leaned into the finger that had been poking him in
the chest. "Do you really think, Dr. Galpas," he asked
blandly, "that these decisions you have made are the same
as the decision whether or not to starve to death? You are
very brave to make them, of course," he said expansively,
ironically, "but have you had to decide whether stealing
or smuggling or eluding the border guards is better or
worse than watching your children cry themselves to sleep
at night because they are hungry or cold or merely hopeless?"

"I am not ignorant of the world's problems," she said.

He shook his head. "I think you are," he said slowly.
"I think, Doctor, you are ignorant of many things."

Chapter 4

"I thought I might find you here."

The voice came from the rocks at Olivia's back, and they both pivoted to face it. Rafe's gun was in his hand before Olivia could think to be afraid—or relieved—that one of Cervantes's men had found them.

But the voice just laughed. "A little late for caution now, Rafael."

Out of the corner of her eye, Olivia saw Rafael relax and lower the gun to his side.

A man stepped out from behind the rocks. "You two were arguing so loud, I could have taken you out any time in the past ten minutes."

"How long have you been there?" Rafe asked, tucking his weapon back into the waistband of his black jeans. He was a little chagrined that his partner had been listening to the scolding he'd been getting from Olivia. And more than chagrined that Bobby had come upon them without Rafe knowing it.

"A couple hours. I watched you come up the mountain."

He stretched and yawned, just as though there weren't a town full of lawmen hunting for the three of them this very minute, Olivia thought, incredulous.

"I was taking a little nap before the yelling started. Hello, Dr. Galpas. Would you like some water?"

Olivia tentatively reached for the offered canteen. So he knew her name, too. "Yes, please," she said. She drank, while Rafael's partner grinned at her. He seemed to take her presence in this godforsaken spot as nothing at all to be curious about. Olivia carefully handed back the canteen. "Thank you."

"I'm Roberto," he said to Olivia. "But everyone calls me Bobby."

"Very nice to—" Olivia stopped herself. What did one say when introduced to a criminal? She should know that by now. "—meet you," she finished lamely.

Rafe shook his head. She'd just been on a forced march and was being introduced to what she must assume was her second drug runner of the past twenty-four hours, and she still sounded as if she were having drinks with the First Lady. He hated rich people. He really did. They were completely out of touch with reality.

Rafe wrenched his focus back to the matter at hand. "A couple hours?"

"Our camp has been raided."

That got his attention. Rafael cursed violently. "Did they dig up our communications equipment?"

Bobby glanced blandly at Olivia, then raised his eyebrows at his partner. "Not yet, but they're poking around," he said. "Even if they don't find it, I don't think we're going to get to it anytime soon. They have four men posted. And two of them are carrying some very nice semiautomatic machine guns."

"What about the bikes?"

"I think we're walking from now on."

"Hell." Rafe dragged a hand down his face, rough now with a day-old beard. He wanted to get back to the ocean, wash the sweat and the smell of Cervantes's blood from his body. "I stashed mine outside the compound. It's in the brush. Or was."

"It's gone by now," Bobby agreed. "You must have had twenty men crawling after you last night."

Rafe swore again, more softly this time. They needed the motorcycles now more than ever. The quick little dirt bikes had been perfect for outrunning Cervantes's goons and their expensive, unwieldy sports utility vehicles. He and Bobby had been able to slide in and out of nasty confrontations without much more than shouting to show for it, and the rough desert had provided the perfect escape routes. No one had been able to follow them across the rock-strewn animal trails and down the washed-out arroyos.

They'd be on foot, now, unless they could scrounge a couple of bikes somewhere. And Rafe knew that would be next to impossible. They'd brought the bikes in across the border; replacements would likely have to come from there, as well, and Cervantes was too well-primed for Rafe to risk the time it would take to make it back to San Diego, or even into La Paz or Cabo San Lucas, for new bikes.

Although it *would* mean getting rid of Olivia Galpas. He could deposit her neatly back into her tidy little doctor's life, and forget all about her.

Someday.

No. No time for that, either. They'd just have to make adjustments. If they could get to their communications equipment, and radio in some assistance from the *federales* with whom they were working on this bust, then maybe the Mexicans could provide some transportation.

Unfortunately, that was a big "if."

Olivia watched Rafael carefully. "Who raided your camp, Ernesto? Why?" she asked. "Do you keep drugs there?'' That seemed incomprehensibly stupid. ''And what did you mean, communications equipment?''

Rafe didn't spare her a look. ''Nothing,'' he said.

Bobby smiled at her, though. ''Satellite phones,'' he explained casually. ''Very expensive to replace.''

''She knows enough,'' Rafe snapped.

Bobby shrugged. ''I wasn't the one who brought it up.''

''Why do you need them? To communicate with your buyers?''

Rafael grabbed her arm, led her to the edge of the clearing. His grip was unyielding, but he settled her gently onto the rock where she'd been sitting earlier. ''Now is not the time for another moral lecture, *princesa.* Sit here and be quiet, while Bobby and I figure out how to not get all three of us killed in the next half hour.''

Olivia put her hand on his wrist to keep him from walking away. ''Why don't you just leave? Walk out right now? I'm sure you could hitchhike down to La Paz.'' She wanted to plead with him, but she knew he would only scoff at her desperation. ''It's only a couple hours south, and it's a big enough town that Ernesto would have a hard time finding you there. Go. Get away from here.''

He studied her hand for a moment, then looked up at her. ''Why do you care whether he finds us or not?''

Olivia gave him a dead-on stare. ''I don't care,'' she said, almost truthfully. ''I just want to go home, and I figure the easiest way to accomplish that is for you two to disappear.''

''And what do we do with you?''

''Leave me. They'll find me eventually.''

She let go of his wrist and eased off her sandals, as though that would settle the argument that she should be left behind. She began to weave her hair back into its customary braid, briskly and brutally detangling it with her nimble fingers.

''We had to have left quite a trail last night,'' she added.

He looked down at her feet and flinched. He sat down

next to her and, without a word, began pulling his own shoes off.

She blinked at him. "What are you doing?"

"My shoes are too big for you. They'll rub a dozen more blisters into your skin if you wear them." He yanked off his socks and shook them out. "Put these on under your sandals."

She stared at his socks. "You want me to wear your socks?"

She looked horrified at the prospect. Rafe wanted desperately to hold that against her, but he wasn't entirely sure he'd wear someone else's damp, day-old socks willingly, either.

"They'll protect your feet inside your sandals," he said briskly. He reached down to grab one of her feet, then thought better of it. He knew himself very well. As angry with her as he was, as crazy as he was beginning to think *she* was, he knew if he touched one sore, sad little toe, he'd be lost. He'd be blowing on her blisters and massaging her instep like a lovesick little idiot, until Cervantes walked right up and shot him in the head.

And he'd probably die smiling.

He tried to push the socks into her lap, but she recoiled. "I don't want to wear your socks," she insisted.

"Just take the socks, Olivia," Rafe said.

She wrinkled her nose. "I don't want to."

Okay, now he was a little peeved. "Listen, *princesa,* I know you've probably never worn anything in your entire life not freshly laundered by half a dozen women wearing starched uniforms, but put on the damn socks or I'm going to put them on for you."

She set her teeth. "You know, you have the strangest idea of what my life is like. And I'm warning you about the *princesa* crack."

"You're warning me." Rafe bit the inside of his cheek for courage, then grabbed her left foot and began stuffing it into his sock. He tried not to linger over the small cuts,

but found his thumb stroking them tenderly, anyway, as
her foot disappeared into his too-big sock. "You are certainly brave for a—"

"Don't say it," she snarled, and grabbed the other sock
from his hand. She yanked it on her bare foot, certain she
couldn't take one more second of his gentle ministrations.
The socks were slightly damp with sweat, but they did
soothe her aching feet. She slipped her sandals back on
over them. She almost sighed.

"Thank you," she said reluctantly. "That does feel better."

Rafe nodded, then put his shoes back on over his bare
feet and stood. He held out his hand. "Then let's go. I
want to try to get back and check out the situation at the
beach camp before it gets too hot. We'll have to circle—"

"Rafael, listen to me. Leave me here. It will be safer
for all of us." *Particularly me,* she thought. *Because every
time you touch me I forget what kind of man you really
are.* "They will find me before the morning is out, I'm
sure. I'll be fine here."

He considered her thoughtfully. "You sound very reasonable about this."

Olivia met his eyes. "I'm a reasonable woman."

"And anxious to get back to your fiancé."

She stared him down. True enough, though technically
not the *fiancé* part. She would run as fast as possible back
to Ernesto; he was the only person she knew who would
be able to get her quickly out of the country.

"Yes."

Rafe nodded slowly. "Brave," he said, running his
tongue across his teeth. "Or stupid. Get up. We're walking."

"What possible difference can it make to you now
whether I go back to him?" she asked, a last-ditch effort.

He stared at her. What possible difference? Had he been
the only one involved in those mind-altering, blood-
pumping minutes back in that dark bedroom?

He considered that. Maybe so. Maybe she hadn't felt anything but disgust, being kissed by a man she thought was a drug runner. But *he'd* been involved. Up to his eyelids.

"I'll tell you what difference it makes," he ground out. "The man you're so anxious to get back to? We've been stealing from him. The drugs we move? They're his."

Olivia stared at him for a full minute. "I beg your pardon?"

Her stupefied expression only made him angrier. She was so quick to believe the worst of him, but not of the real criminal.

"Did you miss that part of the conversation back at the *hacienda?*" he snarled at her. "We're stealing from him. We take what shipments we can intercept and sell them ourselves. 'Cutting into his action,' I think you Americans call it."

No man steals from me. Olivia remembered the words perfectly, remembered the look of fury on Ernesto's face when he'd said them. But he hadn't meant what this criminal was implying. He couldn't have.

"You're lying," she said confidently.

"No, Olivia. I'm not." Rafe felt Bobby's eyes on him. Okay, a major breach of regulations, telling her about their mark. He would explain later to Bobby that the woman had driven him completely out of his mind. He simply couldn't go another minute on this planet with her thinking Cervantes was anything but the murdering scumbag Rafe knew him to be.

And if she called him "Ernesto" in that little voice again, he'd do more than breach regulations. He'd haul her back to headquarters in San Diego and show her the file the DEA had been keeping for twenty years!

"Stealing from him?" Olivia said. "Stealing?"

"Stealing," Rafe bit out. "Narcotics. From him."

Olivia looked from one man to the other. "You're stealing from him."

"The lady has quite a gift for restating the obvious,"
Bobby murmured, grinning.

She looked at Rafael. "He's the shark."

Rafe smiled cynically. "He's the shark, Olivia."

She came to her feet. "My God, you're both insane.
Ernesto is no more a drug smuggler than I am."

Bobby only laughed at that, and it was all Olivia could
do not to ask him furiously if he was on some sort of
medication. Laughing? They'd just made the most absurd
accusation about the sheriff of Aldea Viejo—a man even
now searching for all three of them—and he was *laughing?*

Rafael, on the other hand, never changed his expression.
His dark eyes bored through hers. "Now you have felt the
kiss of two criminals, *princesa,*" he said quietly enough
so Bobby would not hear. "You must be appalled."

Olivia swallowed bile. "You're just saying this so I
won't try to escape."

Rafe swept his arm toward the ocean. "Escape," he
shouted, though he was prepared to tie her up to keep her
with him. "You can probably walk back. Go! Be my guest.
It was your idea to come with me in the first place."

"To save your life!"

"I'm saved. You can go."

Olivia looked wildly toward Bobby again. He was still
smiling, and she couldn't bear to meet his eyes. "This
can't be true. Ernesto has been the sheriff of this town for
years," she argued. "His father was sheriff here before
him, a landholder who knew my uncle. A farmer!"

"And the most notorious smuggler in Mexico, until he
died in a shoot-out with the *federales* twenty years ago,"
Rafe added.

Words caught in her throat. No, it was too preposterous.
Ernesto, a smuggler?

"What about all his friends, the people of the town? Do
you expect me to believe they don't know this about
him?"

"Some of them do, I would guess," Bobby said blithely. "His father *was* a farmer, before he started transporting shipments of marijuana in the 1950s, then raw cocaine from the mainland in the 1970s. You don't build a *hacienda* like that on a farmer's take-home pay."

"He made up the story of his family?"

Rafe nodded. "He has the same pedigree as the rest of the men in Aldea Viejo," he said harshly. "His father was simply more brutally ambitious. As is your Ernesto."

"You're a liar."

Rafe studied her for a moment, making Olivia's breath catch in her throat. She braced herself. If he slit her throat, she wouldn't be surprised. He had the look of it in his eyes.

"I am a liar, *princesa,*" he said, ominously, and Olivia backed up one involuntary step. "Sometimes I think I lie about everything. I will admit that to you." He took a deep breath, let it out carefully. His ribs were howling again. "But I am not lying to you about this," he continued finally. "Ernesto Cervantes is a smuggler. A shark. The biggest shark in Baja. And he wants to kill us because we have been eating away at his stash of drugs."

"No," Olivia said again. "I don't believe you."

Rafe shrugged.

"And I'll tell you why I don't believe you," Olivia persisted, furious with them, furious with herself for the kernel of doubt that had lodged like a slug in her breastbone. "Because you're a *criminal.* You lie for a living. That's what criminals do."

"And you know what criminals do, Doctor?" Rafe asked mildly.

"I know they don't tell the truth."

"So why do you believe anything Cervantes has told you?"

Because I was thinking of marrying him, Olivia wanted to cry. *And what kind of woman does that make me? Cer-*

tainly not the intelligent, thoughtful one I've always imagined myself to be.

Rafe watched Olivia struggle with an answer. Just to be courteous, he supplied her with the one he thought might fit. "You believed what he told you because he looks just like what he says he is. He looks and acts like a wealthy, old-family Mexican landowner with a badge. You're so in love with his fine manners and his perfect speech and his *hacienda,* you don't want to know where all the money to pay for those things has come from—"

"Uh, Rafe?"

Rafe tore his eyes from Olivia's. "What?"

Bobby nodded down the hill. Rafe followed his gaze. A Land Cruiser was slowly crawling the hillside, straight toward them.

"Hell," he said. "Doctor?"

She was dazed, he could see. She looked up at him, but her beautiful black eyes were bewildered.

"What?"

"We're going."

She shook her head, and tears began to slide from the corners of her eyes. "I can't go with you."

He palmed her biceps, shook her slightly. "You can't stay here."

She stared up at him while the truth of that sank in.

Of course, she didn't believe this Rafael person, despite the utter credibility in his black eyes. Beautiful, sincere black eyes were just as capable of deception as any other kind, she reminded herself sternly.

She didn't believe Ernesto was a drug smuggler. That was impossible. That would mean she was a complete fool, a dupe, a naive and vain woman flattered into insensibility. She simply couldn't accept that.

But that miserable kernel of doubt was growing at an alarming rate, though she assured herself that was just a reaction to the extreme stress of the moment.

Like the kiss had been.

Like the bizarre impulse to toss herself in front of a madman had been.

Yes, that was it. Oh, it was something of a relief to figure it out. She was simply reacting—badly, she had to admit—to stimulus, to the severe anxiety of the moment. Of *all* the moments since she'd run into this brooding, hawk-faced man in that hallway. Apparently, she had lost all analytical capability and had turned into some kind of lab rat.

And her reaction to this horrible lie? To the news that her would-be fiancé was coming up the mountain to rescue her? Well, she damn well wanted to run, that was all. Like a rat in a maze, surrounded on all sides by grad students with electric prods. Run like hell and worry later about which nut in a lab coat was actually going to zap her.

Rafe shook her again. Her face had gone white, her lips bloodless. "Olivia," he said sharply. "We have to go."

"Yes, I think that's a good idea," she answered numbly. "We should go."

Rafe scowled at her. She was frozen in place, staring over his shoulder as if she were doing algebra equations in her head. *"Princesa,"* he muttered, and, sliding his hand down to her wrist, dragged her along the path.

Olivia's swollen feet kept them from outrunning the slow-moving Land Cruiser—so they hid from it, instead. It was astonishingly easy to do, Olivia thought vaguely. The desert provided the best kind of cover, and her dirty clothes and dark hair and sun-browned arms and legs did the rest. Bobby, too, in his faded, worn brown trousers and khaki shirt, practically disappeared against the desert floor.

Rafe, in his black clothes, was much more conspicuous against the browns and dusty grays and cactus greens of the Baja backcountry, but his uncanny agility more than made up for his dark costume. He led the way through the brush and cactus as though he'd been living in it all his life. Which, Olivia supposed, could be the case. She swallowed thickly.

"Do you need water?" Rafe muttered without turning to her.

She would have been stunned at his extraordinary hearing, except that in the hours since they'd left the meeting place where Bobby had last offered her water, she'd seen him do a hundred extraordinary things.

"Yes, please," she croaked. She was terribly hot and thirsty. She had never experienced the fiercest heat of Baja, because she'd always, as part of her job, stayed at the ocean's edge. They were nowhere near the ocean now. She couldn't even smell it any longer. All she could smell was heated sand and the sweat of three bodies and the imagined stench of her life going up in smoke.

Rafe stopped his inexorable forward march and motioned to Bobby, who thrust the canteen into her trembling hand.

"You should have asked for water an hour ago," Rafe murmured, watching her swallow deeply. He was alarmed at the dusky color in her tanned cheeks, at the absence of sweat on her forehead. He'd been fretting like an old woman over the condition of her little feet for hours. He'd steered her carefully around the worst of the low-growing cacti and chaparral, unable to keep from wincing at every slow, painful step she took. Now he realized she was in much greater danger of dehydration than of anything else.

He scanned the horizon quickly. They'd been holed up here and there since dawn, but the woman needed a proper rest. He'd have to find someplace where they could get out of the heat of the afternoon.

Olivia took a last drink of water. It was warm and tasted of the metal of the canteen, but it wet her throat. "You haven't had anything to drink," she said hoarsely, handing the canteen to Rafael.

He took it, capped it without drinking and tossed it back

to Bobby, who replaced it on his shoulder, also without drinking.

"I spent five years picking avocados, Olivia," he said, using her name absently. "You learn to drink a little in the morning, and then drink most of your water at night. You can work harder in the heat if your stomach isn't weighed down by water."

"You picked avocados?"

He grimaced inwardly at the incredulity in her voice. Yes, he'd picked avocados. He imagined her regular social circle didn't include many former pickers. He took her hand in his and tugged her into a walk. "Just a little farther. We'll get out of the heat for a while."

"You picked avocados?" she asked again, her head fuzzy from heat and exhaustion. That seemed such a noble, difficult task—picking avocados. She wished he still did it. She would never feel ashamed about kissing an avocado picker.

"Yes, I picked avocados," he said impatiently. "I know it's hard for you to believe, but someone has to pick them, *princesa.* They don't show up in your lunch at the Hotel Del Coronado by the hand of God."

"I've never had lunch at the Hotel Del," she said. Why was he so angry? It was not her fault he'd stopped picking avocados to become a criminal. Her high school prom had been at San Diego's famous landmark hotel, but she hadn't gone to her prom. She'd been too busy studying for her SATs. "How do you know about the Hotel Del?"

He didn't answer, but behind her she could hear Bobby chuckle. *Weirdo,* she thought nastily, and trudged along after Rafael.

Rafe found what he was looking for just after the sun rose to its highest point in the vivid blue Baja sky. All morning they'd been listening to the relentless buzz of the Land Cruiser's massive motor. They'd barely managed to stay out of its line of sight, and once or twice they'd had to stop, duck behind a rock outcropping or press themselves into the burning sand to keep from being seen.

Rafe desperately wanted to keep going. He needed eventually to circle back and get to his beach campsite. He had to have those satellite phones to reach his contacts in La Paz, who were tracking Cervantes's shipments as they came across the gulf from the mainland. He was also required to check in every twenty-four hours, or, according to the agreement with the United States DEA, the *federales* were to begin intercepting the shipments on the assumption that he and Bobby had failed in their mission.

He needed to know when the next shipment was due, and where. Rafael was certain his taking Olivia had been the last straw for the wily Cervantes; the man's pride would allow nothing less than the death of Rafe and his *carnal*. Cervantes would stop at nothing to destroy the men who had humiliated him and stolen from him—stolen something much more important to his vanity and his self-inflated reputation than any mere drug shipment.

Rafe needed to be there when Cervantes cracked, when he decided revenge was more important than his personal safety. If Rafe was any judge of a man's character—and he'd made his living being an excellent judge of the character of men like Cervantes—he knew last night's scene had pushed Cervantes right over that fine edge.

Rafe let go of Olivia's hand, squatted in front of the small sand cave and peered in. He stood and whipped off his shirt. Then he knelt again and brushed the floor of the opening with the shirt. When he pulled it back out, three small scorpions clung to the fabric. He flicked the shirt until they dropped to the sand, then ground them under the heel of his running shoe until they were dead. He repeated the process with his shirt twice more, but found no more scorpions.

Olivia watched the whole exercise, fascinated.

Bobby squinted into the hole in the sand hill, while

Olivia stared at the tiny squashed arachnids. "Looks tight," he commented as he straightened.

Rafe crawled into the crevice. It was low, and his hair brushed sand from the ceiling into his eyes as he looked around. But it was marginally cooler, out of the glare of the sun, and provided good cover. Cervantes would have to come straight upon the water-formed sand crevice and actually look in, to see them in the shade the shallow cave provided.

"You get in first," Rafe said, backing out. "Then she can crawl in after. I'll take the first watch."

Bobby laughed, making Olivia's hair stand on end.

"I don't think so, *amigo*. You get in there with her. I'm not about to risk my life crawling into a dark little hole in the ground with your pretty little hostage."

"I'm not his hostage," Olivia said dully.

"Whatever you say, Doctor." He grinned wickedly at Rafe, who scowled back at him. "Still, I think I'll find someplace around here to wait out the light. It's probably better if we split up. Take the canteen for her. I'll be back here at dusk."

Rafe nodded. "Be careful."

Bobby shot a glance at Olivia, who was still staring at the scorpion carcasses. "You, too."

In moments, he blended into the desert landscape—just another wisp of brown in a world of muted color, indiscernible from anything else.

Rafe watched him fade, reluctant to see him go. He and Bobby had been nearly inseparable since childhood, and he always felt safer on assignment with his *primo* by his side.

With a shake of his head, Rafe turned back to Olivia. "I want you to go in first," he said. "If Cervantes spots us and decides to get nasty, you'll be out of the line of fire." When she didn't answer, he looked down at her. She seemed to be in shock. Her color was better after the water, and she was sweating again, but she didn't look at him. "Olivia?"

"Yes?"

"Did you hear me?"

"Yes."

"What did I say?"

"I am to go in first, and then you'll come in after."

"Okay," he said slowly. "So is that what's going to happen?"

She shook her head.

"Why not?"

"Because you just took three scorpions out of there."

"Out of there. Which means they are no longer in there."

Olivia nodded. "But they may have had babies in there, or friends. Wives. Scorpions are polygamous. There may be dozens of wives." She finally looked up at him. "Hundreds."

He saw instantly that she was on some sort of raw edge herself.

It was, suddenly, more than he could do to continue to hold himself apart from her. He gathered her gently into his arms. She was shaking, and she burrowed her face into his chest.

"I hate scorpions."

He smiled. "You picked the wrong country, then, *mi'ja.*"

"I don't think I can get in that little hole. I'm sorry. I know perfectly well I brought this whole situation on myself, but I really don't think I can get in that little hole when I know there are scorpions in there."

"It's not such a little hole, Olivia. I was just in there. And there were no scorpions."

"How do you know?"

"Because they would have stung me," he said reasonably.

Olivia sniffed. She was in no mood to be reasonable.

Lab rats could take only so much, she thought miserably. "They wouldn't sting you," she said.

He felt a dampness on the front of his shirt. She was crying steadily now. He felt none of the normal, male alarm. He'd grown up in a houseful of women who cried at the drop of a hat. "Because I'm too ugly?" he murmured, trying to cheer her.

"No, because you're too mean."

He smiled, watching for the Land Cruiser over her shoulder. He could hear it coming closer. "Have I been so mean to you, *mi'ja?*"

"Yes. And don't call me that name. Don't call me your dear. It's worse than princess."

She fought a losing battle against the tears, and Rafe felt her shoulders shudder. He pressed a kiss on her dusty hair. "All right. I won't call you anything but 'Olivia' from now on. Okay? Just stop crying now, will you?"

"I don't think so."

"You have to. And you have to crawl into the cave. Be brave, Olivia."

"I am brave," she said into his chest. "I'm famous for being brave. Really. People comment on it all the time. But not with scorpions."

He pushed her gently away from him, swiped his thumbs across her cheeks. The tears had made tracks down her dirty face. She was sunburned and dehydrated and filthy, and her dark eyes were sunken into her face and bruised looking. He kissed her ever so gently because he still thought she was more beautiful than any woman he'd ever known.

"You can be brave with scorpions, Olivia. Just think of them as little spider versions of me."

She stared into his eyes. Gentle eyes, now. No firebreathing dragon behind them, full of fury and danger. Her eyes fluttered closed when he brushed his lips over her forehead a second time, then popped back open. She had the strongest, strangest sensation that if she kept her eyes on his, she would be okay. Somehow, she would get out of this alive.

"I can—do that," she said, her voice hitching.

Rafe nodded and stopped himself just before he kissed her again. There was a time to be an idiot and a time to take oneself in hand, he told himself sternly. He could contemplate later why one kiss in a dark bedroom from this woman had affected him more than any sexual experience he'd ever had.

Right now, he needed to get her in that cave before Cervantes came around the next corner.

"You can." And just in case she doubted it, he put his wide palm over her dusty hair and shoved her inside.

Chapter 5

Before she knew it, Olivia was stretched out in the back of the crevice. Her tears of exhaustion quickly dried up as she realized she was inside the very same crack in the earth where just moments before scorpions had been happily storing up painful venom. The chill that slid down her spine shook her all the way to her tightly curled toes.

And worse, the jerk who'd pretended sympathy just so she'd relax and he could get the jump on her was now *not* crawling in after her, as he'd plainly promised he would.

Smugglers, she steamed. You just couldn't trust them.

"Where are you?" she whispered furiously. She scooted to the opening of the cave. If, by any stretch of the imagination, it could be called that, she thought as sand spilled down her blouse. "Where the hell are you?"

"Be quiet," he said as his face appeared against the harsh sunlight. "I'll be right there."

Olivia waited. Thank goodness she'd spent a week in New Guinea the summer before, going down every day in the institute's small submersible. After that assignment, she'd be immune to claustrophobia for the rest of her life. Still, there had never once been a dangerous, pointy-tailed arachnid in that little sub.

Where was that damn smuggler? He couldn't be trusted, but he'd save her from a scorpion—she felt sure about that.

He came back, finally. She could see his legs to his knees. He was dragging something—a shoot of sagebrush, she noted with surprise. Of course, he'd think to brush away their tracks. It hadn't even occurred to her. Lucky thing she was an oceanographer and not spending her life on the lam. She wouldn't survive the first day.

A little bubble of delirium lodged in her throat, and she gagged on it.

"Shh," Rafe hissed at her as he crawled in beside her. His ribs were hurting, but that didn't keep him from noticing when his arm brushed her breast, when his hip settled against the inside of her thigh as she shifted to make room for him. *Oh, yes.* It was definitely wise of Bobby to find someplace else to hole up.

Rafe reached out and leaned the length of sage against the outside wall of the cave, partially blocking the opening. Then he lay flat and scooted back into the cool darkness. With any luck at all, Cervantes, if he even came this way, would never look twice at the crevice in the wall of the hill.

Rafe slid the canteen over, thrust it in Olivia's direction. "Drink as much as you can stand."

She took the water, drank steadily for several seconds.

"Now you," she said, tapping the canteen on his shoulder.

"I'm fine."

"Right. You know, you die on me out here and I'll murder you. How are your ribs?" she asked crossly.

"Better." Rafe took the canteen over his shoulder and drank. He had to keep himself from licking his lips. He imagined he could taste her on the metal rim. "What makes you think you're better off with me than Cervantes? We're both in the same business, you know.''

"I don't think I'm better off with you," Olivia said flatly. "You're just making it impossible for me to go back to Ernesto, aren't you. And I'd obviously rather not die of exposure and dehydration if I don't have to. Why are you breathing so hard if your ribs are better?''

"I ran up the arroyo a ways and brushed out our tracks.''

"Oh.'' She was quiet a minute. "Do you think that will fool him?''

Rafe shrugged—a huge mistake because he felt the softness of her breast against his elbow. "Can you move back any more?'' he asked testily.

"No, I can't. I cannot believe you'd ask me that. I didn't want to get in this hole in the first place.''

"Lower your voice, for God's sake.''

Olivia felt the earth shiver slightly under her body. "Is that them?''

"Yes," Rafe muttered. "He drives that fifty-thousand-dollar tank around this desert like he owns it.''

"He does own some of it.''

Rafe would have liked to give her a glare for that comment, but he didn't want to move again. He was already having to fold his arms to keep from grabbing her, from rolling against her soft breasts in this godforsaken hole. The very thought made him smile.

"What's with the big grin?'' she asked.

"We're a naturally happy people," Rafe said blandly.

For a moment she simply stared at the back of his head. Then the delirium bubble she'd been choking down made its way up from her throat. "You're a naturally happy people?'' she repeated, strangling, clamping her hand over her mouth.

"Yes, now shut up. I think—oh, hell, they've turned down the arroyo.''

He felt her shaking behind him. Her whole body was

trembling. He reached back a hand and clamped it around her knee. "Settle down," he murmured. "They won't see us."

"Mmph," she answered. She could hear the rumble of the vehicle getting closer, but experienced no reaction at all to the sound. No fear, no thought of escape, nothing. She knew why, of course. She'd gone round the bend.

A naturally happy people? This guy was the least naturally happy person she'd ever met. She imagined he had ten distinct gradations of forbidding, at least that many of gloomy, and maybe more than ten of downright irate. She could do a doctoral thesis on the querulous subsurface currents in the man. *Naturally happy?*

She turned onto her side, holding her mouth, vibrating with suppressed laughter. Oh, she was hysterical, all right, she thought. The bizarre party last night, the exhaustion of a twelve-hour chase, the ludicrous whopper about Ernesto—all had combined to make her insane. *A naturally happy people?* She'd never heard anything so funny.

Rafe watched the truck move slowly into the small canyon where he and Olivia were hidden. He could see Cervantes clearly. The man was talking on a cell phone, his eyes scanning the hillside. Rafe took a sharp breath as Cervantes squinted in the direction of their hiding place. He felt Olivia roll to her side behind him. He slid his hand around her knee to the back of her calf and squeezed reassuringly. She was making a distressed sound at the back of her throat, and he was afraid she'd start screaming at any moment. He stroked the muscle of her calf to soothe her, while watching Cervantes through the cover of the sagebrush.

The driver got out and kicked through the sand, glancing every few seconds back at Cervantes.

Rafe smiled grimly. At times during the past three months—and certainly at times during the past twenty-four hours—he'd have sworn he had the luck of the damned.

But as he recognized the face of the man with Cervantes, he decided a little good fortune had finally come his way.

The driver was making an excellent show of looking for tracks in the sand, but was actually managing to erase most of them. Rafe watched him keep a close eye on his boss in the car. When he knew he was being watched, he'd squat and look thoughtfully at the ground, or peer into the brush or at the near horizon.

Rafe almost laughed in relief. No wonder the three of them hadn't been caught last night. It had seemed like a miracle at the time, one he hadn't been anxious to question—but this explained it. At least one of the *federales* who had infiltrated Cervantes's operation was on the job. And making a good hash of it.

The driver looked around for a minute more, then got back in the vehicle and eased it into drive. Rafe could hear Cervantes shouting at him, and shouting at some poor sap on the other end of the phone at the same time.

The man was not mincing words. Rafe half hoped Olivia would hear the tirade, though she was obviously terrified enough as it was. Cervantes undoubtedly had never shown the lovely doctor this rough side to his disposition. The stream of obscenities alone was enough to sully his reputation on both sides of the border as an elegant ladies' man.

And his face. Rafe took some satisfaction in looking at his face. Cervantes's features were swollen grotesquely, his nose a purple mass stuck between two black eyes. Rafe grunted quietly. The bastard would think twice before he ever again put his filthy hand on Dr. Galpas's breast.

Rafe was close enough to see the sweat trickling down the fold of Cervantes's jowls. The elaborate SUV undoubtedly had air-conditioning, but Cervantes wouldn't use it because of the risk of overheating the vehicle while the windows were down.

Sweat, old man, Rafe thought. *Sweat about every single thing that's happened. Get yourself all worked up.*

The SUV finally inched off down the wash, Cervantes

screaming profanities into his phone. The driver, bless him, was tensely, almost exaggeratedly scrutinizing the landscape.

It took them fully ten minutes to reach the end of the arroyo, where they stopped for another few minutes. Deciding which way to go, Rafe knew. He waited patiently while they made their decision. He didn't mind the wait, wouldn't even have noticed it except that he knew Olivia was probably holding her breath in fright until they were gone. Half his job was waiting; interminable stakeouts and year-long sting operations and court cases that dragged on for weeks. He was very, very good at waiting.

Rafe didn't much care which way the SUV went. He knew Bobby was out of sight and was now satisfied that the three of them could avoid the noisy, poorly organized searchers by heading out after dark. For one thing, Cervantes himself was making enough of a clamor to give even the most inexperienced quarry ample warning. And since they were also receiving a little help from the boys in khaki, Rafe was confident Cervantes wouldn't catch them. Until they wanted to be caught.

Cervantes and his studiously hapless driver finally chose to move north again, and the SUV swung widely to the right.

Rafe shifted slightly so he could look at Olivia. At least she'd stopped that terrible shaking.

"Olivia. They're gone."

She was wound into a fetal position, her eyes tightly closed. She didn't answer. Shock, Rafe guessed. He ran his hand down her calf to cradle her foot. Through the sock he'd given her he could feel the swell of flesh around the tight straps of the sandal. Poor princess, he thought as he loosened the strap of the sandal. She'd had a hell of a couple days.

"Olivia," he whispered again. "It's all right. They've gone." Still no answer. Rafe grasped her ankle and shook it lightly. "Dr. Galpas?"

Good God, she'd fainted from fright.

Well, that was just typical. The princess had fainted dead away at the first little sign of trouble. Shook herself with fear until she collapsed. He squinted down at her in the dim light of the cave. A woman like Olivia Galpas was not built to withstand much more than your average spoiled house cat, he thought, forgetting that a moment earlier he'd been more sympathetic to her plight.

"Doctor," he said sharply. He angled his wide shoulders in the narrow confines of the crevice, going painfully down on one elbow. He waited a second until the pain in his ribs subsided slightly, then raised his hand. "Come on, *princesa*. I know it's probably not your favorite thing to do, but it's time to face reality." He patted her cheeks a couple of times.

Olivia murmured, low in her throat. Rafe let his hand rest against the soft skin of her gently rounded cheek for a moment, watching her long lashes flutter. No harm in that, he told himself. She was in a faint. She'd never remember he'd stroked the line of her jaw with his thumb, curled his knuckles into the indentation below her cheekbone.

As he watched her, she made another small sound. Coming around, was she? He snatched his hand back, and plastered his perpetually perturbed expression on his face, the one he knew made her furious.

But she didn't come out of her faint. She gave a delicate little snort, instead, and began to snore.

He stared at her, astonished. "Are you asleep?"

She didn't answer, of course. But her nose twitched slightly, and she began to snore in earnest.

Rafe laughed in surprise.

Not fainted, not scared out of her wits, not paralyzed with fright. Asleep—as though she hadn't a care in the world.

As though she trusted him to take care of her while she

slept. Abruptly, he stopped laughing. Watched her sleep for a minute.

"Dr. Galpas," he whispered, "what am I going to do with you?"

She murmured faintly again and tried to find a more comfortable position on the hard ground.

Rafe carefully levered himself to a semi-sitting position—cursing quietly as he dislodged another shirt full of dirt down his back—and gently eased the strap open on Olivia's other sandal.

She sighed in her sleep.

"Stupid woman," he muttered, massaging the arch of her foot through the thick sock. "Stupid sandals."

He stretched out beside her as she sighed again. Fingering his ribs through his shirt and bandage, he decided nothing was broken. But he wasn't anxious to see the bruise that probably covered him stem to stern.

He let his breath out slowly. No sense trying to wake Olivia and get her moving. She obviously needed the sleep, and he was tired, too. He rolled against her and closed his eyes to take a nap.

But as his body pressed against the sleeping woman, his heart began to pick up speed in his chest. He shifted slowly to face her, aware of her soft, full mouth, half open, only inches away. His hand, as if in a dream, stroked slowly down her back to rest gently on the small curve of her hip. He thought of the past few years—how he had shunned women, no matter how good looking or how friendly. His single purpose in life was revenge. It had consumed him. Maybe there was something more important, he thought, his hand idly caressing the lovely hip.

Just as Olivia's eyes eased open halfway, he closed his own and breathed her scent of seashells, the ocean.

Olivia could feel her own heart stirring as Rafe's slow-motion hand continued its casual caress. His light touches sent out invisible currents that warmed her deep inside. For so long, her life had been void of such emotion—full of scientific study, writing papers, going to all those parties where rooms full of men stood around talking about ocean currents. They were desperate for women at institute faculty parties, Olivia knew. Sometimes she felt like calling the geek police and having all her co-workers arrested. Anyone with breasts and a pulse could be the belle of those balls.

But Dr. Olivia Galpas was, in addition to being young, smart, and possessed of (lovely) breasts and a (strong) heart, the only Hispanic woman in the whole institute. And she'd been the showpiece of every provost cocktail party and university barbecue since she'd hung her MIT doctorate on the wall of her tiny office. Dr. Eames, who was in charge of general funding for the institute, had even taken to tossing her in front of the local and international press to announce important discoveries in the fascinating world of oceanography—something Olivia might have resented had anyone ever bothered to show up at the press conferences. Not a lot of people were interested in minute changes in water temperature in the Indian Ocean. Even the infamous, glamorous El Niño had lost its shine after a year or so.

Olivia Galpas was a novelty in the white male world of oceanography, just as that wide swath of super-heated ocean water had been a novelty when it first showed itself. Olivia had been fervently hoping that everyone would get sick of her soon, as well.

Well, not everyone. She had spent time with Ernesto, enjoying his charm, being proud to be with such a distinguished man. But her heart had never beat even one eighth-note faster. He was dashing, but somehow cold. And now she was learning the truth about him, realizing what a nightmare a life with him might be.

Then there was this bandit—a man whose inner goodness she sensed, no matter what he said about himself. A man who wanted to save her, to nurse her feet, to touch her so protectively.

Engulfed by his tenderness, she leaned toward him. His eyes drifted open partway, and they began a long, slow delicious kiss. She felt his gliding tongue as his two hands folded around her breasts.

A feeling of exhilaration swept through her, and she wondered how she could abandon herself to such a stranger, how she could be swept into a kiss that now was making her feel wild. She wanted to tell him what a good man he could be if he would take on a better profession, but the words came out as small sounds of pleasure and her own hands began to slide over his lean body.

Trying to clear his head, Rafe turned his face away, taking quiet, short breaths. *Be professional,* he told himself. *Keep her safe and nothing more.* But her nearness warmed him, drew him to her, let him for the moment escape the obsession with revenge that for too long had consumed all his heart.

Still in a slow dream of exhaustion, they began to reach under clothes and softly explore. In the cool dim light, their hands touched backs, glided around necks, unbuttoned clothes and folded them back. Each time their lips met, the kisses became harder, teeth bumping, tongues wrestling. They lay on their sides under the low cave ceiling, nearly naked against each other, their mouths melting together, unwilling to pull apart. His hand drifted down her tight stomach, over the smooth hip and down her leg. Working his hand gently between her thighs, he eased his fingers tenderly into her delicately flowing juices, silky and warm.

Olivia groaned as his fingers swam back and forth, then pushed in deeper, kneading what she thought must be the bottom of her heart. She felt his hard erection against her, and she reached to stroke it.

Sliding his mouth down her neck, Rafe sucked first one of her hard nipples, then the other.

"Do you want me, *princesa?*" he murmured, as she

began to work her hips back and forth against his sliding hand. "Tell me, tell me what to do."

Curling over him, she put her lips gently to his ear, then let her warm breath, coming faster now, fill it with an answer that came from animal instinct, not scientific textbooks.

"Yes," she whispered with a shudder as desire for this outlaw possessed every nerve and muscle in her body. "Yes," she breathed again, as he writhed his sensitive ear away in a frenzy and their mouths landed back together with new urgency.

He smelled of sagebrush, and she squeezed her eyes closed as his hand quietly worked in her, pushing, pulling, sliding. She clutched him and felt his arousal against her. Lifting her thigh over his, she guided him forward, running her hand between his legs to feel all of him.

"You're so beautiful," he whispered, wanting to say something, anything, to let her know his awe, his unbearable pleasure. Fighting temptation to take her wholly, all at once, he pressed his tip through her soft hair and into her folds where his hand had been. He pushed gently, pulled back, then entered farther.

She could feel him begin to fill her, and she took a sharp breath as he pulled back. Her need rose, and she wrapped her arms around him, urging him to give her more.

But he would not be rushed. He took every kiss, every inch into her, as though it would be his last. In near desperation, she ran her hands down the muscles of his back to his tight buttocks. She pressed her body into him, forcing him to surge forward, to push deeper into her as their legs locked in a tangle. Holding himself back, he could feel her clutch him deep inside, as he began a slow rhythm that she met with her own hips. They kissed each other's ears, necks, shoulders—rocking faster, harder, whispering words that no one understood. When she was on the edge of hysteria, he cried out with a final plunge and felt her contractions.

As the hours passed, Olivia slept in Rafe's arms. He carefully pulled her bra and panties back in place, rebuttoned her blouse, smoothed down her skirt and pulled his own clothes back on as best he could. Off and on he dozed, wary that the search for them continued, but smiling at the thought that he could not wait to inform the princess she snored.

Olivia shifted slightly, moving her shoulders. *Ow!* Was she sleeping on rocks? And why couldn't she move her legs?

She reached out blindly and felt dirt under her hand. Well, for crying out loud, her tent wasn't made out of...

She sat suddenly upright, banging her head on the hard-packed ceiling of the cave and getting a mouthful of sand. And dislodging the man who had been resting against her.

"Ow," he muttered.

Her memory instantly cleared. Suddenly, she felt wary at the sight of this bandit who had overwhelmed her so easily.

"What are you doing?" she yelled. She spat sand out of her mouth. *Oh, very ladylike, spitting,* she thought. *Look what I'm reduced to.* "What are you doing?" she repeated when she received no answer.

Rafe lay blinking up at the ceiling, which was steadily sifting sand into his face. He ran his tongue around his teeth. They felt furry, like the roof of his mouth.

What *was* he doing?

He'd been dreaming of her. One of those woozy, heart-pounding erotic dreams he hadn't had since he was a teenager. His face had been buried between her thighs, and she'd been moaning. He felt a little like moaning himself, he was so aroused.

"Were you asleep?" Olivia asked suspiciously.

"Was I asleep?" Rafe repeated dully.

"How could you fall asleep?" She shifted and tried to sit up.

"How could I fall—?"

Olivia peered out the opening of the cave and gave a little shriek of panic. "Oh, my God! It's almost dark. What time is it?"

Rafe, still flat on his back, raised his wrist to his face and peered at the glowing dial of his watch. Did he know how to read a watch? He couldn't remem—oh, there it was. His brain kicked sluggishly into first gear as some of the blood seeped uphill from his groin to his cranium.

"Six-forty-eight," he answered.

"Six-forty-eight?" Olivia shrieked again. "How long have you been asleep?"

He was going to remind her that she'd been the first to fall asleep, but decided it took too much effort. He tried to lift his head to frown at her, at least, but decided half-way through that *that* was going to take too much effort, too. He closed his eyes again, instead. Maybe, if she'd stop that squalling for a minute, he could get back to the dream...

"Rafael!"

"What?" he snarled.

"I've got to get out of this hole!"

For the first time since he'd dragged her out of Cervantes's party last night, Rafe heard an edge of panic in her voice. The passion that had brought her to a frenzy just hours before was now replaced with another kind of hysteria. Was it fear? he wondered, or a massive change of heart?

He reluctantly gave up the dream and rolled to his side—away from her, in case she could spot his rather embarrassing physical state in the dark of the cave—and peered out the opening.

"Wait here a minute," he said, his voice husky.

"I can't wait." She was crowded up behind him, trying to shove him out the opening. "I have to get out."

"Settle down," he snapped. "I want to look around."

"Well, you'd better do it quick."

"Yes, *princesa*," he said, and slid carefully out of the cave.

"You promised not to call me that," Olivia said after him, wondering at her own exasperation.

Rafe stayed in a squat for a minute, then eased to a standing position, his cramped muscles screaming, his bruised ribs making it painful to breathe.

He listened to the desert for a minute. It was alive with the sound of dusk. A good sign. No growling Land Cruisers to disturb the nightly ritual of animals awakening from the heat of the day.

He leaned over and looked in the crevice.

"Okay," he said, and Olivia shot out of the opening like a bullet from a gun.

"Oh man, oh man," she was muttering. "Okay, this is the deal." She was looking around rather wildly. Rafe stared at her, nonplussed. "I haven't gone to the bathroom since last night, and I really have to go. I'm not particularly interested in you watching me, of course—"

The gracious, imperturbable Dr. Galpas was babbling; it was a fascinating thing to watch, Rafe thought. "—but then again, I don't want to get bitten by scorpions tromping through the cactus, either. So I'm going to go right behind that clump of brush right there, and I want you to turn around and promise you won't look."

Rafe turned around obediently, smiling. "Okay, *princesa*."

She hissed a well-seasoned swear word in English at him, making him chuckle. "You said you wouldn't call me that anymore," she said.

"That's true. But it's such a temptation."

"Resist it."

"I'll try, but I haven't been very good at resisting temptation with you." He scratched thoughtfully at the beard on his face. "I may be reaching my limit again."

"Ha!"

"You don't believe that?"

"I don't believe you've resisted temptation much where anything's concerned. Smuggler."

He chuckled evilly. "You don't know what nasty things I've been tempted to do to you, Doctor. Since the moment I saw you come out of the little bathroom last night."

Olivia stopped trying to smooth the wrinkles from her skirt and stared at his back. She didn't want to think about the things he could do to her.

"I need to wash my hands," she muttered crossly. "I need to wash my hair."

Rafe turned around. "I imagine the facilities are not what you're accustomed to."

She put her hands on her hips. "You know, you are not required to make a snide comment every single time I open my mouth."

"Probably not. But I enjoy it."

She scowled at him. "And you're just a naturally happy person."

"That's true," he conceded.

She came out from behind the chaparral. "Uh-huh." She looked around. "What are we going to do, now?"

"We're going to wait for Bobby."

"What time is it?"

Rafe glanced at his watch again. "Straight up seven."

"Do you think—?"

"No. I don't think. Look, now you turn around."

Olivia glanced down at him. At least, he wasn't sporting that enormous bulge anymore. She'd thought she was going to have a heart attack when she crawled out of that wretched little cave to have *that* staring her in the face.

She whipped around when she realized she was staring. To her mortification, she heard Rafe chuckle again.

"I wouldn't be laughing if I were you," she remarked over her shoulder. "I've seen a lot of movies about the conditions in Mexican prisons."

"I'm not going to prison."

"Drug running is a federal offense in Mexico," she reminded him. "As is kidnapping."

"I didn't kidnap you, Olivia," he remarked reasonably. "You kidnapped you."

"Whatever. Are you finished?"

"I'll tell you when I'm finished. Unless you want to watch me?"

Olivia blushed. "No, thank you." Finally, she heard a *zip*.

"Okay. You can turn around now."

She turned, kept her eyes steadfastly on his. "Look, I hate to ruin what is probably the first jolly mood of your life, but you do see this is a pretty impossible situation you've gotten us into, here?"

"You got us into it. I would have been happy to finish the whole thing last night."

"You would have wound up in a pool of your own blood on the floor of Ernesto's bedroom, you idiot!"

Rafe smiled. "I didn't say it was going to finish well. I just said *finish*."

Olivia growled in frustration. "Okay—one, stop smiling. You're making me nuts."

"What does that mean, 'making me nuts'?" he asked, just to watch her spark. His imprudent good mood was really starting to get out of control, he thought happily. He couldn't logically think of a single reason he should feel this cheerful. Except that Olivia Galpas, who *snored,* was in his clutches.

"If I didn't know better, I would think you knew," she mumbled in English. She tossed up her hands. "Never mind what it means. Let's try and concentrate on how we're going to get out of this mess."

"What mess?"

"What mess?" She gaped at him. "What *mess?* I'm starving, thirsty and filthy. I have missed my flight home. For all intents and purposes, I have been kidnapped from the home of a prominent local law enforcement officer. If my boss finds out…good heavens, if my family finds out, I'll never be let out of the house again.'' She pointed accusingly at Rafe. "And you *say* you're stealing drugs from a man who, from what I witnessed last night, would like to kill you with his bare hands.''

Rafe rubbed at his front teeth with his finger. "That's true,'' he conceded amiably enough.

"We're miles from the beach.''

"Yep.''

"And I'm assuming Ernesto controls that little airstrip outside town where I was supposed to catch a puddle-jumper to La Paz this afternoon.''

"Again, correct.''

She eyed him suspiciously. "Do you know what a puddle-jumper is?''

He rolled his eyes. "Do you imagine I've never watched television?''

"Okay. Whatever.'' She chewed on her cheek for a minute. "Did I forget anything?''

"Your skirt is ripped, you have sand down your blouse and your feet hurt,'' he pointed out helpfully.

"That's right. And you should get your ribs looked at by a proper doctor.''

He grinned at her. "If you weren't such a proper doctor, I could get that sand out for you.''

It was her turn to roll her eyes. "You could use a bath,'' she said bluntly.

He nodded. "You, too.''

Her eyes narrowed on him. "And your feet are beginning to smell in those leather shoes.''

"Yours, too.''

"Because of *your* socks,'' she huffed, insulted.

Rafe laughed. "Very nice. I save your pretty little feet from all kinds of bad, crawly, scratchy things by offering you my socks, and you disparage them right in front of me.''

"You wouldn't have had to save my feet if you hadn't dragged me halfway across Baja last night."

"I wouldn't have done that if you hadn't tossed yourself into my arms in front of two hundred people."

"Well, I wouldn't have had to do that if you hadn't jumped Ernesto."

Rafe's dark eyes blazed. "He was pinching your—"

"I know what he was doing," she interrupted quickly.

"Yes!" He jabbed his index finger at her. "And I didn't see you stopping him, even though your mouth was still wet from another man. What kind of woman are you?"

"I didn't know you were still in the room!"

His mouth dropped open at that. "What difference does that make? You only would have stopped him if you'd known I was still there?"

"No! I *never* would have stopped him if I'd known you were still there!"

He threw his hands in the air, looked toward heaven. "She is trying to make me crazy," he said.

"Now, listen, Rafael—"

His head dropped forward suddenly. "Quiet!"

Olivia's mouth snapped closed.

Rafe cocked an ear, closed his eyes. "Back in the hole," he whispered.

"Oh, no—"

In the blink of an eye, he was beside her. How did he move like that? she wondered briefly. He grasped the back of her neck with one strong hand, her wrist with the other.

"Now, wait a min—"

He didn't wait for her to finish. He wrapped one foot around her ankle and pushed her. She went to her knees, and he dropped beside her. For the second time in just a few hours—and for only the second time in her entire life—Olivia was forcibly shoved in a direction she definitely did not want to go.

"I don't think—"

"Shut up. Get in."

When she continued to balk, he turned her face so she could see him. His black eyes were just one tick off deadly.

"Right. Now."

Okay, well, there was just no arguing with a man who looked at you like that, Olivia thought, and scrambled obediently back into the cave.

Rafe scooted in after her, pulling the sage over the opening as before, although it was considerably darker now and Olivia found it hard to believe anyone would even see the low crevice, much less peek in. She certainly wouldn't if she were passing by, and she considered herself unusually curious about these kinds of natural formations.

"Rafael," she began, but his hand clamped over her mouth before she could finish. Smugglers were not only untrustworthy, she thought, furious with him. They were also unforgivably rude. He hadn't let her finish any of the last six sentences she'd started.

She bit his palm. Hard. He didn't release her, just leaned forward and took her earlobe between his teeth and clamped down. Hard.

She squealed against his hand.

"If you don't be quiet, *princesa,*" he whispered into her sore ear. "You're going to get us both killed. Now let go."

Olivia opened her teeth.

"That's better." His hand hurt like hell. The little fiend had practically bitten through his skin. He leaned back slightly. "Are you going to be quiet?"

Olivia nodded, her eyes never leaving his. He could just see the glow of them in the waning light coming from the opening of the cave.

Rafe slowly removed his hand from her mouth. He dug the thumb of his other hand into the palm, pressing down on the bite mark. He shook his head, disgusted with himself. He could barely move, he was so turned on. Pathetic.

Olivia couldn't see him very well, but she knew he was furious. It practically radiated off him.

The low rumble of a vehicle—a big one, Olivia thought,

from the vibrations under her bottom, and close—finally reached her. So, it wasn't Bobby, after all.

She felt a little sick.

If what Rafe had said about Ernesto was true, the bandit had most likely just saved her life. No matter that he did it for his own reasons—reasons she hadn't quite figured out yet—it was still a very decent thing to do.

And for his trouble, she'd bitten through his hand.

She tapped him on his shoulder, found the muscle there as tense as a bowstring.

"Rafael," she whispered.

"Shh."

"I'm sorry I bit you."

Rafe said nothing.

"Did you hear me?"

"Be quiet, Doctor." *And for God's sake, stop blowing in my ear.* He shifted uncomfortably.

"But I want to say—"

He turned as quickly as he could, given the tight space, the sore ribs and the rushing of blood from his extremities to his groin.

"Olivia, shut the hell up."

"Okay, I just wanted to say—"

Whatever it was she was about to say, she forgot in an instant as his mouth came over hers.

"Quiet," he mumbled against her mouth. "Just be quiet."

As his lips slid over hers, he thought to himself, *Oh, yeah.*

Chapter 6

Olivia was too surprised for a moment to react.

Not that Rafael appeared to care one way or the other. His mouth—oh dear, that mobile, magnificent mouth—simply worked away at hers just as though there were not a couple dozen men looking for them, at least two of whom were just outside.

Or, maybe, just as though there were.

What was that study she'd read in Senior Biology, about danger being an aphrodisiac?

Rafe slid his tongue along her bottom lip. "Open your mouth," he ordered softly.

No, she couldn't do that. She was supposed to be thinking about something. Something about why he was so excited. About why she, too—like a rocket had gone off in her toes and was surging up toward the top of her skull—was suddenly so excited.

He dragged his teeth across her lip. "Open," he said roughly. "Kiss me back."

And there was another reason she couldn't open her mouth. What was it, what was it?

Dear God. This man was a dangerous criminal. It didn't matter that he was less dangerous than some, that he did what he did for reasons he justified. He still did something illegal, something she abhorred in both practice and theory.

She pushed at him, but her limbs were pathetically weak. "Rafael," she said. Rafe merely tightened his grip on her. "Rafael."

She was saying something against his mouth, he knew. He just couldn't for the life of him figure out what it was. He was desperate for her, felt as though he'd never been more desperate for a woman than he was now. In the dim distance he could hear the rumble of one of Cervantes's tanks, but the sound only seemed to fuel the fire already burning out of control in his system.

He'd risked his life for this woman; she'd risked hers for him. No matter that she would never in a million years belong to him, belong in his world. No matter that she thought the worst of him. The adrenaline of the past day was zipping through his bloodstream like a drug.

He pushed her onto her back, cradling her head in his palm so she wouldn't be in the dirt, and lay on top of her. He didn't feel the sand sifting down his back, didn't feel the ache of his bruised ribs or the sting of his blistered feet. He only felt the softness of her thighs under his pulsing body, and thrust forward, grinding himself against her. For the first time in his entire sexual memory, he was ready to climax before so much as unzipping his pants.

"Rafael." He heard her gasp. He thought she wanted more, and he so wanted to give her more. He wanted to give her everything. He slid down her body and bit her nipple through her blouse and bra.

Olivia arched beneath him, unable to resist the drag of lust that pulled at her like an undertow.

Rafe heard the truck stop just outside the cave. It only made him more aroused. If these were to be his last moments, then he'd die planting his seed in this soft, beautiful—

"Rafe!"

Rafe froze.

"Rafe! For crying out loud, are you in there?"

It was Bobby. Rafe panted heavily into Olivia's face. He was afraid to move suddenly, afraid he'd embarrass himself beyond redemption.

"Yes," he said hoarsely. "We're in here."

"Thought so," Bobby said. "Get out. I've got something to show you."

There was a long silence from outside, while Rafe tried to gather his wits.

"Hold on a minute," Rafe said, not in any hurry to see Bobby or the vehicle he must have stolen. "We'll be right out."

Olivia looked down. Somehow, of their own volition, her knees had dropped open, her legs wrapping tightly around Rafe's hips. The front of her blouse was wet; it had come untucked from her skirt, and the back was probably filthy.

She pulled her lips through her teeth and bit down, closed her eyes tightly.

"Olivia?"

Tears leaked out the corners of her eyes. She couldn't hold them back. She'd so wanted to be able to stop him, but her body had betrayed her. She'd been writhing beneath him, a smuggler, a criminal, as aroused as she'd ever been in her life.

While her mind screamed imprecations, her body seemed not to care in the least what kind of man it coupled with.

Rafe's breathing was nowhere near normal, and every ounce of blood in his body was still pounding south, but he thought it best to try and make some effort toward getting off this woman and getting out of the cave. He shifted slightly, cutting off the moan that pushed past his clenched teeth.

"Olivia, we have to get out of here," he said carefully.

He felt something wet and warm drop onto his wrist where he held Olivia's head in his hand. "Olivia? *Mi'ja?*" he whispered, and brought his free hand to her face.

She was crying.

He rolled off her with something akin to panic, and came to his knees, hunched over in the narrow space. He was struck dumb for a moment, alarm and confusion swamping him.

"Are you hurt?"

Olivia shook her head.

"Are you...scared?" He was at a loss.

Olivia shook her head again. Rafe could barely see the small movement in the deepening dusk.

"Then why are you crying?"

Even as he asked, the truth hit him like a swift jab to his gut.

The princess. The damn princess. The daughter of San Diego's finest Mexican society family was upset because some nobody from the *barrio* had had his way with her in a squalid little sand cave.

Poor little princess. She'd probably never been on her back before with anyone who didn't have a doctorate or a Lexus or a condo on the beach.

Damn her. She certainly hadn't been crying when that bastard Cervantes had his hands on her.

Every lifelong insecurity about his place in Olivia's sort of world swamped him in that instant, made him forget that he'd forced her to believe the worst about him, that he'd terrorized and bullied her for his own purposes. In his mind, he was back in the *barrio,* running barefoot from immigration officers, keeping the secret of his parents' illegal status a dark and mortifying secret. Waiting for the day George would come back and redeem them all. And

Olivia Galpas was in the castle by the sea he imagined waited for her.

Damn her.

He locked his jaw against the self-doubt, bit down until it became a quiet, indignant rage. He was no longer a child, no longer a nobody.

"Pull yourself together, *princesa*," he said coldly. "I would have expected a little more control from a woman with your…experience."

Ah, a blow. Olivia felt it right between the eyes. His voice had gone flat and cool, and even in the dim light she could see his sharp features were honed by his customary scorn. Well, who could blame him for thinking the worst of her? She certainly thought the worst of herself.

It was her fault, all of it. Every mad thing that had happened since the day she'd arrived in Baja California. She'd been so enamored of Ernesto, so impressed by his manners and his attentions that she'd never looked beyond them to find out for herself the truth of the man beneath. And now she didn't know what to believe.

She'd been fascinated by this Rafael from the instant she'd seen him in that hallway, had let him kiss her, had kissed him back. She'd tossed herself in front of him, practically forcing him to use her to escape the *hacienda* and Ernesto's bloodthirsty goons, and now…this.

"My experience?" she whispered.

Rafe was deranged now. He felt like a caged animal. He wanted to claw his way out of the cave, away from her tears and his unmanly vulnerability, and run. Pace. Howl.

"Yes, Doctor." His hands were clenched into fists, his arousal finally subsiding. "With making love to criminals."

She stared up at him. "I've never made love to a criminal. Except you." If that had been anybody but Bobby out there she would have done it, Olivia thought. It left her reeling to admit it.

Rafe spoke through his teeth. "You're an idiot not to believe me about Cervantes."

"I've never made love to Cervantes."

Why that should ignite some small ember of relief in his heart, Rafe didn't know. It didn't matter whether she'd slept with Cervantes, he told himself harshly. It meant nothing to him that she hadn't. Nothing.

All that mattered was getting her out of here. He knew his partner well enough to speculate on Bobby's plans. They'd forget about trying to get the communications equipment on the beach, would instead drive the two hours to La Paz under cover of darkness. There, they could make direct contact with their informants, and get Olivia on a plane for the States at the same time.

It was a good plan, and one Rafe suddenly knew was critical to execute. He had to get her away from here, away from him. There was something about her that made him crazy, something that made the pure and simple fact that he'd known her just a matter of hours completely inconsequential.

"It doesn't concern me one way or the other, Doctor. We have to get out of here," he continued coolly. "We're going to get you to La Paz tonight. You can catch a plane in the morning."

A plane? She rolled onto her back, let her tears slide into her ears. *Home.*

She nodded. If she couldn't fight, couldn't defend herself against this man and his sudden change of mood, the least she could do was move. If she could manage to get out of this horrible little hole, she could be in La Paz in a matter of hours, and then the nightmare would be over. She slid to her knees.

"Okay," she croaked. "I'm ready."

But as they crawled from the cave into the faded evening light, Rafe and Olivia stopped in their tracks. Two armed guards stood with rifles pointed directly at them. Bobby, his hands bound behind him, sat in the back seat of a Land Cruiser, smiling sheepishly with his teeth together, eyebrows lifted.

"I didn't have much choice," he said, as though offering an apology.

When the larger guard ordered Rafe to drop his gun, Bobby from behind him shook his head, then nodded quickly at the second guard and gave an exaggerated wink. Realizing the second guard was a *federale,* Rafe walked forward, gingerly placed his pistol on the ground and nodded almost imperceptibly back to his partner.

Bobby suddenly kicked at the car door with a blood-curdling scream. As the big guard spun around to handle the troublemaker, Rafe snatched back his pistol, sprang forward and swung his weapon like a baseball bat into the back of the guard's head. The uniformed man dropped boneless, liked pile of dough, into the sand.

"That's my man." Bobby squealed with delight. "Give him a job to do, it gets done. It may take him nineteen hours to come out of a cave to do it, but it gets done."

Olivia, puzzled as to why the second guard was so passive, turned to him. "Who are you?" she asked.

"He's an old friend of mine," Bobby broke in, jumping out of the truck so the guard could untie him.

Rafe tied the unconscious henchman's hands behind his back and dragged him into the cave. To maintain the *federale*'s cover, Rafe tied him, too, gave him a lighter blow to the head—just enough to make a convincing lump— and dragged him into the cave, leaving a clear drag mark.

"We'll call and have them find you by morning," Rafe promised the *federale,* who nodded to say he'd be fine.

The road to La Paz from Aldea Viejo was paved most of the way. Unfortunately, they didn't take that road. They took every other one, however. Or so it seemed to Olivia.

They weaved their way down the coastline like drunken sailors, taking first one impassable dirt path, then turning onto another willy-nilly. Olivia closed her eyes after the

first few hairpin turns and washed-out gullies. She
stretched out on the back seat and pretended she was on a
sort of dusty roller coaster. Good practice, she thought dizzily. And she'd need practice in not facing reality if she
was ever going to get over the past few days here in par-
adise.

Olivia stared at the richly upholstered roof of the Land
Cruiser. It swayed, or she did. She couldn't tell which. But
she had to hang on to keep from getting spilled onto the
floor. Bobby drove just as she'd expected him to. Like a
madman. And he whistled most of the time, as though all
this were nothing more than the greatest of adventures.

After the first hour or so, though, Olivia began to appreciate the sentiment behind the whistling. No one was
talking, and Bobby was just covering up that fact with a
little incessant noise.

She sat up again when the road became particularly
rough, and Rafael looked back at her in surprise.

"I thought you were asleep," he said, his voice gruff.

"I didn't want to end up pitched into the front seat,"
she replied.

Rafe turned back to stare out the window. She'd caught
him off guard, or he never would have looked back at her.
She looked terrible in the dim illumination the dash lights
gave off: circles under her eyes, her cheeks sunken from
lack of food and water.

"Where are we?"

"Beats me," Bobby said, grinning at her in the rearview
mirror. "But we're heading south. I think."

"About half an hour out of Pinchilingue," Rafe said,
shooting his partner a glare.

Olivia gazed out the window to the complete darkness
beyond. "I can smell the sea. If it were light out, we could
see the island of Del Espiritu Santo. I did readings there
one summer when I was in college."

Her sad little voice caught at Rafe's hardened heart.

Damn her again. Rafe pitted his eyes against the night, willing La Paz closer.

"I don't know about you guys," Bobby said after a minute, "but I could use some food."

"What time is it?" Olivia asked.

Rafe looked at his watch. "Nearly ten."

"We've been driving almost three hours," Olivia said, mildly surprised. Perhaps she had dozed off for a while and hadn't known it. "Why so long? Aldea Viejo is only one hundred and fifteen miles from La Paz."

"Not on these roads," Bobby said. He swerved around a boulder the size of a Volkswagen in the middle of a washed-out path. Olivia felt the Land Cruiser shudder slightly as Bobby caught the back fender on the rock as he flew past. He laughed almost maniacally, and Olivia smiled in spite of herself.

"You're certainly taking good care of Ernesto's car," she commented wryly.

"I'm planning to drive it into the ocean in the morning," Bobby replied. "If I can find the ocean."

"Are we lost, then?"

"Probably not."

Rafe shot Bobby another frown. "Cervantes is likely watching the main road into La Paz," Rafe explained without looking at her. "That's why we're taking all these back roads. It takes longer, but it's safer."

"Plus, it's much harder on the vehicle," Bobby said cheerfully, "which is just an added bonus."

"We'll get something to eat in Pinchilingue," Rafe said. His own stomach was still knotted up, but he imagined the princess had to be starving.

She was. It had been more than twenty-four hours since the buffet at Ernesto's party. Olivia continued to stare toward the sea. Twenty-fours hours? That didn't seem like any time at all, really. And yet her life had been completely turned upside down in that short time. She'd barely had time to think. About much of anything, actually.

But now that she had a moment or two, questions popped into her frontal lobe like rifle fire.

Like why a small village police force owned a fleet of expensive Land Cruisers. Olivia smoothed her hand over the buttery leather upholstery. And why that hadn't occurred to her before now.

And why Ernesto needed fifteen men in uniform when Aldea Viejo was about the size of a San Diego housing tract—but with fewer people. He'd told her during those walks on the beach that his men were trained to catch the drug runners that used the coastline as a drop-off point between mainland Mexico and Tijuana. But she'd spent three weeks cruising up and down that coastline, and she'd never seen any of Ernesto's men on the water.

Why hadn't that occurred to her, either?

And another thing. Why in the world was she driving along the coast with two known outlaws, trusting them to get her to La Paz and on a plane home? She slumped back into her seat. Why didn't she bail out of the moving car at the nearest gully and take her chances with the sea and the desert?

And why the hell did the surly one with the perpetually grim expression appeal to all those little fantasies she obviously had been storing up without knowing it about tall, dark and dangerous men?

What was that syndrome—? Stockholm Syndrome, in which captives imagined themselves attracted to their captors, no matter how absurd that attraction would seem in the course of their normal lives.

She had Stockholm Syndrome.

Only, she wasn't technically Rafael's captive. She knew he was rescuing her as much as he was holding her hostage. He was taking her to La Paz so she could go home, and in keeping her was ensuring Ernesto's ire would never cool; endangering himself and Bobby and making certain they could never go back to Aldea Viejo.

She frowned at her reflection in the side window. There

was another explanation, then. She wasn't a stupid woman. She'd never before allowed her instincts or her emotions to rule her head. So why were they screaming at her now?

She shifted her eyes and stared at the back of Rafael's head. His short hair stood up in spikes. He had the shiniest hair, she thought. Even after all they'd been through, it practically shimmered. She absently fingered the loose braid over her shoulder.

All her life, she'd taken the wisest course. Not always the easiest, by any means, but always the wisest. Every brain cell she'd ever owned was counseling her now, cautioning her, admonishing her. It was an audible roar inside her head.

But her instincts and her emotions told her something entirely different. They pleaded with her to look at the man sitting so rigidly before her. To really look at him. There was something more there than her mind could comprehend, and her instincts and her emotions seemed to have no trouble deciphering it.

She was exhausted with the struggle. Soon enough, she thought, it would be over. She'd be on a plane home, and Ernesto Cervantes, whatever part he played in this drama, and this Rafael person would go back to their wretched lives and their bitter vendetta—and she'd never know what happened to them.

With a little sigh, she toppled back onto the seat. "Wake me when we get to Pinchilingue," she murmured, and fell asleep to the pitch and jerk of Bobby's mad driving.

The familiar scent of the sea woke her. Olivia sat up in her seat and looked around. They'd stopped at a small cantina on the edge of a typical-looking Baja town. Olivia could hear the water.

Bobby leaned nonchalantly against the hood of the Cruiser. Olivia suspected that nonchalance was as much a cover as the determined cheer. Rafe was nowhere to be seen. She pushed open the door and stepped outside. Another smell assaulted her nose, weakened her knees. Meat. And tortillas. And spicy salsa. She was ravenous.

"He'd better buy a lot," she said.

Bobby, as she knew he would, smiled broadly.

"We'll drive off to a quiet spot and cook him if he doesn't. Rafe tacos."

Olivia shook her head, but couldn't stop the smile that slid over her face. "You are so weird."

"Do you have to use the facilities?"

Olivia glanced at him. For a smuggler and an outlaw, he was certainly well spoken. *Facilities?* It was almost absurd to call any bathroom between Rosarito and La Paz anything so genteel as the "facilities."

"Yes."

"Okay. Come on."

"I know how to go by myself."

"I should hope so," he said, shuddering. He looked horrified, and Olivia had to smother another smile.

"You just want to keep an eye on me."

He slid her a sideways leer. "Sort of."

She wasn't falling for it. "I won't call Ernesto, you know."

"I didn't think you would."

"And I won't call the police."

Bobby looked around, chuckled. "I doubt there's any to call."

Olivia shook her head. "All right. Just come on, then. I want to wash my hands."

She used the bathroom at the back of the cantina, while Bobby dutifully stood guard outside. Whistling.

The "facility" was spotlessly clean and, unfortunately, had a mirror. Olivia stared at herself, dumbfounded. Not in her entire life, not once, had she ever looked so...awful.

Her hair was filthy, her clothes were worse. Her face was tracked with dirt and tears and small, vivid scratches. She dragged her fingers down her cheeks in shock. She was going to have to come up with one hell of a story to explain this when she got home.

Using the trickle of water that flowed from the sink faucet, she made what reparations she could to her face and hair and hands. She stared in dismay at the rest of her. The bottom of her dress was ragged where she'd ripped the bandage for Rafe's ribs. Her knees were dark with dirt, her ankles white with salt and sand.

And her feet. She groaned out loud. Her feet were encased in thick black socks that slumped forlornly around her ankles, and were stuffed like sausages into frayed and broken sandals. The sandals had come unbuckled somehow, but her feet were so swollen she hadn't even noticed.

No one in their right mind would let her on the plane looking like this.

Bobby pounded on the door of the bathroom. Olivia jumped at the sound.

"Are you done?"

"Is the food ready?"

A slight hesitation. "Not yet."

"Then I'm not done."

Olivia heard a bark of laughter and rolled her eyes. "Lunatic," she muttered under her breath.

After a minute, another knock came. "Food's done."

Olivia took a last look at herself. She'd made her dress much worse by attempting to sponge it off, but at least she had been able to wash herself and rinse out her mouth. She felt marginally better. Smelled infinitely better, she thought.

Bobby escorted her dutifully back to the Land Cruiser. The food was in a brown paper grocery bag on the front seat. Rafe was still nowhere to be seen.

Olivia dug into the food herself, handing Bobby a fat burrito, taking a taco for herself. She ate steadily for a minute, then asked around a bite, "Where is he?"

"He's making some phone calls," Bobby said.

Olivia stared at him. "Phone calls? Who is he calling?"

Bobby smiled. "You think just because we live an alternative lifestyle, we don't have people to call?"

"Alternative lifestyle?" Olivia nearly choked on her last bite of taco. "I'm assuming that means something different here than it does back in California."

Bobby tipped his head back and roared with laughter. "I hope so, too," he said.

Olivia watched him carefully, her eyes narrowing. He got that, did he?

"Bobby, where are you from?"

"Originally?"

"No, since last night. Yes, originally."

"Tepehuanes, in Durango."

"You were born there?"

Bobby nodded, rummaged around the sack for a taco. "Born and raised."

"That's funny. I know someone in Tepehuanes. He's about your age, in fact." She picked a name out of the air. "Tomas Escovar."

Bobby opened his mouth, bit off half the taco. He chewed slowly, watching her. "Don't know him," he said after he swallowed.

"That's funny," Olivia said, her eyebrows raising. "He's the doctor in the clinic there. Tomas Escovar? You've never heard of him."

"There is no clinic in Tepehuanes." Bobby shook his head, smiling. "You're not very good at this, Doctor."

Olivia frowned at him. "Well, it's my first time."

"Tomas Escovar? You could have come up with something better than that. How about Juan Sanchez? Or Jesus Martinez?"

Olivia chewed on her bottom lip, considering. "Those names are too ordinary. I wouldn't have known whether you were lying or not."

Bobby lifted a shoulder. "You still don't. It would have been worth a try." He ate the rest of his taco in one bite.

"I guess." Olivia sighed, took another taco from the

bag. The tortilla was warm and soft. "These are good. Do you know this place?"

"No."

"You have never been here before?"

Bobby gave her a patient look. "No."

"Do you go into La Paz very often?"

"No."

"Because it would take too long on your motorcycles?"

"Dr. Galpas?"

"Yes?"

"What is it, exactly, you want to know?"

Olivia worked her lip a little more. "Okay, here's the deal. I'm leaving Baja in the morning, right?"

"That's the plan."

"And I've already said I won't go to the police, or to Ernesto."

"And we appreciate that."

"But, Bobby, I just don't think I can go home without…knowing."

"Knowing what?"

Olivia levered off the bumper of the truck and began to pace. "I don't know. Why you never speak a word of English, but somehow make jokes that sound vaguely American? Why you live on the beach and ride dirt bikes around and tweak Ernesto Cervantes by stealing from him when he clearly outguns you and out-mans you?"

Bobby's chest puffed out. "Out-mans us?"

Olivia shook her head. "You know what I mean. And why you both seem so smart and capable, and still do something so stupid and dangerous for a living. Why Rafael—" She stopped abruptly.

Bobby smiled at her. "Why Rafe, what?"

"Why one minute he appears to be this horrible hardened criminal, and the next he's risking his life and yours to get me to La Paz, and he looks at me as though he's hurt that I think less of him for running drugs across the border." She met Bobby's eyes. "I'm a scientist. Everything in my world makes sense, even when it all seems like random data and inexplicable, unrelated occurrences. None of this makes sense, Bobby. You don't make sense, Rafael doesn't make sense, and the way I feel certainly makes no sense.''

Bobby shrugged. ''I don't know how you feel, Doctor, so I can't tell you why it makes no sense to you. But I can tell you, we're doing what we have to do down here.''

Olivia put her hands on her hips. ''Right there!'' she exclaimed. ''What you said right there! What do you mean, 'down here'? Down here from Durango? This is *up here* from Durango. See?''

''Bobby!''

Olivia whirled to face Rafael. He was glowering at his partner. ''That's enough,'' he said through his teeth.

Bobby grinned. ''She coerced me,'' he said.

Rafe walked over and opened the back door for Olivia. ''I'll bet.'' He looked at Olivia. ''Did you eat?''

''Yes. It was—''

''Use the bathroom?''

Olivia huffed out a breath. ''You guys are certainly—''

''Did she?'' he asked Bobby curtly, leaving Olivia with her mouth open.

He'd better stop interrupting every sentence, or she was going to have to take steps, Olivia thought.

Bobby lifted his shoulders, amused with both of them. ''I guess so. I didn't go in with her.''

Rafe turned back to Olivia. ''Get in.''

''You know—'' she began menacingly.

''Get in, Olivia. Right. Now.''

Olivia squinted at him. ''That's not going to work on me forever, you know.'' But she got in the back of the Land Cruiser.

Rafe shut the door and motioned Bobby to follow him. They walked several paces away from the vehicle. Rafe turned his back to Olivia, who he knew was watching them avidly from the backseat.

"Arrieta says Cervantes has something big coming in, night after tomorrow."

"How big?"

"Four hundred kilos of rock, maybe more."

Bobby whistled long and low.

"He's getting word through to Cervantes that we know about it, that we plan to pick up our 'share' at the drop-off."

"How's he doing that?"

"Through one of our guys on the inside." Rafe looked up as a patron left the cantina, waited patiently for him to pass. "I don't know how they pulled it off, but one of the *federales* was driving Cervantes around today. They got to within about fifty yards of where Olivia and I were. If it had been any of Cervantes's men, I think we would have been bagged."

"You think Cervantes will bite?"

Rafe glanced back at Olivia. "I think he's pissed enough now, yeah," he said wryly.

Bobby followed his gaze. "She's been convenient, hasn't she."

"What the hell is that supposed to mean?"

Bobby gave Rafe a steady look. "It means she came along and worked things up a little in Cervantes's tidy little world. It means we were making a little slow progress during the past three months, and a lot of very fast progress the past twenty-four hours. It means she's helped the investigation."

Rafe took a deep breath, realized his hands had gone to tight fists and his legs into a fighting stance. He would have taken apart his blood brother, his own cousin, if he'd intimated Olivia had been a convenience for *him*. A sexual release or something.

In that regard, she had been anything but convenient.

In fact, Rafe was very much afraid he was never going to get over how inconvenient Olivia Galpas had become, in every way.

Chapter 7

La Paz was wide awake when they sneaked into town. They'd ditched the Land Cruiser near a dump site on the outskirts of the city, though Bobby had argued vehemently for heading to the coast and driving it into the gulf.

"Why don't we go right to the airport?" Olivia asked.

Rafe didn't answer her, just got out of the cruiser and started walking.

Bobby turned to Olivia. "If we park the cruiser at the airport and someone spots it and calls it in to the local police, we're screwed. They'll call Cervantes and he'll know we're here. We'll all be in jail before he even leaves the *hacienda*."

"Oh." Olivia looked forlornly at her socks and sandals. Her feet were only just beginning to return to their normal size. "So, more walking?"

"More walking," he confirmed happily, and motioned her in front of him.

The three of them, looking terribly conspicuous to Olivia's thinking, walked into town, using the alleyways when they could, tracking across open yards and through parking lots when they couldn't.

Rafael walked ahead of her without speaking. He was, Olivia decided, still upset about what had happened in the cave. She'd finally had enough time to think about how annoyed she was about that. He'd been judging *her?* Ha!

Bobby walked behind her. His casual stroll was belied by his darting eyes. Every time Olivia glanced back at him, he was smiling pleasantly, his hands in his pockets, looking for all the world like a man out for an evening constitutional. Harmless.

Until she looked at his eyes.

They seemed to take in everything. Olivia knew if she stepped out of line, he'd be on her in an instant.

In fact, Olivia was beginning to suspect that of the two of them, Bobby might actually be the more dangerous. After all, anyone with an ounce of sense and decent eyesight would see Rafael's nasty disposition and physical menace coming a mile away. Bobby, on the other hand, could probably kill you while you were still laughing at one of his jokes.

Olivia shivered at that thought.

"Cold?" Bobby asked her.

"No, I was just—*oof!*"

She'd slammed into Rafe while looking back at Bobby. It was like hitting a cinder-block wall. Only warmer. She could feel the lump of his bandage under her cheek, wondered how his ribs were.

"Are you cold?" Rafael asked her.

"No. I'm fine."

Rafe looked down at her, skepticism in his dark eyes.

"I am not cold," she said slowly.

He scowled at her for a moment more, then turned without speaking and began walking again.

Olivia looked over her shoulder at Bobby, rolled her eyes. "Unpleasant man," she whispered conspiratorially to the smuggler behind her, and speculated briefly on just

how her life had so deteriorated that she was having small
confidences with drug runners.

Bobby grinned back at her, pinched his nose between
two fingers. "In more ways than one," he said.

"I heard that, *vato*," Rafe muttered.

They made their way toward the town square. Alleys
slowly became as crowded as the sidewalks, and there
were no more dusty back lawns to cut across. They began
to blend in with people already on the street.

"What night is it?" Olivia asked, when for the third
time she had to haul herself tight against a wall to allow
a group of people to pass.

"Saturday," Bobby said. "Date night."

Olivia pivoted on her heel. "There it is again!" she
accused. "*Date night?* What kind of thing is that for a
Durango man to say?"

Bobby just grinned at her, pushing her shoulder gently
to turn her back around. "Keep walking, Doctor."

Olivia knit her brows. "You know, I seem to walk
wherever and whenever you guys tell me, but I never know
why."

"We're getting a room for the night," Rafe said without
turning his head.

Olivia stopped again, stared at the back of Rafael's head.
"What?"

"We're getting a room." He realized she wasn't behind
him any longer and turned. She continued to stare blankly
at him. "A motel room? Do you have them in the United
States?"

"Are you insane?"

"You ask me that so often, *señorita,* I am beginning to
wonder," he said, and started walking again.

"I have to get home," she said, running to catch up
with his long strides. She jogged beside him. "I have to
get a plane out of here."

"How do you plan to do that when the airport is
closed?"

Olivia shook her head frantically. "The airport is closed? Why didn't you tell me that?"

He stopped, and she took two more steps before she realized he'd planted himself on the earthen sidewalk. "You're a PhD, are you not?" he asked mildly. "I assumed you would be able to figure out for yourself that the airport in La Paz, Baja California, would be closed at midnight. This is not LAX."

"I thought we were coming into town to get a taxi."

He started off again. "We're not. I need some sleep and a shower." He glanced down as she trotted up beside him. "And I assume you want to find something else to wear home in the morning, presuming we can get you a flight out."

"Oh, yes. I guess that would be easier to explain to my family than having to—" She stopped again. Rafe and Bobby stopped, as well, at the horrified look on her face. "I don't have my documents."

"You're okay," Bobby said. "You can fly into Tijuana and have someone collect you there and drive you across the border."

Since he was the only one who answered, Olivia looked at him, her eyes wide. "I don't have anything, though. Not my driver's license or my credit cards or any money. They won't even let me on the plane without identification. And how will I pay for my ticket?"

Bobby put his hand on her shoulder. "Rafe has lots of money. He carries it with him in big wads."

Rafe watched Olivia study him for a moment, her horrified look turning to one of aversion. He wanted to shake her. Right after he punched Bobby in the mouth. *Big wads.* What a yutz.

It's not drug money, princess, he wanted to tell her. *I get a paycheck the same as any working stiff. From the same government that funds your ocean experiments, in fact.*

Of course, he said none of that, but the muscles in his jaw worked with the effort not to.

She would let him buy her a ticket home, Olivia decided finally. Then, when she got home, she'd donate an amount equal to the price to a drug rehab shelter in San Diego. That would make it even, she thought miserably.

"Okay," she agreed, stretching out the word as a measure of her reluctance, "but what about actually getting onto the plane? A one-way ticket paid in cash for a woman with no identification is going to get me strip-searched."

Bobby closed his eyes dreamily. "We can only hope," he said. Rafe's head snapped around, but Bobby ignored him. When Olivia didn't laugh, though, he touched her lightly on the arm again. "We'll think of something in the morning. Once you're cleaned up and have some new clothes and use that American accent and that pretty smile of yours, no one will even think to question who you are." He let his eyelids droop suggestively again. "They may strip-search you, anyway, for the fun of it, but they won't ask for ID."

"Very comforting."

"Can we go, now?" Rafe asked roughly. "Or do you two want to hold hands here on the street until Cervantes actually drives past on his way to the fiesta?"

Olivia sighed and began walking. Bobby held back a moment, long enough to punch his cousin, hard, in the biceps. "She's had enough."

Rafe lifted a single brow. "Has she?"

Bobby's mobile mouth pursed in disgust. "Look, I don't know what happened in that cave back there, but whatever it was, she's holding up better than you," he said. "Ease up."

Rafe grabbed Bobby's shirtfront. "I don't need you to tell me how to talk to her."

Bobby stared him down. "I think you do."

Rafe eyed his partner a moment more, then let go of his shirt and backed up a step.

Bobby made a show of brushing out the wrinkle Rafe had put in his already hideously wrinkled shirt. "You should never have gone to that party."

"I know," Rafe replied shortly.

"I told you that."

Rafe once again struggled against punching his cousin in the face. "You were right," he admitted through clenched teeth.

"She would have married Cervantes and had an heir to the empire on the way before we busted him, and you never would have been the wiser. She could have come to the trial eight months pregnant and cried into a little hanky, and you wouldn't even have noticed her."

"Shut up, Bobby."

"If it's any consolation, she'll be gone in the morning, *carnal.*" He started off after Olivia. "Then we can get back to work," he tossed over his shoulder.

Rafe stared after them for a minute.

She'd be gone in the morning and they could get back to work.

Gone in the morning. Gone forever.

"Forget it," Olivia said.

Bobby squinted at her—trying to look mean, Olivia thought. And failing.

"You don't have a choice."

"I *do* have a choice. I'm not sharing a room with you."

"Come on," he wheedled. "We'll just sleep together. Just sleep. Nothing else. I promise."

Olivia had to laugh. "I've heard that line before."

"Come on, Doc."

Olivia worried her lip, looked over at Rafael. He was sliding bills across the worn counter of a registration desk. She didn't want to know where the money came from. Then again, maybe it was left over from when he was a picker. That wouldn't be so bad.

Olivia, amazed at herself, tore her gaze from him,

looked around blearily. The motel was tiny but clean, and in the thick of town, where their coming in tonight and their going out tomorrow was not likely to be noticed. She ran her tongue around her teeth, resisted scratching under her hair. She needed a shower in the worst way, but she didn't exactly relish the idea of sharing a bathroom with Bobby the smuggler, here.

"Why can't you guys take one room and I have one to myself?"

"You know why."

"I'm not going anywhere without you. I don't have any money." She pinched a fold of her skirt and lifted it an inch. "And I'm not really dressed for dancing, anyway."

"We can't leave you alone."

"You think I'll go to the police. Even after I've said I wouldn't."

Bobby shrugged.

"I'm not going to," she insisted. "Look, you don't know me very well, but allow me to let you in on a little secret about myself. I'm a practical woman. Eminently. I want to go home. I want to go home more than I've ever wanted anything in my life. I'm perfectly willing to let you guys and Ernesto do your own thing down here until at least one of you ends up in jail. I'm not going to go to the *federales* and risk spending another minute with you and *Señor* Congeniality over there."

"I thought you loved Baja," Bobby said, sounding wounded.

She bared her teeth. "I can't believe this."

"It's for your protection, too."

"Ha!"

"It is," he insisted. "Cervantes could track us here any time."

Olivia frowned. "You're just saying that to scare me."

"So, it scares you, does it?" Bobby grinned. "Had a little time to think during the leisurely drive down in the local police vehicle?"

"Oh, leave me alone, will you? I just want a shower. If I had a thousand dollars on me, I'd give it to you if you would just let me have a shower."

"Have you checked your pockets? You might have a thousand dollars on you and not know it—"

"Shut up, Bobby," Olivia said looking back over at Rafael. He was leaning against the registration counter, patiently awaiting the outcome of her argument with Bobby. A plastic shopping bag dangled negligently from one finger. He hadn't had that a minute before. She hoped he hadn't robbed the desk clerk.

She glared at him. She knew he fully expected Bobby to convince her to docilely take this order, just as she'd taken all the other orders he had given her.

Sort of.

Well, tough. If she was going to suffer, so should he. He could sleep outside her room all night, if he was so worried she'd turn him in to the police.

"Tell him, no dice."

Bobby dropped his head to his chest, groaned. "Just do it."

"No. I want my own room. If he doesn't trust me, he will just have to sleep outside my door."

Bobby shook his head, his chin brushing his chest in defeat. "Please?"

"No. And stop looking like that."

"You don't know how mad he gets."

"Yes, I do."

"Fine." He glared at her. "But I thought we'd established a certain rapport, here, Doc."

"Okay, now you're just saying stuff to make me crazy. 'A certain rapport'?"

"We use that phrase all the time in Tepehuanes," Bobby insisted. "It's an old Indian saying."

"It's French," she called after him, as he walked over to Rafe.

"She's not going for it," Bobby said.

Rafe chewed on the inside of his cheek. "She wants her own room," he repeated. He met her furious eyes for the first time since he'd crawled out of the cave. Better furious than disdainful, he thought. He could fight with furious.

"You can't blame her," Bobby was saying. "She hardly knows me."

"Better you than me, you would think," Rafe said thoughtfully.

"What am I, a eunuch?"

Rafe bit back a reluctant smile. "I don't worry about you. You know I'd kill you. After I made you suffer for a while."

Bobby gave Olivia a quick once-over, just to make Rafe suffer. "Yeah, well, I still have needs, man," he said.

This time Rafe had to smile. "You never will again if you touch her, my friend. I'll cut off your needs and feed 'em to the sharks."

Bobby chuckled. "Man, you have got it so bad."

"I'm just looking out for a countrywoman," Rafe stated blandly. "What else does she want?"

"Just her own room. She said you could sleep outside her door, if you like."

"Did you tell her to forget it?"

Bobby nodded. "But she's stubborn under all that girly hair and those big eyes. You can see how she made it to the top of her profession. I'll bet those guys at Scripps never knew what hit them."

"I'll bet they did," Rafe said. "Okay."

"Okay, what?"

Rafe didn't answer, just stalked to where Olivia was standing, mutinous and terrified.

"You can't leave the room," Rafe said curtly.

"I won't," she promised.

"There are no phones inside."

She narrowed her eyes. "I told you. I'm not going to call anyone. I'm not an idiot. Whatever else Cervantes is, and I'm by no means convinced of anything, *amigo,* he's also a sheriff, and I assume he will have called his cronies in La Paz by now. If I call the police, the likelihood is I'll be held in Mexico until all this is straightened out, right?''

"Yes," he said slowly, "but I meant that you can't call from room to room. If someone comes to your door, you won't be able to call me."

She lifted one small, dirty fist to his face. "I can pound on the wall."

That little hand, raised so bravely, just about broke through his anger.

"Fine," he said, his jaw working. He started toward their adjoining rooms. "We'll get you clean clothes in the morning when the shops open."

"It'll be Sunday," she reminded him. It had only just occurred to her.

"Then we'll get you clothes when the shops don't open," he muttered.

They reached the door to her room. Rafael opened it and went inside. Olivia followed him, turning on the wall light.

"You're going to steal clothes for me?"

He went into the bathroom, placed the shampoo and soap he'd bought from the desk clerk on the counter. "Would you rather go home looking like a street hag?" he called.

"A street hag? Listen, Mr. Charm, I don't want you to steal for me."

He came back into the room. "What difference does it make, Olivia? You know what I am—or you think you do." He wrenched open the closet door, checked inside. "What's one more crime?" he said, seething inside. He closed the closet door ever so carefully. He wanted to rip it off its hinges.

"You can't steal from these people. It's not the same as what you do with the...other thing. You can't go into some woman's little shop and take a dress that she needs to sell to put food in her children's mouths."

Nor would he have. Ever. He was not opposed to a little breaking and entering, of course, but he would have left money for whatever he'd taken. Enough and then some. Did she really think he was so anesthetized to the plight of the poor in Mexico?

He shook his head slightly. Well, of course she did. She thought him guilty of far more serious crimes than insensitivity.

Better that she did, actually. Better for everyone involved.

He squared his shoulders, summoned up a sneer. "You should have become a judge instead of a doctor, Olivia."

Olivia narrowed her eyes at him. He wanted a fight, did he? She was just fed up enough to oblige him.

"A judge! Look who's talking. You were pretty quick to judge me for what happened in that cave back there." She'd worked up a good head of steam over it, too. It was better than being miserable. "You've been furious with me ever since, as if you have any right!"

Rafe stared at her. "Me? Judging you?"

Olivia widened her eyes and bobbed her head. "Who do you think? It was just the two of us in there. I don't remember anyone else accusing me of having 'experience'!"

"You were crying!" he accused.

"So what? Excuse me for being a little overwhelmed. I've never made love to a criminal before," Olivia shouted.

You still haven't, Rafe wanted to yell back at her. Unless she counted the kisses she shared with Cervantes. But he kept his mouth clamped shut. He knew she wasn't in league with Cervantes, had known it since she'd thrown herself in front of him at the *hacienda.* But until she was safely on a plane to the States, it was too great a risk telling her the truth about his and Bobby's assignment, their quest. God only knew what the bastard would do to her if he somehow got hold of her again.

Not that he would, Rafe vowed silently.

"Well, life is full of surprises, *princesa*," Rafe said tightly.

"It certainly has been lately," Olivia conceded. "What happened in the cave…if you want me to say I'm sorry for something, you can forget it. This isn't 1850s Spain, you know. I don't have to apologize for a perfectly natural physical reaction. Besides, it was just as much you as me. More," she finished defiantly.

"Natural physical reaction?"

"Yes. I can't seem to help how my body responds to you. It doesn't make any sense," Olivia said. "So, too bad for me and too bad for you, chemically speaking, because we obviously have nothing else going on here."

"Wait a minute." Rafe shook his head to clear it. "Let me get this straight. You were crying because you were embarrassed by how you responded to my kissing you?"

"Not embarrassed!" Olivia protested vehemently. "Appalled! My head knows what a colossal mistake it is, being attracted to you. My body just seems to be taking a little more time to figure it out."

Oh, he couldn't hold out. Couldn't resist. The smirk he wore slid away. How could she be so honest about it? How could she reveal so much? He felt the same about her; his body craved her like a drug, even though his head told him how utterly hopeless it all was.

His entire life was about concealment, and her simple candor undid him.

Giving in to his own body, giving in to his heart, he placed his palms flat against the wall on either side of her, leaned in. "Listen to your body, Olivia," he urged. "Forget what your head tells you. It's wrong, anyway," he murmured. He didn't dare take her mouth. Her blouse had drooped below her collarbone, exposing soft, tanned skin. He kissed her there. "I'll never see you again after tonight," he said against her body.

The thought of that made his throat close curiously.

Even if he did see her, by some odd chance, it would never be the same. She would be back in her ivory tower, among the swells of San Diego Latino society. Dr. Olivia Galpas. And he would still be a peasant. A law-abiding peasant, but a peasant nonetheless. Never again would she be weak in his arms, her lashes soft on her cheek, her breath coming unsteadily.

"Olivia," he whispered, and kissed her where her lashes lay.

"No."

He heard that *no*. Perfectly. He pushed against the wall until he could look into her dark, flashing eyes. "Don't say no."

Was it only sexual desperation she saw in his eyes? she wondered fleetingly. She thought she saw more. Yearning, perhaps. Loneliness. She shook off the sensation, steeled herself. How could a man so criminal, so corrupt, touch her so deeply? What was wrong with her?

"I have to."

After a minute, he closed his eyes, sighed.

"Okay," he said finally.

She wanted to weep. In relief, and regret.

He stood back, looking everywhere but at her. "Don't go outside. For any reason."

Olivia shook her head. "I won't."

"Okay," he said again, stalling for time. He hated to leave her here. He heard Bobby rattling around in their shared room. A shower awaited him in there—and a soft bed, the first he'd slept in for weeks. But he couldn't bring himself to leave her alone. "Will you be all right?" he asked roughly.

"I'll be fine. I've spent a lot of time in little motel rooms at the ends of the earth."

He nodded. Of course she had. She was a well-traveled, well-respected scientist, a woman with all the experience in the world. It was ridiculous that he should be feeling so protective.

Only, she'd been in his care for too long now. In his care, in his head, definitely in his libido. Working slowly and inexorably into his heart—brave, smart, beautiful woman.

"Rafael," she said.

"I'm going," he said, and walked toward the door. It was better this way. He didn't deserve a woman like her, any more than Cervantes did. She stood at the light switch, watching him. He stopped next to her, but kept his eyes on the door. "I'm sorry, Olivia. For everything."

Then he was gone, leaving her with her breath stopped in her lungs and her heart beating like a wild bird against her chest.

It was hot in her room when Olivia woke the next morning. And bright. She sat straight up in her narrow, sagging bed and blinked in the direction of the thinly curtained window.

"Oh, no."

It had to be mid-morning, at least. She could hear the sounds of street life outside her door; of men and women long awake and going about their business. She was supposed to be on the first flight out of La Paz this morning— that was the plan.

Apparently, she'd slept through the plan.

She whipped the worn sheet from her legs and scooted out of bed. She took another quick shower just to make up for the two or three she'd missed, and combed out her hair. It had dried on her pillow during the night and one side was flat while the other puffed out in a wavy mass, but she hardly noticed. She began to plait it tightly to her head, smoothing out the odd bumps as she went. She'd wash and dry it again when she got home.

Her fingers fumbled in her braid.

Home. It seemed impossible she'd be home today. Had it only been three weeks since she'd arrived in Mexico, three weeks since she'd met Ernesto? Less than three days since she'd met Rafael?

Both men had changed her life profoundly.

Home seemed almost unreal to her now. Oh, she could picture it perfectly: the bougainvillea that swept along the iron railing on the second story; the view of both the ocean and the eucalyptus trees of Balboa Park; the sound of her brothers and sisters running across the tile floors toward some mischief that she, as the eldest sister, was bound to disapprove of. She loved the house almost as much as she loved the people in it. It was why she'd allowed her parents to convince her to stay there when she wasn't on a tiny boat in the middle of some ocean somewhere. It was convenient, beautiful, and the only place she'd ever really wanted to live.

But it wasn't real anymore—not the way it had always been when she'd come back to it after a long assignment.

This seemed real, she thought, looking into the mirror. It was insanity, and she told herself she couldn't wait to see it end, but this was real. Being with Rafael was real. The tense conversations and whispered words and powerful kisses—those were real. They scared her, and they had to stop—today—but they were more intense, more stirring, than anything she'd ever had with any other man.

It was only the danger, she knew. The thrill of the unknown. The circumstances. She *knew* it. Her excellent brain, which had never failed her, told her. But it simply didn't seem to matter.

She scrubbed her teeth with her finger and dried her mouth. There was no sense even thinking about it. The fact was, it was nearly over. This morning she'd get on a plane and leave Mexico. And Rafael and Ernesto—bad guys, good guys, whichever they were—would be nothing but an ache of regret in her heart and a stab of shame in her gut.

She padded back into the tiny room to gather up her

filthy clothes and put them, reluctantly, back on her clean body.

Her dirty clothes were gone.

On the bed, where she wouldn't be able to miss it, was a bag. Attached to the bag with a staple was a handwritten receipt for one dress, a pair of panties and a bra, and one pair of white socks.

Olivia sat down on the edge of the bed, clutched the bag to her naked chest and told herself under no circumstances was she to cry.

Chapter 8

Rafael and Bobby were already dressed and waiting for her, when she left the motel room, dressed in the not-stolen clothes. They looked dreadfully uncomfortable in their own starchy new clothing, and they smelled faintly of chemical dyes and mothballs. But Bobby no longer looked like a reprobate from clown college, and Rafael looked cooler, dressed in a white cowboy shirt and denims instead of a black turtleneck and black jeans.

Her own dress was plainly fashioned and of an unappetizing orange color, but it felt marvelously clean against her skin. She wished Rafael had thought to buy her a little makeup, but she decided she could get around having to explain to her mother why she had left the house without mascara by having someone pick her up in Tijuana and take her by her office first.

She was willing to take just about any precaution to keep her mother from knowing about the past three weeks.

She spread out her arms. "Ready?" she asked.

She looked beautiful, Rafe thought. Pretty and bright as any American tourist, in that silly dress.

He'd pounded on the door of a small shop in the heart of La Paz early this morning, until someone had come out of the back and opened the door. He'd flashed a fistful of American cash through the window first, to make the decision to open up on a Sunday morning a little easier for the shopkeeper.

The man had had a miserable selection of mostly ancient, mostly dusty, mostly men's work clothes. The dress Olivia wore was the single article of women's clothing he could find that he thought might fit her. It was a terrible color, but she looked wonderful in it. Her hair gleamed, her face glowed. She looked as she had when he'd first seen her.

"It fits," he said.

She looked down. "Yes. Thank you. And for...for the other thing."

He nodded. *The receipt.* It had been a little gift. Maybe it would help to ease the shame he knew she felt about being with him.

He glanced down at her feet. "What about your socks?"

Olivia held out the balled socks. "My feet aren't swollen anymore. The sandals are fine."

"That's because it's first thing in the morning. They're bound to hurt by this afternoon. Keep the socks."

"I don't have anywhere to carry them. Besides, I'll be home by this afternoon."

Right. Why did he keep forgetting that? She wouldn't be with him by this afternoon. She'd be hundreds of miles away, laughing about her adventures over margaritas in some San Diego hot spot, most likely. Rafe took the socks and stuffed them in the front pocket of his jeans.

The sun was already beating down on them, and the dust from the unpaved side streets was a haze that would only get worse as the day progressed. Rafe scanned the street briefly.

"We'd better get going. We need to get through town and to the airport before *siesta*. We want to be as inconspicuous as possible."

"Lucky she's wearing that orange dress, then," Bobby observed.

"It was the only one they had in her size," Rafe said sharply.

Olivia looked down, fingered the fabric. "It's bright," she conceded. She looked up at Rafe. "I don't have to put the other clothes back on, though, do I?"

"No. It's fine." He glared at Bobby, who snickered. Rafe suspected it was becoming Bobby's mission in this situation to appear as obnoxious as possible. Rafe, as his superior officer by one grade, would have to tell him later what a damn good job he was doing of it.

"How are we getting there?" Olivia asked.

"We'll have to take a taxi."

There were plenty around. March was a good month for tourists in La Paz. Sun worshippers from the north were still chasing the Baja desert sunshine.

Rafe jerked his head toward the main plaza, and Bobby loped obediently off to flag down one of the taxis that cruised for sightseeing or shopping tourists.

Olivia looked around, pretending interest in everything but the man in front of her. "I've always liked La Paz," she mused quietly. Rafe watched her. It was his last chance to memorize her delicate features, her exotic, almond eyes, the creamy tint of her skin. He'd had such a short time with her, and he wanted to remember everything.

"You can't come back here, Olivia," he said after a minute.

She gazed up at him, the sun and the statement making her blink. "What do you mean, I can't come back here?"

"Until Cervantes is dead or behind bars, you can't come back to La Paz. He'll know you've been with me. He'll know I've told you about him. You can't come back to Baja at all."

Olivia's heart dropped like a brick in her chest. She felt suddenly as though she'd been running again and couldn't catch her breath. "I have to come back," she choked out. "I...I have to come back next fall for a follow-up study."

Rafe shook his head. "Unless Cervantes is in jail, or someone's killed him, it won't be safe."

"Rafael," she said urgently, "you don't understand. I'm in Baja all the time. For the next six years I have to be here twice a year. We're doing current studies in the gulf. Data has to be taken on a regular basis."

"Someone else will have to take it."

"No one else can take my data," she cried, feeling desperate. Rafe seemed to look around to ensure she'd attracted no attention, but Olivia ignored the significance of the look. "That would mean giving up my promotion, my team."

Rafael's expression hardened. "Then give them up, Olivia. If you come back here before he's put in jail, he'll kill you."

"No." She shook her head frantically, as though if she denied his words forcefully enough, they would not be true. "He won't. Even if what you've told me is true, I'm an American citizen."

He gave her a scornful look. "Don't be stupid."

Olivia stared up at him. "This is insane. I have to come back to Baja in just a few months. It's my job."

"Is your job more important than your life?"

"Yes! No, I mean, that's not a question I can even answer."

Not a question she could answer? Rafe thought he detected the slightest red haze in his normally clear vision. Not a question she could answer?

"Are you out of your mind?" he whispered furiously. "Your life cannot be separated from your job?"

"My job is my life. It's my whole identity. It's everything I've worked for since I was a child." She gripped his arm. "Rafael, you can't understand. I have worked so

hard for credibility. It has taken me years to make people
understand how serious I am. How smart I am. And still
I get trotted out to press conferences and cocktail parties
as the token Latina.

"This was my first team, my first assignment in charge.
Not as the assistant scientist, but as the boss. I know it
was mostly because of my Spanish, my connection with
Mexico and the fact that my name opens some doors here.
But I earned it, too, with long days on a thousand different
boats in a dozen different waters. If I have to tell my colleagues that I can't go back to my job in Baja because I
got mixed up with a bunch of drug-running Mexican bandits, I will never get another team or another assignment
of my own again."

He glared at her, putting every ounce of menace into
the look. If she wouldn't listen to reason, maybe she'd
respond to good old-fashioned intimidation. He understood
what she was saying, of course. He, too, had dedicated his
life to a very specific goal. He'd earned every promotion,
when often the brass had thought of him as just another
barrio boy who could translate for the border patrol.

If, after all that work, someone had tried to tell him he
couldn't come to Mexico, couldn't come after Cervantes,
he would have told them to go to hell—and he'd have
come, anyway.

But this wasn't him. This was Olivia. And the thought
of Cervantes finding her, hurting her, made him nuts.

"I don't care if you never get another assignment," he
said, wearing his fierce, implacable stare. "I don't care if
you never take another current reading in your life. I don't
care if you get fired, if you have to wash dishes to make
a living. You are not coming back to Mexico until Cervantes is behind bars." He poked her in the chest with his
middle finger. "And *then* only if I call you personally and
tell you it's safe to come back."

She stared at him, dumbfounded. "What are you talking
about?"

He realized too late what he'd said. He straightened, raked his fingers through his hair, buying time. "What am I talking about?" he bluffed. "I'm talking about your life, Olivia."

"No." She frowned up at him. "I mean, why would you know when it was safe for me to come back? Why would you call me? Why would Ernesto go to jail, and not you or Bobby? What did you mean by that?"

He looked around for their taxi. Where the hell was Bobby? "I only meant that you have to take this as seriously as I do. You don't know what Cervantes is like, Olivia. You've only seen that smarmy charm of his."

Olivia's brows snapped together. "Smarmy?" He'd never spoken a word of English to her, but he tossed words like *smarmy* around?

"He's insane, Olivia. And not just the regular kind of insane. I'm talking about a man who kills people without a second thought. Who terrorizes his little town until they're afraid to so much as talk to the police or the drug agents out of fear for their families. He's not like the rest of us," he added, intentionally including himself in the rundown of moral degenerates, if only to erase that dangerously considering look from her face. "He's not in it just for the money, although he makes more of that than most small countries. He's in it for the power. If he finds out you know about him, or if he even suspects it, which I imagine he already does, your American citizenship and your PhD and your family name aren't going to mean anything. He'll put you on a little boat and set you on your precious gulf—and you'll never be seen again."

"I am just as dangerous to you, Rafael. Why haven't you put me on a boat and set me adrift? Why are you helping me? I could just as easily turn you in, make the police suspicious of you."

Rafael couldn't possibly answer that question. He didn't have a clue. Even if he had been the kind of man she thought he was, even if she had posed that kind of threat to him, he would still be sneaking her out of the country, would still be keeping her safe. He couldn't imagine doing anything else.

So he didn't answer. He only looked down at her, at her hair and how it gleamed in the sunlight, at her lovely face and the brilliance in her eyes and the strong, stubborn set of her chin.

He lifted a hand, brushed back a strand of thick hair that had escaped its ruthless braid. *"Princesa,"* he said. "If anyone has been set adrift, it is me, I think."

A horn blasted, making them both jump.

Rafe broke eye contact first, watched the taxi Bobby hired pull to the curb, while Olivia watched Rafe.

The man quite simply devastated her. Just when she had him pegged—a desperado, a drifter, a ruthless smuggler— he turned out to be something entirely different. He pushed her and bossed her and dragged her around, scaring her out of her wits most of the time. Then he tipped up her chin or brushed back her hair, and he'd be someone else. Someone who moved her.

He was moving her, now. In more ways than one.

"Hey!" Olivia snapped, as Rafe practically tossed her into the back of the cab beside Bobby, giving curt instructions to the driver as he scooted in next to her.

They drove in silence out to the airport, which was really not much more than a single runway and a tiny terminal.

The taxi dropped them off, as Rafe had instructed, at the entrance to the terminal parking lot. After the driver gave them all a curious once-over, he circled around and parked behind several other taxicabs to wait for the next wave of American tourists to come filing out of the terminal, eyes blinking in the sun.

Rafe, Olivia and Bobby stood on the asphalt in a small knot, Olivia sandwiched carefully between the men. Bobby and Rafe faced outward, surveying the parking lot.

They nodded at one another briefly, and Bobby faded into the low-growing windbreak trees that ringed the lot.

"Where is he going?" Olivia asked.

"To the terminal."

"Is this all necessary? I mean, Ernesto doesn't seem to be the kind of man who could or would operate covertly. If he were here, wouldn't he be here with some of those Land Cruisers he likes and fifty men?"

"Probably," Rafe grunted. "And if you don't stop calling him 'Ernesto,' I'm going to have to gag you."

Olivia ignored the threat. She'd found, over the past few days, that his threats held no real peril for her. "Then why do all this?"

"Because Cervantes isn't the only sheriff in Baja, Olivia." And except for a handful of Mexican federal agents, no one knew he and Bobby were not actually drug runners. He didn't particularly care to be shot down in the line of duty while trying to buy Olivia a plane ticket. Not much glory in that for his family, Rafe thought.

"Oh," Olivia said. She watched him as he followed Bobby's wary progress through the trees toward the terminal. Every few seconds he would focus on the taxi drivers, who were out of their cars now, smoking and chatting. His beautiful black eyes were never still.

"How can you live like this?" she said, almost to herself.

He didn't look at her. "You get used to it," he said.

"I couldn't get used to it."

He flicked his gaze over her. "You've had a choice, *señorita.*"

Ah, the other Rafael, now. The snide, irritable Rafael. She wanted to be angry with him, but she suspected he was trying to provoke her. She didn't have the heart to rise to the bait.

"Everyone has a choice, really."

Rafe didn't respond to that. Mostly because he wasn't sure he believed it was true.

"Come on." He grabbed her hand and started walking toward the terminal.

Olivia looked around for Rafael's partner. "Where's Bobby?"

"He's inside. Everything checks out all right. We can go in."

"How can you tell?"

"Because Bobby told me."

"How? I can't even see him."

"It doesn't matter if you can see him, *princesa*," Rafe said absently, keeping his eye on the cabdrivers as they passed. "I can see him."

"You guys have some sort of secret code, don't you."

Rafe laughed shortly. "No. But we grew up together. You get to where you can communicate pretty well without having to say much. Very useful in our business."

They entered the terminal. It was not air-conditioned, and felt warmer inside than it did outside. Olivia was grateful for her summer dress, orange though it was. She still could not see Bobby, though, and that fact gave her the funniest little tickle on the back of her neck. She'd had that tickle before...oh, right. Well, maybe she did have women's intuition, after all.

"Where is he?" she whispered.

"You don't need to whisper, Olivia." He looked around. "There's no one here."

"Then why doesn't he come out?"

"Because that's not the plan."

"Then what is the plan?"

Rafe sighed. "I know you like to know everything, Dr. Galpas. But try to curb that impulse just this once."

"Fine. But what if there aren't any flights to Tijuana today? Then what?"

"Then we make a new plan." Rafe read the departure schedule above the Mexican Airlines counter. "But there is a flight out, this afternoon." He glanced at his watch. "Three hours from now. Are you hungry?"

"Uh, yes. I am."

"Okay. Let's go."

She dug in. This man had been dragging her all over Baja for two days now. She didn't want to go another step without knowing where she was going.

"Wait a minute. What about my ticket?"

"We're not going to buy it until the last minute. If Cervantes or anyone else is looking for you, it's too easy for them to check with the airline agents. If they know you're holding a ticket for the 2:45 flight, they'll just wait around here until you show up to get on the plane."

"But if the plane is sold out?"

He raised his eyebrows. "What do you suppose the chances are of that?"

Olivia looked around the sleepy little airport. There were only half a dozen or so other people in the whole place: two ticket agents behind a counter, a slow-moving older man cleaning out ashtrays in the lobby, and a small knot of tourists enquiring, in very loud English, about their lost luggage, which had somehow ended up in Guadalajara. It occurred to Olivia that the taxi drivers would have a very long wait for a fare.

"And if it's sold out, we just wait for the next one. Or you go out on the 4:24 to Cabo San Lucas, then take a flight from there tonight. They run planes back and forth to Tijuana all the time down there."

"You're not concerned by this?" she asked him. "You're not concerned that we have to hang around for three more hours like sitting ducks, while Ernesto is looking for us?"

"Concerned?" He felt a petty satisfaction that some of Olivia's fears had transferred away from him, at least partially, and onto Cervantes. Whether she wanted to admit it or not. "Are you concerned?"

She opened her mouth. Nothing came out at first, she was so astounded by his relaxed attitude. Wasn't this the man who brooded over every little thing? "What if he finds us?"

"Then he finds us. We'll deal with it then. I'm kind of surprised he hasn't tracked us down already," he added calmly.

"Oh, God."

"Look, Olivia, there's nothing more we can do. We're at the airport, we know when the flight is, we've ditched the Land Cruiser and we have new clothes." He smiled. "What else is there to do but to have lunch?"

"Worry. Obsess. Plan for contingencies." She met his mild stare. "Okay. I guess you're right."

He gave her a patient smile. "I can rise to the occasion when I have to."

They bought tacos from one of the small travel trailers that worked every town in Baja. It was parked just outside the east entrance to the parking lot, awaiting the airport workers and cabdrivers and occasional intrepid tourist that made up the bulk of its business. Olivia and Rafe stood under the scrawny awning of the trailer and ate from paper sacks.

Olivia finished a second hot-sauce-soaked taco and peered into the sack. "Is that it?"

Rafe grinned. "Want more?"

"No. I was just wondering if you were going to take any back for Bobby."

"Don't worry about Bobby's stomach. He always manages something."

"What are we going to do until 2:45?"

Rafe took her by the hand again. It was starting to feel very comfortable, holding hands with this woman every time they took more than two steps in any direction. He wondered how long it would take him to forget the feel of her small hand in his. He frowned. Fifty, sixty years ought to do it.

"We're taking a *siesta*," he said, and tugged her toward the trees.

"A *siesta?*" she asked incredulously as, once again, her sandals filled with dirt. She hopped along awkwardly behind Rafael, trying to kick the dirt from her shoes at every other step.

"When in Rome, do as the Romans do," Rafe said.

Olivia stopped dead in her tracks. "What?"

Rafe yanked on her hand until she fell in behind him again. He was glad she couldn't see his flash of a grin. "That's an old Mexican saying."

"It is not," she muttered. "Any more than 'a certain rapport' is. I think you and Bobby watch too much American television. You're losing your culture."

"This looks comfortable."

"It does?" Olivia looked around. Nothing but sandy dirt and scrubby trees. "I can't believe you expect to take a nap out here."

"Safer than inside. And cooler." He scouted for a low spot on the other side of the embankment that circled the parking lot. "Here's a good spot." He hunkered down, pulled her to her knees next to him.

"It's dirty," she said, not even bothering to object to being yanked to the ground. Again. Perhaps she was developing a tolerance, the way people did to malaria. "What about my dress?"

"It's mostly sand, *princesa*. It'll brush out." He let go of her finally, crossed his arms beneath his head and lay back. The rise of the embankment provided cover from anyone looking for them from the direction of the airport parking lot and terminal.

Olivia stared down at him. "Are you really going to sleep?"

"Unless you want to fool around," he said. He opened one eye, looked up at her astonished face, and closed it again. "No, I suppose not."

"We're out in the open, here, Rafael." She snapped her head back to watch a plane descend almost on top of them. The noise made her ears ring.

"Not really," he said, after the plane hit the runway. "The trees hide us from above, the embankment hides us from the terminal, and unless someone decides to come by and water these things, I doubt anyone is going to be walking by."

"What about Bobby?"

Rafe opened his eyes and gave her a brief glare before closing them again. "Stop worrying about Bobby. He doesn't need a mother."

"Fine." She chewed on her lower lip for a minute. "Do you have your watch set so we'll wake up?"

"No."

"Will you wake up?"

"I don't know. Probably."

"That's not funny. I have to get back to the States. What if someone tried to call the motel in Aldea Viejo and found I never came back after Ernesto's party?"

"I don't think that motel has a phone," Rafe said reasonably. "Besides, what would they think if they did know?"

"I guess they'd think I stayed with Ernesto," she offered quietly, after a minute.

Rafe made a sucking sound with his front teeth. "There you go," he said tightly.

Olivia drew her knees to her chest. "I probably would have," she said. "Eventually."

"Stayed with him?"

"Married him."

Rafe took the blow like a man. It was, after all, no more than he'd expected of her. But his hands went to fists behind his head. He'd have shot them both before he'd have let Olivia marry that dirtbag. "Lucky for you I happened along, then."

Olivia shot him a wry look, though she knew his eyes were still closed. "Yes, you've been very lucky for me," she said blandly.

Rafe didn't answer. His breathing had evened out, but

Olivia knew he wasn't asleep. Didn't really think he intended to sleep. She knew his methods well enough by now to know they were merely killing time as safely as possible before her flight.

As he had for days now, he was keeping her safe. Baffling, but true. She wished she could figure it out. Take the data in front of her and make sense of it. It was what she did best. What she lived for.

She hugged her knees, listened to people talking as they spilled out of the terminal behind her. Their voices were a low hum of mixed English and Spanish, and she decided the little plane must have come in from the border. She hoped some of the passengers took taxis into town; their driver had looked like he could use the money.

"Rafael, why are you doing all this for me?"

"All what?"

"Getting me here, buying my ticket home. If what you've told me about Ernesto is true, you're saving my life."

"You saved mine."

"Oh. That's true."

"Besides—" he began, then abruptly stopped.

"Besides what?"

"Nothing."

"Besides *what?*"

Rafe watched her. A couple of hours more and she'd be gone. He'd never see her again, and she'd spend the rest of her life thinking he was a drug runner and a lowlife. He didn't think he could live the rest of *his* life with that.

It was foolish, telling her the truth, but he'd done many foolish things since he'd run into Dr. Galpas two nights ago. He'd kissed her, had breathed in the scent of her, had lain on top of her so every impression of her body was molded to his, never to be forgotten.

"Besides," he began again. "Since we actually made it to the airport, and you'll be leaving soon—"

"We weren't supposed to make it to the airport?"

"Yes, we were supposed to, but there were many mitigating factors that could have prevented us. Anyway, since we're here—"

Olivia peered at him in the shadows the trees made. "Mitigating factors?"

"Will you pay attention? I have to tell you something."

"But mitigating factors? What kind of smuggler are you, anyway?"

"That's what I'm trying to tell you," Rafe said somewhat impatiently. No wonder the woman became a scientist. She asked questions about everything. "I'm not who you think I am."

"Who are you?"

His jaw worked for a minute while he lay before her. Oh, dangerous waters, these. In more ways than one, he was just beginning to realize. For his mission, and his heart.

"It may be a little hard to believe." He sat up slowly, pushed his hand through his hair. "I'll tell you what I'm not, first. I'm not a—"

He didn't finish his sentence, because Bobby slid down the embankment almost on top of him. Rafe was on his knees before Bobby even came to a stop.

Olivia stared at them both, stunned by Bobby's sudden appearance.

"They're here," Bobby said, breathless.

"Where?"

"In the terminal. In the parking lot."

"How many?"

"What are you not?" Olivia asked Rafe. She knew she should be somewhat concerned about the reappearance of Ernesto Cervantes in her life, but she really wanted to know what Rafael had been going to say. It seemed vital he tell her what he was *not*.

They ignored her. "Eight guys and Cervantes," Bobby said. "They came in two vehicles. One guy's guarding the cruisers, the others have split up through the airport. One guy's searching the parking lot.''

Rafe and Bobby hit the dirt and slithered up the embankment. ''Uh, Rafael?'' Olivia called in a loud whisper. ''Before you do anything rash, you were saying something before—?''

Rafe wasn't listening. He was busy scrutinizing the parking lot and the front of the terminal. ''Where's his backup?'' he whispered.

Bobby shrugged. ''Guess he didn't call anybody in.''

''Dammit.''

They slid backwards down the embankment.

''Why is that bad?'' Olivia asked in a low voice, looking from one man to the other. They certainly seemed serious. Even Bobby. Perhaps she should pay attention to the matter at hand. ''Isn't it a good thing he didn't bring any more police in on this thing? That's fewer people to contend with.''

She didn't stop to consider why she wasn't scrambling up that embankment herself, flagging down the boys in khaki and flinging herself headlong into Ernesto Cervantes's burly arms.

''Normally, we'd be happy with that,'' Bobby answered. ''But we got you, now, Doc.''

''Me? What do I have to do—? Oh, I get it.'' A shudder lifted the hair on the back of her neck. ''He doesn't want me to talk to any other police officers. You two he can shoot as drug runners from his district. Me, he'd have a tougher time explaining away.''

Bobby tapped her temple with a blunt index finger. ''You're not as dumb as you look, Doc,'' he said.

''Thanks.'' She turned to Rafael. ''Now what do we do?''

''So you believe us, Doctor? About your shark out there?''

Olivia pulled her lips between her teeth. She hadn't realized how much she'd come to depend on these two, how much she'd come to trust them. "I guess I do. Though I'm sure to regret it."

Rafe grinned briefly. "I'm sure you will, too." He looked her up and down, consideringly. "I kind of regret that dress, myself," he said. "The dirty white one would have been better."

"For what? What are we going to do?"

"Well, *princesa,* first thing we're going to do is ask you the basic question every man asks a woman sometime in his life."

Her throat went dry. "Which is?"

"You ever stolen a car?"

Chapter 9

Olivia's palms were sweating. So was her neck. She thought it very likely that she was sweating in the roots of her hair. She had never been so terrified in all her life.

She was creeping along behind a known criminal, a drug dealer, on her way to steal a taxicab so they could get away from a man who, for all she actually knew, really was a law-abiding peacekeeper. A man of character and principle who was only concerned with justice and her well-being.

Only, he wasn't. Rafael had told her he wasn't. Rafael—who'd seduced her in less time than it usually took her to pick out her work clothes in the morning, who was as dangerous a man as she'd ever known, who didn't appear to give a damn about justice or anything else that didn't put money in his pocket—had told her Ernesto Cervantes was a terrible person who would happily kill her. And she had—reluctantly, unwillingly—come to believe him.

Her life, she decided, was wildly out of control.

Rafe came to a sudden halt at the edge of the parking

lot. The trees partially concealed them, Olivia knew, but it would only take one glance from the felonious-looking man standing next to Ernesto's dusty Land Cruiser to end this whole mad plot.

She began to tremble, and found, to her horror, that she was completely unable to swallow. She put her free hand—Rafe was holding the other one, as usual—to her neck and clawed frantically.

Rafe looked down at her. "Stop that."

"I can't swallow," she rasped. "I think something's wrong with me."

"Steady, *princesa,*" Rafe whispered. "It'll be over in a minute."

"That doesn't comfort me."

He squeezed her hand. "Come on, Bobby," he urged under his breath. "Come on."

Olivia heard an odd grinding sound, then the faint *ping* and *crash* of metal against metal—like pots and pans banging together—She turned her head just in time to see the taco trailer go over on its side, making a horrific racket. She stared, wide-eyed.

How in the world had he done that? Of all the diversions she'd imagined Bobby creating for them, turning over the taco trailer was not one of them.

Rafe, unbelievably, chuckled. "Good boy," he said. He yanked Olivia abruptly forward. "Come on."

They ran like mad toward the taxi stand, while Ernesto's lookout and the parking lot searcher started toward the taco stand to investigate the sudden, strange disturbance. The taxi driver was walking numbly in that direction, as well. As diversions went, Olivia supposed it was an excellent one. No one seemed to be able to believe their eyes. One madman was running in circles around the overturned trailer, screaming imprecations and brandishing a long pair of metal tongs as if they were the sword of David.

There was, of course, no sign of Bobby anywhere near the ruckus.

There was one cab left. It belonged, Olivia saw, to the hapless driver who had brought them in. As Rafe shoved her in the driver's seat and climbed in after her, she made a mental note to write down the number of the cab so she could make some sort of reparation after she got home for the fares he was bound to miss. She groaned aloud. Rafe's lifestyle was racking up quite a bill.

"Keys," Rafe muttered, reaching under the steering wheel. He laughed again as the engine roared to life. "God, I love Mexico! Hold on."

Tires shrieked as Rafe shot out into the now nearly empty parking lot. As they whipped past Ernesto's pair of thugs and the astonished, slack-jawed taxi driver, Olivia closed her eyes and shrieked a little herself. Rafe had very nearly run over all three of them.

He careered the wrong way out the front entrance, just as gunshots exploded behind them.

"Open your door," Rafe shouted at her.

Olivia obeyed without thinking, shoving the door open with her shoulder, as Rafe abruptly slowed the car. Off balance, she slid to the floor, her head almost connecting with the blurred rush of pavement.

Rafe grabbed her ankle. "I told you to hang on," he yelled, as she struggled to right herself.

"You told me to open the door," she screamed back.

Bobby, laughing like a loon, was running next to the car. With one leap, he was inside and slamming the door shut behind him.

Olivia lay sprawled at his feet, her butt on the floor and her limbs sticking up in four different directions.

"Hey, Doc," Bobby said. "You need a hand?" He hauled her back up onto the seat.

"Get her head down, for God's sake," Rafe snarled at Bobby. He took a quick glance in his rearview mirror. "Okay, they're after us."

Bobby promptly shoved Olivia's head between her

knees. "Stay down there, Doc." He fumbled around her hips. "There a seat belt in this hunk of junk?"

Olivia grabbed her knees and tensed every muscle in her body. The car was bouncing crazily up and down in exact counterpoint to the sharp turns Rafe was taking toward downtown La Paz. She thought, somewhat hysterically, that she'd add a little extra in her check to the cabdriver for new shocks. Even wedged as she was between the two men, she was in imminent danger of ricocheting right through the roof of the cab. Bobby kept his hand on the back of her neck, forcing her to stay low. She was grateful for it when she heard the back windshield shatter into a million pieces. She felt glass patter on her back and saw it hit the floor.

"You gotta love those old windshields," Bobby commented conversationally. "They just break right out. Easier to see through that way. I hate the ones that just crackle. Safety glass, I think they call it."

Rafe didn't answer. He sped past a slow-moving produce truck, then accelerated through an intersection without slowing down. Olivia heard the squeal of brakes behind them, then a peculiar, bursting sound.

"Oooh." Bobby sucked a breath through his teeth. "Watermelons. That'll be tough to clean off the road."

"Hold on," Rafe mumbled unnecessarily, and took a right turn on what Olivia would have sworn were only half the wheels usually required for that kind of maneuver.

She closed her eyes. The floor was starting to blur in front of her eyes. "I think I'm going to throw up," she said quietly.

"Do you get car sick, normally?"

She stared at him. He was examining her face with casual curiosity as they screamed headlong into the middle of afternoon La Paz in a stolen car, with the sheriff of Aldea Viejo and eight of his henchmen in hot pursuit.

"No, not normally," she said, hoping he caught the sarcasm. She'd hate to have to point out the obvious. She'd really rather spend her last minutes on the planet throwing up her trailer tacos and praying for forgiveness for whatever the hell it was she thought she'd been doing the past three days.

"Huh," Bobby said thoughtfully. He felt her forehead. "Maybe you have the flu."

Rafe performed another violation of both the motor vehicle code and the laws of physics. "Yes, maybe I have the flu!" Olivia hollered in Bobby's face. "Do I have a fever?"

Bobby grinned at her. "I don't think so. Do you feel hot?"

"I feel slightly hysterical," she yelled.

"Maybe you should see a doctor." He angled his head so he could look up at Rafe. "Can we stop at a clinic?"

Rafe didn't so much as glance down at them, hunched together under the dash. "No."

Bobby looked back at Olivia. Their faces were inches apart, and Olivia could see the twinkle in Bobby's eyes. She could have killed him for it. Then again, she didn't feel like throwing up anymore.

"He says we don't have time to stop now, but maybe in a little while."

"Thank you," Olivia said through gritted teeth.

"I just hope I don't catch it," he said, shaking his head. "I *cannot* afford to get the flu right now. My job is just crazy."

"You are completely out of your mind, aren't you," Olivia asked, staring at him.

"What do you mean?"

Olivia gave him a long look, then turned her head back to the floor. "Never mind."

Bobby sat back up, grinned over at Rafe, who paid him no attention whatsoever. "Your girlfriend is going to barf," he said cheerfully.

"She'll have to do it in the car," he muttered distractedly, focusing intently on the road ahead of him. He'd lost the two Land Cruisers a street back, but he expected them to pop up again at any moment.

He slowed the car considerably as they reached the outskirts of town. There were pedestrians everywhere. And even if the sidewalks had been empty, the narrow, confusing streets of La Paz were no place for a car chase. Someone was going to be killed, and the way Rafe's luck was going, it would not be Ernesto Cervantes. Rafe jerked the cab into a tight alleyway, brought it to a screaming stop.

"Everybody out," he said, and shoved open the driver's door, his gun already in his hand. He took hold of Olivia's wrist and hauled her out of the car. She fell into him.

"Are we stopping?" she said, white-faced and wide-eyed.

Rafe examined her face intently for a second. "Do you need to vomit?" he asked.

She blinked at him. "No."

"Then, come on."

And again, they ran. If her life hadn't been in danger and she hadn't been shaking with fear every other minute, the past three days would have constituted an excellent workout, she thought as she was pulled through the streets. She only wished she'd worn better shoes.

She didn't ask where they were going this time. It really didn't matter, as long as they eventually ended up someplace where she could stop for a minute and let the fight-or-flight adrenaline bleed off and her system settle.

Funny, that's all she wanted now. The meaning of her entire life compressed into a single desire. She just wanted to feel safe again. She didn't want to be chased, she didn't want to listen for the sound of running feet or gunshots behind her, she didn't want to look over her shoulder.

She no longer yearned for anything so impossible and abstract as to go home. She knew in her heart she'd be trapped in Baja until she died; she accepted that. She just didn't want to have to run another step.

But she did. Because Rafe had her hand in his and she realized she would have followed him anywhere. He and his cousin were the only people she could trust in all of this madness, the only ones who could provide her the safety she required.

They'd risked their lives a half-dozen times in the past forty-eight hours to keep her safe. Or to keep her from Ernesto, anyway. Olivia instinctively knew that was the same thing.

Rafe and Bobby could have hidden in those desert hills for weeks and never been found. They hadn't needed to steal one of Ernesto's Land Cruisers to drive her to La Paz. They hadn't needed to be at the La Paz airport, sitting ducks for the police and Ernesto's men. They hadn't needed to dump over a taco trailer and steal *another* car and drive like lunatics so she would be safe. They could have faded into thin air. She'd seen them do it.

But they hadn't faded into thin air. They'd done everything they could to keep her alive. Criminals or not, she wouldn't leave them now for the world. Her survival instincts had thoroughly overridden her common sense.

They stopped running when they hit the streets, and Rafe and Bobby tucked their weapons back into their waistbands. The three of them tried to blend in with the strolling tourists and the busy townspeople. They ducked through stores, going in the front, heading out the back, doing everything they could to disappear.

It was not enough, Rafe knew. He caught a glimpse of one of the Land Cruisers as it slowly patrolled a side street, the driver and passengers—not Cervantes this time—squinting intently into the faces of passing pedestrians.

Rafe stopped dead at a shop window, when the vehicle turned onto the street where they were walking. He watched the reflection of the cruiser as it slipped past, keeping his body between Olivia and the street. Bobby had gone into a crouch the instant Rafe had stopped, ducking his head, blending into the scene. Olivia stood frozen with dread, expecting any moment to feel Rafael's big body shudder at her back as a bullet ripped through him.

"Where's Cervantes?" Rafe muttered, as the vehicle turned down the next cross street.

Bobby rose casually, shrugged.

Rafe pushed his fingers through his hair. "We'll have to hole up again."

Bobby sucked on his teeth. "Day after tomorrow's the nineteenth," he said enigmatically.

"I know what day it is, *vato*."

"What does the date matter?" Olivia asked, her voice trembling. She wanted to go again, get out of the open, but neither man was making any move. So she stayed still, trapped between Rafe and the storefront, while he and Bobby talked to each other without taking their eyes off the reflection of the street.

"We have to be back in Aldea Viejo before the nineteenth," Bobby said. "We're intercepting a shipment."

"You know," Rafe said in disgust, "why don't you just tell her the national soccer scores while you're at it?"

Olivia had turned her head, was staring at him in horror. "You'd go back? For a shipment of drugs, you'd risk your life?"

"That's what I do, *princesa*."

"Oh, my God." She looked at him for a moment more, then broke from his grasp and began walking, alone, down the street.

She didn't finish a third step before she was whirled back around to face him. "Where do you think you're going?"

"I'm going to the police."

"I don't think so."

"I am, Rafael. You two are obviously too stupid to protect yourselves, much less me. I'm going to the police. I can't imagine every single one of them knows and cooperates with Ernesto." She tried, unsuccessfully, to wrench her arm from his grasp. "I'm sure I'll be safer there than

I am with you two lunatics," she said as patiently as her roiling stomach and her pounding heart would allow. "I'll just give them your description and your last known whereabouts, and they'll come by and arrest you and save your stupid lives for you."

"Olivia, you're not going to the police," he said, his expression stern. "And I am not going to stand here on the street with you and argue about it."

"No, honestly." She tried to convince him. "You'll be safer in jail. You're obviously not well."

"Olivia."

"Let me go, Rafael."

"No."

"Let me go, or I will start to scream. That will undoubtedly bring both the police and Ernesto's goons to the scene in short order. We'll let everyone just shoot it out here on the street, and whoever wins gets the drug shipment and the Land Cruisers and whatever's behind door number three!"

Rafe began tugging her in his wake again. "You won't scream, Olivia. You never scream." It was one of the many things he'd come to admire. Along with her stubbornness. He knew the little princess would go to the local police and rat them out. She'd think she'd be saving their lives, but all she'd accomplish would be to ruin years' worth of good DEA undercover work. He wasn't letting her near a police station, here or anywhere else, until this thing went down.

He'd just have to *really* kidnap her this time.

She twisted her wrist, giving herself a skin burn. "Let me go," she warned through her teeth. They passed Bobby, who was smiling fatuously. Olivia bared her teeth at him. "I'm screaming, Rafael. I'm screaming."

He didn't even turn around. "You're not stupid, Olivia. You won't scream."

Olivia filled her lungs to capacity. The piercing sound that came from that pretty little bow of a mouth shocked

all three of them, and made several people on the street
jump in surprise.

Rafe jerked her body close to his and clamped his hand
roughly over her mouth, cutting off the scream. He put his
nose to hers. "You're going to get us all killed," he hissed
ferociously. "I trust you not to be so stupid, Olivia, and
then you do something like this. It's very disappointing."

"Very disappointing," Bobby murmured in agreement
from his perpetual place at her back.

"Now, you have two choices," Rafe continued, while
Olivia stared at him from above his hand. "I can clip you
on the jaw right now and carry you unconscious in that
orange dress through the streets of La Paz, thereby ensuring all three of us end up as shark food. Or I can let go,
and you can behave like a sensible adult, and we can try
and get out of here in one piece."

"Clip her on the jaw," Bobby said helpfully.

Rafe ignored his cousin. "Olivia?"

"Mmnnph," Olivia replied.

"Sensible adult?"

She nodded.

"She could be lying, Rafe," Bobby said. "I say you
clip her on the jaw, anyway."

Olivia rolled her eyes, trying to see Bobby so she could
glower at him. Rafe glanced over her shoulder at his cousin
and swore softly.

"I'm counting on you, Olivia," he said, and let go of
her mouth. He kissed her swiftly, firmly. Then kissed her
again, for good measure and because she looked so scared.
"It's okay, *mi'ja*," he said softly, and he pulled her into
a tiny grocery that smelled of fresh fish and sweet bread.
"I am not without friends in this town. All I need is a
telephone."

Fifteen minutes after Rafe used the store owner's phone,
a tiny hatchback pulled to the curb in front of the store.

Bobby, at the window, checked out the street. "Okay, let's go."

Bobby and Olivia scrambled into the back seat, and Rafe sat next to the driver. Not a word was exchanged as the car threaded through the streets. Olivia didn't even bother to look out the window. It really didn't matter where they were going, anyway. Rafe and Bobby were going back to Aldea Viejo for a drug shipment.

After several minutes of silence, the driver looked at Rafe in disgust. "A taxicab?"

Rafe shrugged, glancing in his side mirror to determine if they'd been picked up by either of Cervantes's drivers. "It was all we had to work with."

The driver snorted. "And the taco trailer?"

"That was a stroke of genius, I thought," Bobby offered brightly from the back seat.

"Did you? Then *you* deal with the man who owns it."

"I gave the guy a hundred dollars American to let me do it," Bobby said indignantly, leaning forward in his seat. "He even helped me push it over."

"He is not the owner, idiot," the driver said.

Olivia stared at the back of his head. She wished she could see him. How in the world had he already found out about all this?

"How'd they know we were in La Paz?" Rafe asked.

The driver sniffed. "I don't know, for sure."

"You've got a leak, *amigo,*" Bobby said.

"Big news," the driver said sourly. "Anyway, we found the Land Cruiser yesterday. We didn't run it, but someone must have recognized it and called Aldea Viejo."

"If he didn't drive those damn conspicuous monsters," Bobby said, flopping back onto the seat in annoyance. "Everyone knows them."

"Yeah, that's what's been wrong with this whole deal. *You've* made every right decision—it's the Land Cruiser's fault you've almost been caught a dozen times," the driver said scornfully. "Starting with you, *vato,*" he said to Rafe.

"Kidnapping a female American marine biologist was a great plan."

"I'm not a marine biologist," Olivia said dully.

"I didn't kidnap her, she kidnapped me. And she's an oceanographer," Rafe added.

The driver shook his head. "Whatever. I got a report from the party, Camayo. Apparently it looked very much like you had a gun to her head."

"I wouldn't have shot her," Rafe said evenly. "Besides, if you guys had been able to find anything out from the inside, I wouldn't have had to go in."

The driver glanced over at him. "I can't believe you got nabbed. What a loser."

If Olivia didn't know better, she would have sworn Rafe looked embarrassed. "Mitigating factors," he mumbled.

"Oh, my God," Olivia said softly.

They ignored her. "What have you got for us?" Rafe asked.

"You know, you want the damn moon."

"No. I want a boat. That should be a hell of a lot easier to get."

"Well, I got you a boat."

"Good. We can get back to Aldea Viejo by tomorrow afternoon. When's the shipment scheduled on Tuesday?"

"Who knows? According to our source, the boat's leaving the mainland today. Barring bad weather, that could put him in at Aldea Viejo any time after sunrise Tuesday."

Olivia huffed out an astonished breath. Of course, she thought. *Of course.* How could she have been so blind?

"You can hold Dr. Galpas in La Paz until Wednesday?"

"I don't know why you don't want her going out on the next plane. Seems it would be a hell of a lot easier on everyone involved if she was back home safe and sound in the States."

"Not if Cervantes has contacted his people in San Diego," Rafe argued. This was a point he would not concede under any circumstances. Until Cervantes was actually facedown in the Aldea Viejo sand with handcuffs on his wrists and Rafe's foot on his neck, Rafe wanted to know exactly where Olivia Galpas was.

"If she makes a fuss, she can cause a lot of problems for us, Rafael," the driver said quietly, glancing suspiciously back at Olivia. "We're not technically supposed to hold American women in Baja against their will."

"Just do it," Rafe said shortly. "She's liable to blow this whole thing for us if you don't."

Olivia started to nod to herself. She caught Bobby's eye. He had the audacity to smile knowingly at her. Oh, she was going to murder them both. With her bare hands.

"Fine, but if I get fired, I expect you two to put in a word for me with—"

"Will you shut up?" Rafe snapped. He shook his head. "I swear, no one can keep their mouths shut anymore," he muttered to himself.

Except you, Olivia thought, furious, shaken.

She spent the rest of the trip to the Sea of Cortéz—and she knew they were heading in that direction, she could practically feel it in her bones—trying to calm down. It would be easier to kill them, she thought, if she kept a cool head.

The driver pulled into a dirt parking lot that abutted the sea. One dingy dock jutted irresolutely into the calm waters of the gulf. Tied to the dock was a fishing boat Rafe wouldn't have trusted to take him across the orca tank at Sea World.

He got out of the car and walked down to the boat, carefully avoiding gaps in the disintegrating dock, through which he could see chunks of seawater. Olivia, Bobby and the driver followed.

"Very nice," he said.

"You called me half an hour ago. If it has fuel and starts on the first try, count yourself lucky, *vato.*"

Olivia looked at the driver for the first time. He was a smaller man than either Bobby or Rafe, with a wildly thick head of hair and an unscrupulous air about him. He looked as though he'd fleece his own mother and laugh while he was doing it.

Just like Rafael. Just like Bobby.

Olivia tipped her head back and took a deep breath of ocean air. It was so obvious. She had been unforgivably obtuse.

"I guess we don't have much choice," Rafael was saying. "But I'm going to remember this, Manny."

"Yeah, and I'm going to remember you dumping the lady marine biologist on me," Manny replied.

"I am not a marine biologist," Olivia said evenly. The three men looked over at her in surprise, as though they had forgotten for a moment that she was there. She pinned Rafael with a look. She hoped she hid the hurt she felt, but didn't have much confidence. It didn't matter, she supposed. "In fact, I'm no more a marine biologist than you are all drug runners."

The driver of the little hatchback rolled his eyes dramatically. "Wonderful. Now she's pissed. That'll make this whole thing easier."

"Shut up, Manny," Rafe said sharply.

Bobby, for once, did not smile at her, and Olivia was grateful. She didn't think she would have been able to combat both Rafe's furious scowl and Bobby's silly grin at the same time. She ignored Manny completely as he paced the dock in short bursts, swearing and wondering aloud how much trouble she was going to give him.

"How could you?" she whispered.

She might as well have screamed it, Rafe thought. The accusation went through him like a knife.

"What are you talking about?" he asked, his face expressionless.

She stared at him, her eyes dry, her heart pounding a hole through her chest. "You can stand there, after everything, and ask me that?"

Rafe resisted the urge to drop his gaze. "I'm just trying

to establish what it is you're saying, Olivia,'' he said calmly.

She watched him for a moment, then smiled thinly. "You have no soul, *señor*. At least, I was right about that."

Bobby grabbed Manny as he paced. "Come on."

"What? I'm not getting on that boat."

"Neither am I until you prove it seaworthy, Manuel, my friend," Bobby said, and practically tossed the smaller man on board.

Rafe and Olivia never broke eye contact. "You're a cop," she said, her voice flat, her eyes flat.

Rafe didn't acknowledge the statement. "You were better off not knowing," he said.

"No, you were better off with me not knowing."

"It would have put the entire operation in jeopardy."

Olivia squeezed her eyes shut. "And you couldn't have that."

"I couldn't have that," he insisted. "Bobby and I have been planning this sting on Cervantes for over a year. We've been in Baja since before Christmas. There are eight other DEA guys down here, as well as Manuel and a dozen Mexican *federales* working with the agency. You don't know how important this is."

"How would I have jeopardized all that?"

"Come on, Olivia. Have you forgotten all those evening walks you and Cervantes took together? How the hell did I know how close you were getting?"

"Were you watching me at my camp?" She thought she might be sick.

"No."

"Then how did you know about the walks?"

"We have four guys inside his organization. When he started hanging around your camp at the beach, they let us know."

"That's how you knew my name," she breathed. Oh, so many things made sense now.

Rafe nodded tersely. "I had you checked out."

"Lovely." She gritted her teeth. "If you had me checked out, you knew who I was. You knew I would never have been involved in whatever it is that Ernesto does."

"Did I? The first time I saw you two together, he was announcing your engagement, for crying out loud!"

She didn't flinch when he shouted at her. She could not imagine he was any angrier than she was. "That was Friday. This is Sunday. A lot of things have happened since Friday, Rafael," she said, her meaning clear. "A lot of things."

Rafe kept his distance, when what he really wanted to do was go to her. He breathed fire and spoke harshly, when what he really wanted to do was beg her forgiveness.

"I was going to tell you at the airport."

"When you thought I was leaving Baja," she said.

"Yes."

She shook her head. "Because you didn't trust me not to tell Ernesto."

Rafe swallowed thickly. "I could not endanger the operation," he repeated. "Or you. If Cervantes got to you, you would talk, whether you wanted to or not, Olivia. There are too many lives at stake here in Mexico, back in the States. It's a complex, covert operation. If it all fell through now, when we're so close—"

"Would you have let Ernesto get to me?"

"No." He would have done anything to keep her safe. Anything but give up his revenge for Cervantes, he thought. And maybe even that. "He would have had to kill me to get to you, Olivia."

"I know." Olivia laughed roughly. "Isn't that funny? I think I knew from the minute I stepped in front of you in that bedroom at Ernesto's house that you would keep me safe."

Rafe didn't say anything, just watched her try to blink

back tears, steady her breathing. The struggle nearly broke his heart.

"But you did not have that same faith in me," she continued after a moment, her voice cracking slightly. "Even though you actually knew who I was, Rafael. Even though I never told you a single lie, or hid who I was. I trusted you in spite of everything you did, in spite of everything you made me believe about you. And you didn't trust me at all."

"That's ridiculous. I didn't tell you because it would have endangered you as well as everyone else in the operation."

"So instead you let me believe I was— That this thing between us was—"

"What did you want me to say? It's okay that you're attracted to me because I'm not really a criminal?" he yelled, defenses back up.

He was so focused on her, so intent on her every word slicing through him, that he didn't see the Land Cruiser until it was almost too late. A small flash of movement caught his eye. "Bobby," he roared. "Start the boat and shove off."

Olivia turned to stare at the men behind her. She could not imagine why they were here. She heard the boat clamor to life, as the men began to run toward her.

"Olivia!" Rafe shouted, and rushed at her.

She turned back to him just as something icy hot and dreadfully painful exploded through her arm. She fell forward into Rafe's arms, stunned.

"Oh, God. What—?"

"Olivia!" Rafe shouted as he scooped her into his arms. Blood seeped from her body onto his.

Blood. Good God, *Olivia's blood.*

Rafe forced himself to stay calm, to think clearly. He turned and leapt onto the deck of the already moving boat, throwing himself on top of Olivia as he hit the slick surface. Bobby was at the helm, gunning the engine the instant Rafe and Olivia were on board. Manny was hauling in the dock rope hand over hand, yelling obscenities into the warm air.

Rafe lay perfectly still, curled around Olivia's body. He stopped his breathing for a moment so he could listen to hers, compelling his body to remain inert, a physical protector.

All he wanted to do was return up the dock and exact retribution on the man who had put a bullet in Olivia.

Ernesto Cervantes.

Chapter 10

Bobby steered the fishing boat into the sea. Behind them, on the dock, Cervantes and his men stood helplessly by as the little boat headed into the waters Olivia loved.

"Could you get off me?" Olivia mumbled weakly, her face pressed firmly against the nonslip deck of the boat.

Rafe rolled off her and knelt at her side. "Manny!" he shouted. "Get below and find me a first-aid kit."

Manny stood with the rope still in his hand. He apparently hadn't been shot at very often in his small-town police career, and he appeared quite unnerved.

"I don't know if there's even one on the boat," he said.

Rafe tore his attention away from Olivia. "Well," he said, his lips stretched back from his teeth, "look for one."

Manny scrambled below with all the haste Rafe's intimidating visage could instill in a man.

Rafe leaned back over Olivia. "Okay, *mi'ja*. You're going to be okay." Good God, he was shaking like a leaf. Where the hell was Manny with that first-aid kit? "Manny!"

Bobby turned from the helm for a moment. "Is she hit?"

"Yeah."

Bobby began to swear, too, low and steadily.

Olivia looked up at Rafe's furious face. She'd heard more cursing on this little boat in the past ninety seconds than she'd heard in five years on ships across the globe.

"I think someone shot me," she said.

Rafe stroked back her hair with a trembling hand. "Yes, *mi'ja.* Someone shot you."

"Am I going to die?"

"No," Rafe promised fiercely.

Olivia smiled. "Because you keep calling me 'my dearest.'"

You are my dearest, he wanted to say. "Don't worry," he said quietly. "I'm not going to let you die." He smiled gently. *"Princesa."*

"That's better," she sighed, her eyes tightly closed. "I don't think it's too bad. It kind of hurts, though."

"I'll bet it does." He reared back. *"Manny!"*

"Yeah, yeah, I found it."

"What the hell took you so long?" Rafe snarled as he snatched the kit from Manny's hands and tore into it. "Couldn't you hear me?"

"The Coast Guard in Long Beach could hear you," Manny answered. "Is she bad?"

"I don't know yet, you moron." He leaned down, kissed Olivia lightly on her mouth. "I'm going to touch you. Try not to move."

"I'm not moving," she assured him. "I think when you landed on me you quick-sealed me to the deck, here."

Rafe took a deep breath, began to carefully palpate Olivia's chest. Her blood was spattered rather than oozing, and he had no idea where the bullet had entered, or if it had exited.

"Rafael, why are you feeling my breasts?"

"I don't know where you were shot, Olivia."

"Well, you could ask me."

Rafe put his hands on his knees, wiped the sweat from them onto his jeans. He was sick with nerves. Pathetic. He'd seen men with their heads literally blown from their shoulders and he'd never felt this woozy before.

"Where are you hit, Olivia?"

"I'm not sure. Feel around my breasts a little more. Maybe I was wrong."

Behind Rafe, Manny laughed. Rafe spun around and glowered at him. "Get the hell away from me," he warned in a low voice. "Olivia, seriously, where are you hit?"

"I think my upper arm, the inside. It hurts like mad there."

Rafe gently lifted her arm. "I'm going to rip your dress, sweetheart."

Olivia chuckled back in her throat. "Okay. Only don't take advantage. Remember how mad I am at you."

He stared down at her. He was about to throw up with remorse and anxiety, and she was making jokes? If she hadn't already been shot, he might have strangled her.

"I won't," he promised. He slipped his fingers under the sleeve of her dress and tugged. The fabric ripped right along the seam, exposing the bleeding, wounded flesh where Cervantes's bullet had shot cleanly past her upper arm.

Rafe sucked in air through his teeth.

"Is it that bad?" Olivia asked, and tried to raise her head so she could see it. Rafe put his hand on her forehead and pushed her head back down.

"Don't look at it," he said weakly.

"Good heavens, it doesn't *feel* that bad," Olivia said. "Are you going to faint?"

Rafe gave her a retiring look. "No," he said, as though the idea were too absurd to contemplate, when, in fact, he did feel a little light-headed.

He took a deep breath, pulled himself together. "The

bullet grazed the back of your arm. I don't think it went through any muscle, just skin and fat," he said.

"*Fat?*"

"I'm just going to clean it out and then bandage it. I'm sure it'll be fine. We'll get you to a hospital—" he meticulously poured some rubbing alcohol into the shallow groove the bullet had made and swallowed bile when she blanched "—and they'll probably look at it and say, oh, it's practically nothing, and send you on your way."

"Rafael."

"Okay, that's done. All I have in this stupid kit is rubbing alcohol. Dammit, dammit. *Dammit,* Manny! Why don't you do something about the conditions on this boat?" he shouted over his shoulder, making Olivia jump.

He turned back to Olivia, practically cooed at her. "But that'll get it clean enough." He tore a length of bandage with his teeth. "It'll be fine. You'll have a little scar to tell all your friends about at cocktail parties. Just a little scar." He wanted to lean over and kiss it. "I'm going to wrap this bandage around your arm now, so I'll have to move it a little."

"Rafael."

"It's going to hurt when I move it, but not as much as the alcohol. I don't know where Bobby's heading this heap, but I'm sure there'll be a hospital there, wherever it is. Don't worry, Olivia. Don't worry."

"Rafael!"

He blinked down at her. "What?"

"Stop blathering. You've said more in the past three minutes than the whole time I've known you." She lifted her expertly bandaged arm. It hurt like the fires of hell, but she wasn't about to tell him that. He already looked green around the gills. She'd never have pegged this fake smuggler as having a weak stomach for blood. "It's better already. I was just surprised, more than anything. And you knocked the wind out of me when you accidentally fell on me getting in the boat."

"I didn't accidentally fall on you," he said, embarrassed that she'd caught him panicking. He was, after all, very proud of his natural *machismo*. He'd never before lost it so thoroughly. "I landed on you on purpose because they were shooting at us, *princesa*."

"Ah, now I know I'm going to be okay," Olivia said, sitting up. "You're sneering at me again."

"Because you say stupid things. I was not blathering." The idea of it, now that she wasn't bleeding any longer, was laughable. He gathered up the medical supplies in something of a huff. "Take an aspirin."

Olivia obediently took the pills from his hand and swallowed them one at a time, dry. Anything to stop the fire in her arm. Lord, who knew getting shot was so excruciating? In the movies, when someone said they'd been grazed by a bullet, they always acted as if it were nothing at all. This felt like *something*.

Nevertheless, she smiled up at Rafael. "I'm glad you're a cop, you know."

He stopped packing the kit and stared at her. "Why?"

"Because you can arrest Ernesto for shooting me."

"You saw that, did you?"

"I saw him raise his gun. I couldn't believe it. Three days ago he was pinching my—"

"I know what he was doing," Rafe snapped irritably. "You look pale. Will you lie down?"

"I don't think so. Right this very minute, Ernesto and his boys are probably hopping aboard some sleek little cigarette boat and will be upon us any time. I should stay awake for that, I think."

That, unfortunately, was all too true. "Bobby?"

"Yeah?"

"Where the hell are we going?"

"South."

"South, where?"

Bobby stared at the horizon, moved his shoulders. "Damn if I know. I just figure if Cervantes takes off after us, he'll think we're headed back up to Aldea Viejo, which is north. That's why I'm headed south.''

"Uh, Bobby?"

"Yes, Doc?"

"Do you know what you're doing?"

"As in, can I drive a boat? Very nice. I just saved your life, if you didn't notice. Again.''

"I did notice. Thank you. But do you know how to read a coastline, a chart? Get to where you need to go on the ocean?''

"Yes."

Olivia smiled at him.

Bobby lifted his chin defiantly. "Pretty much.''

"Because I can do all that for us.''

"I can do it!" Bobby said.

"You've just been shot," Rafe objected at the same time.

Olivia gave them a patient look. "Okay, listen, boys. You've been dragging me all over Baja for three long days. I have gone along without much objection because I realized you knew what you were doing. But Bobby, you're not headed south, you're headed east. And Rafael, you look like you're going to toss your cookies any minute. Now, whether that's from being shot at or seasickness, it doesn't really matter.''

"It's not from being shot at!" Rafe declared, wounded she'd think so little of his courage. "I've been shot at a hundred times.''

"Be that as it may, if you two don't let me help you, you're going to end up in Mazatlan tomorrow morning trying to find someplace to dock next to the cruise ships. And the little operation you've got going here will be completely undone.''

"It's undone, anyway," Rafe said. "We're taking you to Cabo San Lucas to the hospital there, and then getting you on a flight home.''

Olivia put her hands on her hips, forgetting until she felt

the searing pain that she had a hole in her arm. Or a very deep scratch, anyway. She lowered them promptly. "What about the shipment of drugs you're supposed to intercept day after tomorrow?"

"There will be other shipments."

"All right, that's probably true. But correct me if I'm wrong. Your whole tweaking of Cervantes's pride these past couple of months has been leading to this moment, right? He's chasing you around Baja like a lunatic. According to your friend here, he knows you're going to try to steal this big shipment on Tuesday, also right?"

"It took him shooting you to stop calling him 'Ernesto,' I see," Rafe said deliberately.

Olivia ignored him. He could narrow his eyes at her all he wanted. He could brood and glower and pout until the sun came up. She was taking charge of this boat. She turned to Bobby. "Also right, Bobby?"

Bobby rolled his lips over his teeth and nodded solemnly. *"Sí, Generalissimo."*

"You have him exactly where you want him. It seems to me if he's willing to risk prison, local censure and embarrassment, and an international incident to shoot at *me,* he'd be willing to take just about any chance to get you guys."

"She's right, Rafe."

"Shut up, Bobby. Olivia, you don't know what all this entails."

"Yes, I do. I've spent ten years assessing data presented to me. I may have been a little slow on the uptake with you two, but I was deliberately mislead by all parties, so I can't really be held accountable for false conclusions." She glared briefly at Rafael. "But now that I've had a few minutes to think about it all while I'm not being shot at, I have to conclude that you haven't arrested Cervantes before now because he lets his flunkies do all the dirty work. You need to annoy him enough that he'll take any chance to get rid of you. Including implicating himself by over-seeing his own shipment of illegal drugs."

Rafe scowled at her. "Forget it, *princesa*. You're not going anywhere near Aldea Viejo."

Fine, he was as unreasonable as he always was. *The mule.* She turned to plead her case with Bobby. "And I figure I have assisted you in this scheme by humiliating him by getting myself kidnapped at my own engagement party. From that little murder attempt on the dock back there and the cross-country chase, I would surmise he now suspects I know all about him and the relationship between the three of you. He's desperate to keep his secret life safe from both Mexican and American authorities, but he's also furious and wants revenge. It's the perfect time for you. Right?"

"She's right," Bobby said again.

Rafe dug the heels of his hands in his eye sockets. "I cannot believe this."

"I can get you to Aldea Viejo before Tuesday," Olivia said.

"What about the sleek little cigarette boat?"

Olivia rubbed her hands together, and winced at the pain. "Oh, I think we can get around that little problem."

"How?" Manny asked.

Olivia grinned at him. "How long have you lived in Baja, Manny?"

"All my life, *señorita*."

"And how many times have you cruised this coast-line?"

Manny considered. "Dozens of times, I would suppose," he said.

"Well, Manny, I have you beat." Olivia looked at Bobby, then locked her gaze on Rafe's exasperated face and smiled. "By quite a bit."

There had to be a hundred fishing boats on the water between La Paz and Aldea Viejo during the spring fishing months, Rafe decided. A hundred fishing boats and maybe half that many whale-watching boats and dive boats, and dozens of people just tooling around for fun.

Olivia didn't let any of them get within a million miles of them.

She took the helm as if she owned it. Rafe tried very hard to resent her for that—it was, after all, something only a princess would do with such temerity. But she was so impressive he couldn't have held a grudge if his life depended upon it.

Against his objections, she'd turned the boat north. Bobby had stood behind her until the sun went down, protecting her place at the helm.

Rafe was still a little shaky from watching Cervantes shoot at her, still a little nauseated from the spatter of blood on her awful orange dress. When he closed his eyes, he could see the pattern of it against the cheap fabric. He tried not to close his eyes much.

But it was more than an unwillingness to cause her any more physical pain that kept him from insisting she turn the boat south, to Cabo San Lucas. Rafe had fumed and seethed and paced, but he'd seen the perfect wisdom of her plan. She knew this coastline better than anyone he knew, Mexican or American, and the places she didn't know from experience she could read in an instant.

She ducked them into coves Rafe wouldn't have noticed if he'd been looking right at them. When any other craft got too close, she maneuvered the little fishing boat behind rock outcroppings or into water Rafe thought far too shallow, or on the other side of sandspits, so that anyone who wanted to get too close would be beached. Rafe was wildly, annoyingly impressed.

All the while she faced the wind and water with her chin up, muttering to herself, her bandaged arm forgotten. Rafe watched her like an overwrought brood hen for signs of fatigue, of pain, but as the hours ticked by and she outsmarted or outran every other boat on the water, she seemed to grow stronger, more confident. The color in her cheeks rose, and her eyes shone and danced.

God, he was in love with her. Passionately, madly in love with her—with the emphasis on *madly.* How he could fall in love in three days when he'd never fallen in love once in nearly thirty years was a mystery he'd spend the rest of his life trying to figure out. But he loved her. His heart ached just looking at her, standing at the helm of the crappy little fishing boat as confidently and happily as if it were the Queen Mary and she were the monarch it was named after.

He closed his eyes against the shot of misery that analogy invoked.

She *was* royalty, in every way that counted. Born to better things than he could even imagine.

She thought she was attracted to him, but he knew that was ridiculous. It was the danger and the excitement she'd responded to back in Cervantes's bedroom and in the little sand cave—not the man. And no wonder; she'd probably been coddled all her life, kept carefully safe from men like him. Dangerous men, poor and beneath her. The first chance she had to go slumming, to experience that adrenaline burst of risk with a man entirely unsuitable, she didn't even recognize it for what it was. She thought it was chemistry because chemistry was the only thing a scientist like her could conjure up to excuse her own reckless behavior.

She didn't know the difference.

But he did.

He loved her. He'd probably go through his life loving her. He'd marry some girl from the neighborhood and have a couple of kids and live out his life wondering every day where she was in the world, if she was happy and safe. If she loved someone else, someone appropriate. The thought of it made his throat close.

Dusk fell, and Olivia had Manny pull out the spotlight used for night fishing and hook it to the boat's battery. She didn't like being this close to the coastline at night, but there was a risk on the open water, as well. It would be much easier for Cervantes to run them down on open water. Their small boat had more gumption than she would have guessed, she thought proudly, patting the steering wheel with some affection, but it could never outrun anything bigger than an inflatable with a good outboard motor. Better they take their chances with a spotlight and her memory of this part of the gulf's rugged coast, where there were a thousand places a small boat could hide.

Rafe was watching her, she could feel it. He'd been watching her all afternoon. She struggled not to rub at her eyes or stretch her back or yawn, knowing he'd take the first sign of fatigue as an excuse to make her stop. She didn't want to stop. She wanted to get as close to Pico Cupula tonight as possible. They could get fuel at the little village there in the morning, and then motor up to Aldea Viejo by Tuesday morning.

She hoped.

Olivia knew boats better than she knew almost anything else, and though this one was sound enough now, anything could happen before Tuesday, particularly if she continued to push it this hard. Which, obviously, she would.

She had to get Rafael and Bobby to their rendezvous with that drug shipment on Tuesday. She had to.

It had come to her sometime between the instant when she'd turned on the dock to see Ernesto Cervantes—a man who'd kissed her!—leveling that lethal-looking pistol at her, and the instant when she'd instinctively turned to Rafael to see that, ·as usual, he was hurtling himself to her rescue.

She and Rafael had something together. Something strange and uncomfortable and risky, but something. More than she'd ever had with anyone else. And if putting Cervantes behind bars was the only thing standing in the way of figuring out what that ''something'' was, well, then, she'd use her considerable intellect and her significant skills to make sure that happened.

Olivia tilted her chin to the bow of the boat, filled her lungs with sea air.

"Come on, *princesa*," Rafe said, coming up behind her. "That's far enough. Find someplace to park this frigate for the night."

"I wanted to get a little closer to Pico Cupula tonight," she argued.

"You'll miss it completely if you don't wait for morning. We'll end up in Rosarito."

Olivia laughed.

Rafe shook his head ruefully. "Okay, now I know you're tired. Pack it in. You're laughing at my jokes."

She leaned back so their bodies touched, smiled when he stepped forward and pressed himself against her, covering her hands on the wheel with his.

"That's not so strange," she murmured. "You're a naturally happy person. I guess it's rubbed off on my dour personality."

He rested his chin on her head. Couldn't resist. "How's your arm?"

"Hurts. How're your ribs?"

"Sore."

"You shouldn't have flopped down on top of me like a flounder. Probably cracked them again."

He nuzzled her neck. Couldn't resist. "A flounder? I was saving your life, ingrate."

Olivia dropped her head back and closed her eyes. She rubbed her hair against him, catlike, loosening more strands of hair from her long braid. "Mmm. You've spent a lot of time doing that the past few days."

"And for my trouble you call me a flounder."

"Well, you said I had fat arms."

He lifted his head, looked at her pretty profile. "I did not!"

"Yes, you did. You said that bullet went through my fat arms."

Rafe put his face back into the hollow of her throat. Simply could not resist. "You're crazy. I would never say something like that. Even if it were true. I have three sisters. They beat that kind of honesty out of me by the time I was fifteen."

"You have three sisters?"

"Yes." He peered past her shoulder. "Are we turning?"

"Just into a cove ahead. We can anchor there tonight. It's inaccessible except by foot over the Sierra de la Gigantas. I don't think Cervantes is up to forced march over the mountains, even if he knew we were here. Where do your sisters live?"

"One's married and lives in El Cajon, California. The other two are still at home."

"Home?"

"In San Diego."

"I thought you and Bobby were Americans," Olivia confirmed softly. "He uses more American slang than *I* do. You ought to talk to him about that. It's bad for your cover."

Rafe stayed snuggled against her. Her skin was cool in the sea air, and he wanted to warm her. Warm himself.

"We work for the Drug Enforcement Agency out of San Diego."

"A hometown boy," Olivia mused. "What's your last name? Maybe I know your family."

"It's Camayo, but I don't think you'd know my family. And you and I are not from the same hometown, Olivia," Rafe said mildly, then added suddenly, "Do you see that—?"

Olivia had known the rock was there, pushing out of the ocean like a whale snout, long before Manuel had spotlighted it. "Yes. That's our mooring for tonight. The boat's small enough that we'll be almost completely hid-

den. We just have to get around it—'' She pulled her lower
lip between her teeth in concentration. ''Bobby, get the
anchor, will you? We can't tie off. I don't want to scrape
Manuel's nice boat.''

Bobby saluted her briskly and readied the anchor.

''Okay. Drop it.''

Olivia killed the engine and turned in Rafe's arms.
''We'll need fuel first thing.''

''Okay.''

''Do you have enough money?''

He smiled. ''You worry a lot about my finances, you
know that?''

''When I thought you were a drug dealer, I was worried
about spending your ill-gotten gains. I do have my karma
to think about, you know.''

Rafe raised one dark brow. ''Your karma?''

''I subscribe to the idea of karmic debt.''

''I'm sure two hundred years' worth of your Catholic
ancestors are rolling over in their graves right now.''

She kissed him, grinning. ''Maybe. You know, you have
permanent frown lines in your forehead.''

''I do? I didn't three days ago. Olivia?''

''Yes?''

''Does the fact that you're letting me touch you mean
you forgive me for lying to you? Because if this is a trap
and you're just luring me close so you can get a good shot
at me, I should probably let you know you should try and
stay away from the ribs. They need a couple days before
anyone pounds on them again.''

''No, I haven't forgiven you. You haven't even said you
were sorry, as a matter of fact,'' she pointed out. She
rubbed her nose against his shirtfront. ''I just can't seem
to resist you,'' she admitted.

''You know,'' he said, ''I was just thinking the same
thing about you.''

''I'm tired of fighting it. I've been miserable. I don't
want to be miserable anymore.''

Rafe took a deep breath. Apologizing was not something he did well. Not something he did often. "I'm sorry I didn't tell you. I never meant to hurt you. I never wanted you to feel ashamed of…what went on between us."

"I know." She ignored the rustling of their other two shipmates as they scrambled below deck—looking through the galley for something to eat, she suspected. "I know you were just trying to keep Cervantes from finding out about your operation."

"It wasn't only that. I knew if you got involved, it would be dangerous for you."

"That's a pretty lame excuse, Rafael. I've been involved from the first minute I set eyes on you."

He pulled her close, taking care with her bandaged arm. "And I still don't understand that," he said softly.

She snuggled closer. "Me, either. You're surly and you sneer at me and I'm not usually attracted to men just because they're good-looking."

Rafe grinned slowly, terribly pleased. "You think I'm good-looking?"

Olivia rolled her eyes. "And egotistical."

Rafe laughed. "I'm Latino, woman. Ego comes in the blood."

"I know. I have brothers. They think they're gods."

Brothers. Rafe sobered instantly at the mention of her family. It was all well and good to stand with his arms wrapped around this woman in the sea air and the heavy darkness, but there was no use pretending for even a minute that she was anything other than what she was. A woman of family, a woman he could never win.

He leaned back, looked into her eyes. "Olivia—"

Olivia didn't know what had put that solemn look on his handsome face, and she didn't care. Not right now.

"You know what?" she said, interrupting him abruptly. "Don't say anything." She went back into his arms, rested her cheek against his broad chest. "You're just going to hurt my feelings again."

His hand went to her hair automatically, holding her to him. "I don't hurt your feelings, do I?" he asked, surprised.

Olivia laughed. "Well, I am getting used to *princesa*. I just tell myself it's an endearment."

Rafe closed his eyes. "It is an endearment," he whispered, knowing full well the peril to his vulnerable heart of such an admission.

She looked up. "I know."

He shouldn't have kissed her, he knew better than to do that. She'd go back to her life in a few days, back to a life that could never include him. Every kiss he took now would make it harder for him to live without her when she was gone.

But her eyes shone and the boat rocked gently under them and he was so tired of battling against her. So he lowered his head ever so slowly and took her mouth.

The kiss started out wonderfully soft. Really, just nothing more than a press of lips. Her mouth tasted slightly of sea spray, and he rubbed his against it to collect the salt. For minutes he did just that, content with just that. Pathetically grateful for no more than the feel of her tough little body in his arms and the beat of her heart against his chest.

Then, to torment him, she angled her head so that her lips slid sensuously against his, opening fractionally, letting him in by increments. Her tongue came out after that slow opening, and licked at him. He felt dazed by the touch of that small tongue, drowsy with the slow, saturating lust that seeped into his cells. For the first time in days, he didn't feel the nerve-stretching, low-level disquiet of being hunted by a criminal. He didn't feel the anxiety of protecting the woman he loved. He didn't feel consumed by the investigation or worried about tomorrow or even the ache of his bruised ribs.

He just felt Olivia. In every pore and every muscle and every bone. She'd come in through his mouth and permeated his body. And he couldn't even find the will anymore to remember how she would rip his heart out while she was in there.

"I thought I'd imagined my initial reaction to your mouth," she said against him. "It couldn't have been this amazing." She dove in for more.

"Olivia, wait, Bobby and Manny—" he began, almost desperately.

—were coming up on deck.

Olivia and Rafe separated, jumping apart like randy teenagers caught groping by their parents.

Olivia almost laughed. She was nearly thirty years old, a woman with a PhD and a position with the best oceanography institute in the world. She'd been chased, shoved headfirst into a scorpion cave and very recently shot at.

She was damn well going to kiss anyone she pleased, she thought. She moved back toward Rafael.

But then she caught sight of Manny carrying an armful of food, and she decided she'd damn well kiss any man she pleased *after* she ate something.

"What did you find down there?" she asked, incredulous. She hadn't been below deck since she got on this tug, but she wouldn't have bet the boat that there was much more on board than old bait.

"Dinner," Manuel said proudly. "Crackers, olives and two cans of tuna."

"Wow," Olivia said. "Tuna?"

"Maybe the guys who own this boat aren't very good fishermen," Bobby commented, using his pocketknife to pry open the cans.

"Did you find any tackle?" Rafe asked.

"There's some in the hold," Manny said.

"I think I'll see if I can't catch something a little fresher than that for dinner," Rafe said. He went below.

"But there's no stove," Manny shouted down to him. "Where're you going to cook it?"

Rafe came back up a moment later, a surf pole in his

hand. He eased his gun from the waistband of his jeans and laid it next to Bobby. "Watch out," he said. He looked toward the beach, then at Olivia. "How's your arm?"

Olivia smiled. "Pretty good."

He grinned back at her. "Then start swimming, *princesa.* You'll have to schlep for wood while I fish."

Olivia burst out laughing as Rafe dived, fishing rod and all, overboard into the warm gulf waters. "Schlep?" she called after him. "Schlep?" She jumped overboard after him. She was still laughing as she surfaced. "Rafael Camayo, you watch too much American television."

Chapter 11

The swim did them both good. It allowed Rafe's arousal to subside sufficiently that he could walk upright again, he thought wryly. And it got Olivia's dress soaking wet, so that he could see the outline of her panties and the press of her nipples, rucked and stiff from the water, as she emerged from the surf.

It was a petty little pleasure, as grown men went, he supposed. But he took full advantage of it, sneaking glances at her as he fumbled with the fishing rod.

"Cold?" he asked, as she wrung out her hair.

"A little," she said, trying to ignore the terrible sting of saltwater through the bandage. "I'll get some wood." She walked up the beach a little ways, then stopped. "Oh, how are we going to start a fire without matches?"

Rafe studiously chose a lure from the small box he'd tucked into his pocket. "Have a little faith. Smugglers are very resourceful."

Olivia frowned briefly at him, then wandered into the brush that rimmed the beach. In a short time, she'd gath-

ered an armful of dead sagebrush and ironwood pieces.
She dropped them next to Rafael, who was already slitting
open the belly of a small fish on the sand.

"I'm hungrier than that," she commented.

"You know, sometimes you have no common sense,"
Rafe mumbled absently, scooping out fish guts with his
thumb. "It's like you see the bear, and you know the bear
can eat you, but you antagonize it, anyway."

"Eat me?" Olivia asked innocently. "Is the bear going
to eat me?"

Rafe looked up, then, chuckling, shook his head.
"There's just something about being on a beach for you,
isn't there?"

Olivia leaned over and hugged his neck. "There's something about being on a beach with you," she corrected
rather rashly. She didn't care. She was feeling rash. She
was feeling relieved and rash and optimistic. She hadn't
kissed a criminal. Well, she had, but not the one that mattered. "So, what do you think about more kissing? Or are
we going to cook that puny little fish, first?"

"Actually, I'm going to start a fire first, then catch another puny little fish for your highness, then look at your
arm."

"Then we can fool around?"

Rafe laughed again. "Maybe," he said, heaving the fish
guts into the surf. "It depends on your arm."

"If your ribs can take it, my arm can take it."

"My ribs can take it." Though right now they were
being pretty well battered by the pounding of his heart.
How could she stand there in that damp dress, her hair
slicked back from her face and her white bandage practically glowing in the night, and ask him if he wanted to
fool around? He didn't know that he'd ever wanted anything more in his life.

He pulled a waterproof lighter from the pocket of his
jeans and carefully lit a frayed length of dry sagebrush,
cupping his hand around the infant flame until it was

crackling. The rest of the wood caught quickly, and once it was burning nicely, Rafe turned back to the sea for their dinner.

Olivia watched him. Fishing, he used the same economical motion of muscle and bone he used to do everything else. It was no wonder she felt so safe with the man, she thought. He could do everything. She lay back on the warm sand, watched the stars that cloaked the night sky. Drop him in the middle of the Baja desert, and in no time at all he was clearing caves of scorpions and buying dresses on Sunday mornings and catching fish in the dark.

"Don't fall asleep," Rafe said, dropping cross-legged onto the sand next to her. He'd caught two more fish; they were already gutted and rinsed. "We can't sleep here tonight. We need to be on the boat in case Cervantes shows up and we have to make a quick getaway."

"You know," she mused, casually identifying star clusters in her head, "it's amazing to me I didn't peg you guys for Americans the first time I met you, the way you speak. 'Quick getaway?' You sound like an old movie."

"Horsefeathers," Rafe said in English, making Olivia laugh. "How's your arm?"

"He just winged me, speaking of old movies. It burns a little when I move it, but I think the water did it some good. I hardly feel it anymore."

Rafe spitted the fish on a long, smooth stick Olivia had intended to add to the fire. "Fire's pretty hot, but I'm too hungry to wait." Rafe held the fish over the flames. "I'm sorry I didn't see him coming. I should have. I'm used to watching for him."

"As I recall, we were pretty involved just then." Olivia wrinkled her nose. "And he's a sneak. I wonder that I never noticed that about him."

Rafe looked over at her. She was flat on her back, relaxed as a cat, staring thoughtfully heavenward. "You know, I called my office the first day he went down to the beach."

She turned her head to look at him. "Why?"

"I asked them to call Scripps and get you guys yanked off the beach."

Olivia studied him for a minute, then looked back at the sky. "Huh. Lucky for you your foul plan didn't work. I would have hunted you down and smacked you around if I'd gotten yanked from my first command assignment."

Rafe chuckled. "I figured I'd be tougher to kill than you. And Cervantes would have killed all of you if you'd gotten between us."

"I did get between you, and he hasn't managed to finish me off, yet."

"Luck," Rafe grunted.

"Skill," Olivia corrected. "Between your survival instincts and Bobby's thievery and my experience on this stretch of water, we could elude that little weasel for another fifteen years."

Rafe gloated a little over the "weasel" comment. He refrained from mentioning *he'd* known Cervantes was a weasel since he was ten years old, while it had taken her getting shot at to come to the same conclusion. "We just need to stay out of sight for another thirty-six hours."

"Then what?" Olivia sat up, brushed the sand from her hands. "What happens on Tuesday, exactly?"

"Exactly? I never know what's going to happen exactly. Maybe nothing."

He slid one of the fish to the very end of the stick and blew on it until it was cool enough to touch. He then offered it to Olivia, who took it in her fingers and peeled the skin back. She took a bite.

"Needs salt," she said.

"Stop poking the bear," Rafe warned placidly.

Olivia mumbled something too low for him to hear, then giggled to herself. Rafe couldn't help but smile at her. She was pretty damn charming.

Olivia ate steadily, picking out the bones of the fish and

flicking them into the fire. "What do you *think* will happen, then?"

Rafe swallowed a bite of his own dinner. "If he shows up, we wait until he makes contact with his suppliers. Both Mexican and U.S. authorities have known about Aldea Viejo and Cervantes's operation since before Ernesto even took over for his father. The *federales* could have shut down the town, but they never had enough proof to convict Cervantes. We want the Mexican government to extradite him to the States, and to do that, we have to have evidence he's connected to the shipments directly."

"Why extradite him? I mean, isn't that a very complicated thing to do?"

"Very complicated. But he's wanted for crimes other than trafficking inside the United States, and we want him to stand trial on our turf, where his money and position and influence won't get him off."

"What other crimes?"

"He murdered a DEA agent twenty years ago," Rafe said, the words sticking in his throat even after all these years.

"My God, no wonder you want him so badly. He killed one of your own."

More one of my own than you know, he thought, the bitterness he'd held to him for so long rising in his chest.

"He must have been just a boy when it happened."

"He was seventeen," Rafe said tightly. "He'd already been a linchpin in his father's organization for three years when he came across the border for the first time with a shipment of unprocessed heroin. One of our young officers was there to intercept, as part of a regular patrol near the Mexicali border crossing. The officer identified himself as an agent and asked Cervantes to step out of the car so he could search it. Eyewitnesses say Cervantes shot the officer before he had even finished his sentence."

Olivia was watching Rafael closely now. His face, in the firelight, was flat, expressionless. His knuckles were

white around the stick he still held, however, and his eyes
were blazing. Fury, she thought. But something else, too.

Grief? For an unknown officer shot down so long ago?

"Who was he? The officer Cervantes killed."

"My brother. George."

"Oh, Rafe." Grief swamped her—for him, for the child
he'd been when his brother had died. "How terrible. How
old were you?"

"I was ten, almost. Bobby was a year younger. George
was his *padrino,* his godfather, as well as his cousin."

"And you've dedicated your lives to making Cervantes
pay."

Rafe looked at her for the first time since he'd begun
the story. "He was my brother," he said fiercely, quietly.

Olivia met his savage gaze. "You don't have to defend
yourself to me, Rafael. I am only surprised you haven't
killed him already."

Rafe's eyes reflected the flames of the fire. Olivia could
not tell which blaze burned hotter. "I don't want him to
die," he said. He glanced meaningfully at Olivia's bandage. "I want him to suffer."

"And so you became a drug agent. You and Bobby,
both."

"We made a blood pact after George's funeral. I don't
even know if Bobby understood it all at the time, but he
came to understand it, and he's kept the pact all these
years. It's taken us twenty years to get this close—ten
years waiting to grow up, ten years working our way
through the agency." He laughed shortly. "I can't tell you
how many times I've woken up in a cold sweat over the
years, praying some son-of-a-bitch drug runner didn't kill
him before Bobby and I could bring him to justice." He
shook his head. "I know that must sound crazy to you."

"Not crazy," Olivia said. She steadied herself against
the rush of admiration she felt for him. "Not crazy at all,"
she finished quietly.

There were so many ways to exact retribution, Olivia

knew. And Rafe deserved retribution, she thought, for him-self and his family. Olivia understood perfectly what an eldest son meant to a Latino family. More than just a means to ensure the name, an eldest son represented all that was strong and noble about a family. Her own younger brother, the eldest male Galpas offspring, was the apple of even her enlightened, modern father's eye.

But Rafael hadn't turned into the kind of man circum-stance and bitterness could have made him. He'd been pa-tient, intelligent, resourceful. He'd followed the laws of both countries, and done his duty to his family at the same time.

Olivia cleared her throat, willing herself not to tear up. "I respect you for it, as a matter of fact."

He blinked at her. "What?"

"I respect you, Rafael. You could have killed Cervantes a hundred times, I'm sure. I know you could have killed him the other night, in his house. But you've taken this path. I respect you for sticking to it, despite the anger you must feel."

She damn near terrified him, this woman, Rafe thought. She sat innocently next to him, and just when he thought he could handle the way he felt about her, she said some-thing that terrified him. *Respected* him? How the hell was he ever supposed to let her go, when she said things that made his heart swell in his chest and made every single hurdle he'd overcome in the past twenty years seem worth-while, even honorable.

He gave her a scornful look. For his own protection, as much as anything. "My brother was a police officer, Oliv-ia. How could I avenge his death by doing something il-legal?"

Olivia smiled gently. This was the other Rafael, now. With his hard face and his sharp eyes. She scooted across the sand until she was plastered against his side, and took the stick from his hand. She tossed it into the fire, gripped his hand in hers.

"That's true, Rafael," she said softly, laying her head on his shoulder and watching the fire with him. "I'm sure, wherever your brother is right now, he respects you, too."

Rafe felt the oddest sting at the back of his throat. He tried to swallow it down. He slammed his eyes tightly shut before anything unforgivable happened, and held onto Olivia's hand for dear life.

"For a scientist," he said roughly after a minute, "you have some very unscientific ideas."

"I'm a woman, too," Olivia murmured comfortably. "And a Latina." She smiled wryly. "You cannot kill the passionate heart of a Latin woman with anything so simple as science."

Rafe kissed the hair at the crown of her head. Lucky thing, he thought. He'd hate to see Olivia lose her passionate heart.

They sat together for a while, watching the fire die down. Rafe knew they needed to get back to the boat, but he was loath to make any move at all. He felt relaxed, contented almost, for the first time in months, without the perpetual simmer in his gut that reminded him constantly of his duty and his promise to his long-dead brother.

Olivia kept her head on his shoulder, equally unwilling to move. Her dress had dried in the heat of the fire and the breeze that had blown up after dusk. She was thirsty, but otherwise perfectly comfortable. Not cold, not hot. Just…happy.

She'd spent hundreds of nights like this in her life, even before she started working for the institute. Beach fires and clothes stiff with salt and sandy hair were nothing new to her. But she'd never been with Rafael on any of those beaches.

"Are you ready for another swim?" Rafe asked after a while.

She stretched her shoulders, sighed. "I don't think so," she said, and pushed him back into the sand.

The woman crawled on top of him as though she'd belonged there all her life, without a moment's hesitation or abashment. He wrapped his arms around her instinctively.

"Olivia."

"I want you, Rafael."

"I know," he said. He laughed thickly. "I can't believe it."

Olivia smiled. "Me, either. I'm normally a very cautious woman. If we were back in San Diego, you'd have to court me for months before I'd lie on top of you like this."

"I love Mexico," Rafe breathed. "I want you, too, Olivia."

Her toes rubbed the still-damp denim at his shinbone. She framed his face with her small, competent hands, and kissed him with all the passion and tenderness she felt in her heart. "Show me," she whispered.

He didn't need to think how. His body took over, touching her, sliding her dress up her thighs until he could feel the swell of her bottom under his rough hands. He moaned—or she did—when he cupped it solidly; he couldn't tell which of them made the sound.

The calluses on his hands snagged at the delicate nylon of her panties. They were pink, he remembered. He'd bought them only this morning, not allowing himself so much as a single image of her wearing them as he'd stuffed them into the paper sack.

Now he allowed himself an image or two. "Olivia," he said frantically. "Sit up."

Olivia sat up, straddling his waist, careful of his sore ribs. "Take your dress off. I want to see you."

His voice was thick, raspy, sexy. And so deep. It had fallen another octave. Olivia thought she might climax from the sound of it alone.

She took the hem of the dress in her hands and slowly, slowly raised it to her waist. "This dress?" she asked.

Rafe looked from her half-lidded eyes to the pink panties he could now see, quite clearly, in the firelight. "Oh, man."

Olivia laughed lightly at his desperate groan. She'd never done anything very wicked before, and she found she enjoyed the risk. She raised the dress another inch.

He could see her belly button now. Exquisite. His tongue flicked out automatically, so badly did he want to taste that little nub of skin. He stared at her, unable to so much as raise his eyes to hers. "A little more," he rasped.

Olivia bunched the fabric of her dress in her hands. "This much more?"

"Higher, Olivia." He could see the glimmer of nylon where her breasts filled the underside of her bra. "Higher."

Up the dress went, just a fraction of an inch. His fingers were twitching, his lower body jerking upward instinctively. "You're killing me," he moaned.

She whipped the dress over her head and off.

He stared at her for a minute, then reached up with one big hand. Olivia held her breath. Her nipples were already stiff inside her bra, her breasts full.

But he didn't touch her where she was dying to be touched. He traced the bandage on her arm with one finger. "I could kill him for this alone, you know," he said, his voice nothing more than a low growl in the darkness.

She moved his hand away from the wound, placed it on her left breast. He cupped her automatically, and Olivia watched his eyes dilate to pinpoints, following the motion of his hand.

His other hand came up, then, and caressed her right breast. Olivia tipped her head back and let him play. He pressed his palms against her, rubbing, molding, pinching lightly, until her back was bowed and she was grinding herself against his abdomen, looking for relief.

"Take off the bra," Rafe ordered, his dark eyes fixed on her breasts.

She reached back, unsnapped the hooks and let the bra fall to his chest.

His breathing accelerated to a dangerous level. "You

have the most perfect breasts," he said. He cupped them
again, whisked his thumbs across the dark, puckered tips.
"Small and high and proud. Like a queen."

Olivia could do nothing more than whimper. She would
have liked to tell him she was no queen, no woman to be
treated like royalty, but she couldn't get a single coherent
word past her lips. He spent minutes playing with her,
studying her, as though they had all the time in the world,
as though he intended to make her climax simply from
touching her breasts.

But no. He sat up suddenly, scooting her into his lap by
moving those amazing hands down to her bottom and
clamping her hips to his. And then...oh, then, Olivia
thought, dazed. He played with her breasts a little more.
With his mouth.

She was probably going to die. This kind of pleasure
would kill her. He sucked, hard, until she moaned out loud.
Then he moved to the other peak, and sucked again.

He was almost at the edge of his composure. One more
wiggle of that panty-clad little butt over his fly, and he
was going to embarrass them both. He dug his fingers into
her hips to keep her still. The feel of her eraser-hard nipple
between his tongue and the roof of his mouth was more
than enough, without the added stimulation of her writhing.

She was doing something with her hands now. Oh, man,
taking off his shirt. Her fingers brushed his nipples as she
pushed the shirt to his shoulders. He did five quick algebra
equations in his head and tried to remember the batting
averages of at least three San Diego Padres. Then, when
she flicked at them again, on *purpose* this time, tried to
recall the name of the Charger quarterback from 1976 to
1984. *Dan Something*.

"Olivia, slow down."

"No, you hurry up," she implored frantically. She
yanked at the buttons of his jeans.

Rafe grabbed her hands. "You're going to hurt something,'' he said, breathing unsteadily. He eased her to the sand next to him, where she knelt, nearly naked.

He shucked his jeans and briefs in an instant, and knelt in front of her, taking her hips in his hands again.

She looked stunning in the firelight. Her skin was the color of honey where the sun hadn't touched her. He reached up, ran a fingertip from the base of her throat to her navel. ''Beautiful Olivia,'' he murmured.

''You have bruises,'' she whispered. She touched his chest gently.

''I do?'' he said, managing a smile. ''Right now, Olivia, I couldn't even tell you if I had ribs, much less bruises on my ribs.''

''Then you're okay?'' She worried her lower lip, stared at his chest again. ''For this?''

''Look lower.''

She did. And blinked. ''Oh.''

He had to laugh. ''Olivia, are you sure about this?''

She met his gaze. ''I'm sure.''

''Then finish,'' he said.

''Finish?''

He gave her the slow once-over. She felt her skin flush, his dark eyes were so hot. ''Finish.''

She sat back in the sand, slipped her panties down her legs. Then, because it was the most natural thing in the world to do, she lay back, stretching her arms over her head, and let him look his fill.

''Finished,'' she said.

He came over her like a conqueror, no longer wondering how or why, knowing only that he had to be inside her or die. He kneed open her legs. ''I want to taste you,'' he said, almost to himself. ''I've wondered what you taste like. But I can't wait any longer to be inside you.''

She wrapped her legs across his back. ''Then be inside me,'' she urged.

She was so small, and he was not small by any means, and the joining was slow, sweet torture for them both.

He rocked back and forth for the longest time, letting her adjust, talking himself out of spilling inside her quickly, marking her with his seed as his own.

Olivia couldn't take her eyes off him. He was up on his hands, levering his weight off her, his jaw taut and his eyes squeezed shut in intense concentration. The veins in his neck were distended with effort and one slow bead of sweat dropped from his chin onto her chest. He opened his eyes, followed the droplet as it slid between her breasts to rest in the hollow at the base of her throat. He cocked his elbows and, lowering his head, licked it up with one long swipe of his tongue. Olivia whimpered and closed her eyes.

Her hips seemed to rise against his of their own accord. She couldn't bear the slow stroke of him any longer. She wanted speed, heat. And because she'd always been a woman who went after what she wanted, she lifted herself to him again and again, changing the pace of their love-making until they were slamming into each other, flesh against flesh, fast and hot and wild.

Rafe heard her cry out, felt the clench of her body around him. His vision began to gray but he battled it back. He looked down, watched her buck beneath him. She was beautiful, remarkable. *His.* He wanted to tell her he loved her so she would know it as she came.

"Olivia."

She opened her eyes languidly, smiled up at him in wonder and satisfaction. A jolt of sexual electricity zapped every thought from his mind but one.

"Do that for me again," he whispered. And he began to move.

"No," she groaned. She couldn't possibly.

Moments later, she did. And this time he came with her.

"Olivia, we have to get back to the boat."

She lay on her back, pressed into the sand by his big,

incredibly warm body. She ran one limp hand down his damp back. "Can't."

"Have to," he mumbled against her shoulder. But he made no effort to climb off her.

"You're lying on me," she reminded him.

"I know. I'm going to get off in a second. As soon as I can see again."

"Are you blind?"

"Yes."

Olivia chuckled. "Sorry."

"And paralyzed."

"You'll have a hard time swimming."

"I'll have a hard time ever thinking again," he muttered. "Am I crushing you?"

"Mmm. It's nice. Don't move."

He shifted slightly. "I'd better."

She clamped her legs around his, wrapped her arms around his back and hung on. "Why?"

"Can you feel that?"

He was growing inside her. Already. Olivia laughed from the sheer, joyous flattery of it all. "Yes." She moved against him.

"Don't move. Olivia, stop it! We need to—" His instincts took over and his hips began to thrust forward. It felt so…good. "Oh, man," he mumbled, and gave in to it.

It went more slowly this time, and they watched each other carefully, reading each nuance of expression.

He slid his hand between their bodies. Olivia's eyes glazed. "Do you like that?"

"Yes," she breathed. She lifted her head, took his nipple between her teeth and bit down. He moaned. "Do you like that?" she asked.

"Oh. Oh, yes."

It ended quietly, but by no means moderately. Olivia's back arched from her shoulders to her heels as he slid adroitly, expertly against her. His eyes stayed open until the last, and he linked his fingers with hers without knowing it.

He rolled off into the sand afterward, to keep from crushing her again. And to keep some physiological miracle from happening to his body that would keep them from getting back onto the boat.

"We really do have to go now," he said once his breathing returned to normal.

"You go," she said sleepily. "I'm going to take a little nap." She rolled to her side on the sand, her bottom to the dying fire.

Rafe chuckled, ran the back of his hand down her spine. He rubbed her back and watched the stars for a few minutes, while she took a catnap. But he knew they needed to get back to the boat. He shook her gently. "Come on, *princesa*. Time for another little swim. Get your dress on."

"I'll just swim without it," she mumbled. "I don't have the strength to put it back on."

"I don't think so. I'm going to have to blindfold Manny and Bobby as it is. If you climb aboard naked, I'll have to cage them."

Olivia giggled drowsily. "You overestimate my appeal. I'm sure Bobby and Manuel have seen a naked woman before."

"Not in a while. And never one who looks as good as you."

Olivia rolled over to face him. She was definitely awake, Rafe noted with something close to trepidation. And she had a wicked little gleam in her eye.

"Oh, yeah?"

Rafael stared at her in surprise, then shook his head. "No. Forget it. I couldn't even if I wanted to, which I don't."

She crawled over on her hands and knees. Rafe felt his mouth go dry at the sight. Her breasts were too small to swing properly, but what they lacked in heft, they more than made up for in responsiveness. Her nipples were pebbled already.

"Stay away from me," he warned halfheartedly.

"I have stayed away from you. I stayed away for three whole days, when I didn't have to. All your fault, I'd like to remind you."

She wriggled on top of him and stretched out. His hands came up and stroked from her bottom to her neck and back again. He didn't want to encourage her, but he couldn't seem to control his own impulses.

"I don't know what you expect is going to happen here, Olivia."

"Oh, I can think of all kinds of things," she said.

"Didn't you take human anatomy courses in college?"

Olivia's laugh rumbled against his chest. "You know, for the most humorless person I know, you say the funniest things."

"I'm not humorless." He clamped his arms around her and sat up. "You just don't understand my subtleties."

She kissed him, grinning. "Yes, I do. I've determined you have at least three separate gradations of pissed off."

"I'm all strata and substrata," he agreed.

She levered up on her good arm to look at him. "Very un-cop like words to be tossing about, *señor*."

"I took one geology class at San Diego State."

"You went to college?"

Rafe nuzzled her. One wayward, unbiddable hand slid up to cup her breast. He felt a stirring that shocked him. Maybe his human anatomy was not as subject to the whims of physics and blood flow as he'd previously thought. "Mmm?"

"You went—" Ooh, he was flicking at her with his thumb. "You went—?" She was supposed to be asking him an important question. What the hell was it? He shifted her on his lap. "Oh, do that again."

Rafe groaned and chuckled at the same time. "You want to ride me, *princesa?*"

She locked her eyes on his, wrapped her arms around his neck.

"Can you take it?"

"I can if you can."

She grinned. "Then hold on."

Chapter 12

They fueled up the boat in Pico Cupula, and continued up the coast of the Sea of Cortéz. Olivia stayed at the helm, usually with Rafael standing at her back, while the other two men watched the sea and the shore for any sign of Cervantes.

At dusk, Rafe went below for something to eat, and by some unspoken signal Bobby came to stand at her side. "How far?"

"Another couple hours to the beach at Aldea Viejo," she answered. "But I'm assuming you guys want to stop before then, or overshoot it?"

Bobby grinned. "Those little letters after your name aren't just for show, are they, Doc."

"You'd be surprised how often they're *entirely* for show," she answered wryly.

Bobby looked out to sea. "Looks like you outsmarted them, Doc. We haven't seen them, they haven't seen us. You're pretty good at the covert stuff."

"Really? Then why have you and Rafael been plastered to my back all day?"

"Snipers," Bobby said simply. "You can evade the other boats, but you can't stop a bullet coming from shore."

Olivia's jaw dropped. "Are you kidding?"

"I never kid," he said with a completely straight face.

"You know, I don't know why Rafael just doesn't tell me these things—"

"Because Rafael thinks you have enough on your mind without worrying about getting shot at again," Rafe said, climbing the steps from the galley. He punched Bobby, hard, in the arm. "Keep away from her, bigmouth."

Bobby rubbed his arm. "You're just afraid she thinks I'm charming and funny."

Rafe snorted his opinion of that, then muscled Bobby out of his way and took up his place behind Olivia again. Just in case she *did* think his cousin was charming and funny.

He had told Bobby he wanted to keep close to her during the trip up the coast, the primary reason being that they had no idea what kind of firepower Cervantes had along the shore. Cervantes knew they were out on the gulf somewhere, and he knew Rafe and Bobby planned to steal the shipment of raw coke coming in from the mainland Tuesday, so chances were excellent he'd be watching the shoreline.

Thanks to Olivia and her uncanny ability with the little fishing boat, they'd evaded Cervantes so far. But Rafe was taking no more chances with Olivia's life. So he and Bobby had taken turns watching her back all day.

He had to admit, though, it was more than his well-honed survival instincts that kept him close during the long hours motoring up the rugged desert coast. He realized, after tomorrow, he wouldn't see her again. And it made him ache. She would be gone, returned to her high-class family, doing prestigious research, socializing with well-educated scientists. He would be back in his routine of living undercover where a bullet could take his life any day of the week. She could never be happy with a man like that, he told himself harshly. She was from another world. Her life would continue in high society, and he could never hope to be a part of it. Never before and never again would their paths cross, he thought, the ache filling him with sorrow.

"How close do you want to get?" Olivia asked him.

He watched the water over her shoulder, resisting the urge to bury his nose at the curve of her neck. She smelled, as she always did, of the sun and the water and that warm scent that was just Olivia. He knew he'd never smell anything so wonderful again in his life. "I don't know, exactly. I want to be able to get to the beach on foot."

"Okay. I know a beach near here. I spent a week there last fall with a water temperature team. There's an animal path that leads through the dunes that will take you north in a couple hours' walk."

Rafe nodded. "Good. The Mexican *federales* are going to be in the dunes at Aldea Viejo, waiting for a signal from Bobby or I. We don't have any transportation waiting, so we need to be fairly close." Olivia turned her head to study him. He met her eyes. "On the other hand, I don't want to be too close. Cervantes will likely have someone patrolling the beach for miles, waiting for us to come in."

"How are the *federales* going to get past him, then?"

Rafe grinned. "They're already there."

"The moles?"

"Yes, but don't call them that to their faces."

She stared at him. "But if you have people on the inside already, why can't you just arrest him at the *hacienda?* Why risk your lives like this?"

"Because we have four men inside, and he has dozens. Besides, no one has been able to determine whether he keeps any kind of records in the *hacienda.* I told you last night, we have to be able to connect him physically with an actual shipment or we can't get him out of Mexico to stand trial. That's what the past few months have all been about. Drawing him out of his hole.''

"Okay, I can see that. But what about the past few days? Where were your *federales* when we were being chased all over hell and back? And when Cervantes shot me?''

"One of them was driving one of the Land Cruisers, which is how we managed to stand on the street as they drove by and not get nabbed. Two more were passengers in the vehicle with Cervantes. The fourth, I guess, stayed in Aldea Viejo to coordinate. As for being shot at, I suspect the reason Cervantes didn't continue shooting is that our guys interfered in some way, or convinced their boss not to draw a crowd to the dock by blowing us out of the water so close to town.''

"Is that who you called when we stopped for food that first night? You actually called Ernesto's house?''

"No, too risky. We're sort of working independently. I called our guys in La Paz and Loreto to make sure we were all still going for the Tuesday shipment.''

"This is huge,'' Olivia breathed.

"Cervantes is a big fish, on both sides of the border. Everyone wants him, and we know this is our best chance.''

"Okay, now I'm worried,'' Olivia said. Her hands had gone sweaty on the wheel. "There's not much chance of anyone getting out of this whole deal with a few shots fired, is there.''

"Nope.''

Olivia sagged back against Rafe. "Wonderful.''

He circled her waist with his arm. "Don't worry, *princesa*,'' he whispered in her ear. "You just get us close enough in this little dinghy of yours, and Bobby and I will take care of the rest.''

She moored several miles from Aldea Viejo, off a beach that, as far as she knew, had no roads leading to it from the main highway. Rafe and Bobby would have to walk

overland to keep their appointment in the morning. Olivia
chose the place with as much care as she would choose a
home for the rest of her life. She knew if Cervantes came
upon them in the night, they would have little chance of
surviving the attack.

She and Rafe did not swim to shore. Because he had
eaten earlier, Olivia shared the last of the rations with
Bobby and Manny, while Rafe kept watch. Then, as she
had the night before—after she and Rafe had crawled back
onto the boat, dripping wet and giggling like lunatics—
Olivia headed below to sleep.

She paused at the top of the steps leading to the small
galley and single forward bunk.

"Rafael."

He turned from his place on the bow.

"Don't leave tomorrow—" She fought against both
dread and longing, knowing he needed his mind on his
work. "Don't leave without waking me."

Rafe nodded once, then looked back over the water.

Olivia went below, used the tiny head and crawled into
the snug bunk. She thought she would never sleep, but a
day of staring out onto the bright water worked its magic,
and to the familiar rocking of a vessel on water she fell
fast asleep.

Topside, Manny slapped Rafe on the shoulder. "You
staying up? I'll take the morning watch, if you are."

"Fine," Rafe replied. He didn't think he'd be able to
go to sleep yet, anyway. He needed to think.

Not about the morning. He'd been planning that for
months. For years, in one way or another. He knew everything about what he was going to do, how he would act
and react to keep them all alive and make sure Cervantes
was brought down at the same time.

No, he needed to think about Olivia. About how he was
going to let her go.

At midnight, Bobby came to the bow. He'd been sleeping on one of the bench seats at the stern of the boat.

Manny was on the other, snoring loudly. "Come on," Bobby said, yawning hugely. "Get some sleep."

Rafe went to the stern and lay back on the bench seat. It was too short for him, and he had to keep his knees in the air to fit. The cushions were baked hard and rough as hay bales from constant exposure to the sun; the one under his head was cracked, and the crumbling foam felt like pebbles against his skull. He barely noticed. He'd slept under far less comfortable circumstances over the past few months.

But he didn't drift off. His eyes would not close, his mind would not shut down.

She was below, and after tomorrow he'd never see her again.

He lifted his head. Manny was snoring, and Bobby was peering through a small pair of binoculars Manny had scrounged up, using the light of a half-moon to scan the shoreline.

Rafe rolled to the deck, stood up and slipped silently down the steps to Olivia.

She was asleep. He knew it was unfair to wake her; after all, she'd taken on the Baja coast in a tiny fishing boat all by herself today, and had done a damn good job of it. She deserved to rest now.

But he was desperate, trembling with need and regret and desire. He inched his way onto the bunk beside her. She felt warm and smelled so good. She sighed and turned in to him, snuggling close in her sleep.

"Oh, God, Olivia," he whispered. "How am I going to let you go?"

"Hmm?" she murmured.

"Olivia, wake up."

She opened her eyes slowly, like a cat waking from a nap in the sun. "Rafael?"

"I need you."

She blinked once, then opened her arms.

He didn't remove her dress, just flipped it to her waist

and tugged her panties down her legs. He unbuttoned his jeans, freed himself and plunged into her.

He made love to her silently, desperately, Olivia thought, his mouth fused to hers, his hands sliding over her as though he might never touch her again. He didn't wait for her climax, but reared back at the last minute, reaching his own release with an expression that was almost painful. His lips were drawn back from his teeth, and he seemed barely able to contain the low growl that erupted from his chest. Olivia watched him, wondering at the despair etched into every line of his sharp face. All she felt, aside from the lust, was joy.

When he rolled to her side, he touched her delicately, until she was writhing and bucking under his hands. After the glorious peak, as her system calmed, he stroked her belly.

They didn't speak. After a while, Rafe toed off his shoes and rebuttoned his jeans. Olivia pushed her dress back around her knees. Then, hands linked tightly together, they went to sleep side by side.

He knew it was morning before he opened his eyes. He shifted to cuddle Olivia closer, though he was already spooned around her from head to toe.

"What time is it?" she whispered in the dark.

Rafe lifted his wrist to check. "Four."

Olivia stared at the hull of the boat. It was inches from her face. Rafael took up more than his share of the bed. She'd have to get a bigger bed when she got home to San Diego. And, good heavens, her own house. She didn't think she could ever make love with him again and keep from screaming out loud.

If she ever made love with him again. The thought had been there in her sleep, had come to her even as he'd buried himself inside her. What if she never made love with him again? She'd been so confident the night before last, alone with him on that small stretch of beach. Now, when he was just hours away from facing his enemy, she couldn't summon a shred of the same brash conviction.

A shiver started in her stomach, radiated outward until she was shaking uncontrollably.

"Stop it," he said in her ear. "Stop shaking."

"Okay," she stuttered through chattering teeth.

"Olivia, it's going to be all right. You're going to be fine."

Was she? It hardly seemed to matter. "I know," she said.

He clutched at her, thinking if he held her tightly enough, she'd stop shaking. He wanted to go on holding her forever, but he knew he only had a little time and a lot to say.

"Listen, I haven't wanted to use the boat radio in case Cervantes was monitoring the coastal transmissions, but after we leave, I want you to wait two hours, then radio La Paz for help. Make sure Manny knows who you're talking to. He's a local cop there. We think there's a leak in his unit, but he says he has a guy he can trust. Understand?"

"Yes."

"Olivia, stop shaking. I want you to give them the coordinates where we're anchored. Do not get off the boat until someone Manny knows and trusts comes to get you. He has a weapon, but only one. You need to stay hidden here in this cove until someone comes for you, do you understand?"

"Yes." *But I want you to come for me,* she wanted to say. She pulled her lips between her teeth to keep from crying out.

"Good girl. When you get to La Paz, get the first flight out. I don't care where it's going. Take it. You can get a connector wherever you land. If you have trouble at the airport, let Manny take care of it for you."

"All right."

"I have to go." He kissed a spot between her shoulder

blades. He knew if she turned around, offered her mouth to him, he'd never be able to tell her goodbye. Forever.

He slid to the edge of the bunk, unlaced his shoes.

"When—" Olivia cleared her throat of sleep and anxiety, trying to be brave for him. "When will I see you again?"

Rafe steeled himself. "What do you mean?" he asked, feigning distraction. He knew this was best for them both; would allow him his dignity and wouldn't keep her from her real life. If they went on pretending they had any chance together, she'd only end up resenting him for the *barrio* kid he really was, and he'd end up with his heart in a million bloody ribbons.

Olivia turned her head to stare at his back. "When will I see you again?" she repeated dumbly. She had no idea why he would answer in such an odd way.

"Olivia, I don't really have time for this discussion right now."

Her heart went cold even as her mind refused to register his impatient tone, his reluctance to look at her. "What discussion? I just want to know when you'll be back in San Diego. When I will see you." She had to know, because if he left here without a promise, there was a chance he would die out there. If he promised her he'd see her in San Diego, she knew he'd be all right today. He'd never break a promise to her.

He rested his elbows on his knees. "We hardly hang out in the same places, Olivia," he said, the short laugh he gave sounding like the hissing of a snake in his own ears. "If we've gone this many years not running into each other, I can't imagine we would now."

"Run into each other?" Her voice was so soft that he could barely hear her. His hands were in fists now, and his stomach was in knots. "What do you mean, 'run into each other'?"

He leaned back, kissed her lightly on the cheek. "I mean, *princesa,* that you're done slumming and I'm done taking care of you. Where the hell would we ever see each other again? We don't exactly socialize in the same circles.''

She stared at him. "You're a liar."

Rafe sucked in his cheeks. He was botching this completely. Her eyes were huge, liquid, disbelieving. If she didn't start crying soon, he might.

"You're a liar," she repeated. "You're in love with me.''

Rafe shook his head. "No, I'm not."

"Yes, you are." Olivia frowned, her breath coming in short, panicky bursts. "All the data points to it."

"Olivia, before you came walking down that hallway, I'd barely *seen* a woman in months, much less had sex with one. Maybe you didn't input that with the rest of your data.''

Her head snapped back as if she'd taken a blow to the face. Rafe dug his hands into the rough fabric of the bunk to keep from reaching for her.

"You came to me tonight. You made love to me."

Rafe sighed heavily for dramatic effect, while his guts twisted up into a hangman's knot. "What man wouldn't have come to you, Olivia? I may not make it through today, and you're—well, to put it bluntly, you're here. Not that I'm not very sexually attracted to you.''

"My God," she whispered. "You're trying to hurt me. This is the old Rafael, the drug smuggler person you only pretend to be.''

"There's only one Rafael," he said flatly. "And I have to go.''

She didn't say anything, didn't try to stop him. He was both grateful and sorry. If she'd said another word, he might have lost his nerve.

He so wanted to lose his nerve in this.

He paused at the doorway to the steps. Without turning around, he spoke. "Remember what I said about the radio, and Manny.''

She didn't sound like Olivia when she whispered, in English, "Go to hell," but he understood the sentiment. He wanted to tell her he was already well on his way.

Rafe watched the boat zip toward the shore. It was a sleek, powerful vessel, one he knew was designed for just this kind of transport. His eyes searched the beach again. No one there. Not one man.

"Where the hell are they all?" he muttered. The seething in his belly that he'd been living with for months and months was about to drive him insane. Something huge was happening, and damn if he knew what it was. "Where the hell is Cervantes?"

His partner kept a hawk's eye on the boat. It bobbed just offshore, its motor idling, its driver and passenger studying the beach.

Rafe glanced at his watch. It was nearly eight in the morning. Olivia was long gone by now, on a boat or in a car headed back to La Paz. She'd soon be on a plane home, or to somewhere closer to home, at least, than this godforsaken stretch of coastline. He wanted to drop his head in the sand and moan.

"What do we do now?" Bobby asked after several minutes.

Rafe had no idea. He'd had no contact with the moles in Cervantes's organization and he had no way of contacting his people in La Paz or Loreto to make sure the deal was still going down. "We wait," he said. "We've got nothing better to do."

Olivia heard the low growl of a boat engine and scrambled off the bunk and up the steps. Manny was lying on his belly on the cushions of the stern, his gun aimed toward the little boat.

"Get down," he yelled at Olivia.

She hit the deck, her heart thumping wildly. She'd been

sitting below, numbly counting off the minutes until she could use the radio and get the hell off this boat. She had been sure then that her heart had stopped in her chest, that nothing could make it beat again.

Rafe didn't love her. What an idiot she'd been to think he did. He'd never said any such thing, never intimated anything of the kind. He'd lied to her from the beginning about who he really was, but he'd never lied to her about love.

She was a brilliant woman. She was accomplished and well-respected and terribly, terribly smart. Yet Rafael Camayo had been able to take out her heart and stomp it into the sand, and she'd never even seen it coming.

But when the distinctive noise of an incoming boat caught her ear, her heart had started beating again, surprising her, frankly. And now her brain had kicked in, as well, as she considered and discarded a dozen options for evading this unknown threat.

So, Rafael was not the only one with an exaggerated survival instinct, she thought, her face pressed to the rough surface of the deck.

"Rafael, *cabrón*, show yourself, you thieving coward!" The voice was distorted by a megaphone, but Olivia recognized it instantly. It had become very familiar during all those long, chatty strolls down the beach.

Olivia slithered forward on her stomach until she reached the helm. With one hand she reached up, turned the key and pressed the ignition button. The boat, dear old thing, sputtered to life. Manuel turned and stared at her, goggle-eyed.

"What are you doing?" he yelled.

"I'm getting us the heck out of here," she yelled back, and, still in a crouch, pulled the throttle back until the boat began to move. She stood up then. "Hold on," she warned Manuel, and shot the throttle to the limit.

The boat leapt forward, impressing Olivia once again with its power. But it wasn't enough. Not nearly.

The other boat was upon them before Olivia had a chance to maneuver her boat out of the cove and onto open water. It had been a futile attempt, and she knew it, but she wasn't about to allow Ernesto Cervantes to shoot her down like a dog.

"Shut it down," the megaphone voice called to her over the water.

She didn't bother to look over, just kept her eyes on the open water ahead.

"Shut it down, Olivia. We just want Rafael and his partner. You are free to go back to your country."

She could brazen this out. She knew she could. He'd only hit her on that dock because she'd been standing there like a lump. Now she was a fast-moving target. Not only was her boat roaring through the water, but her knees were knocking together so hard she didn't think anyone in the world could get a clean bead on her.

Manny came up behind her. "Stop this damn boat," he screamed at her.

"No. Shoot at them!"

"Are you crazy? They have three men with guns pointed right at you."

"Shoot at them."

"Dammit, Dr. Galpas, if you get yourself killed, Rafe is going to have my *huevos*."

"I'm warning you, Olivia," the megaphone voice said. "You are interfering with Mexican law."

She snapped her head around to glare at him. "You're not the law! You *shot* me," she screamed.

"I was aiming at the drug smuggler, Olivia. I was rescuing you."

"I have had enough of being lied to," she yelled, and turned the wheel just enough to bump the speedboat. She caught a glimpse of the skipper's face as he swung his boat to avoid her. He looked genuinely horrified. Olivia laughed tersely.

"Stop the boat," Manny ordered. "You'll never outrun them."

Olivia worked her jaw. No, she couldn't stop. She knew Cervantes wasn't going to get her off this boat just to let her go. She'd rather take her chances with the Sea of Cortéz. It had always been her friend.

"This is your last warning, Dr. Galpas," Cervantes cautioned her.

She raised her hand and gave him a distinctly American indication that she was unwilling to cooperate.

Cervantes shot the proverbial cannon across the bow. Only it wasn't proverbial, it was real, and Manny hit the deck behind her.

"You crazy woman," he screamed at her. "Kill the engine!"

She did. Shut it right down and stopped dead in the water. Then, while Cervantes's boat zipped past her going full speed, Olivia gunned the boat into reverse.

Manuel was right. She'd never outrun them in this tug, gutsy as it was. She'd have to outrun them on dry land.

Manny got to his knees, stared first out the back of the boat at the approaching shoreline, then back at Olivia.

Cervantes was shouting hysterically at his driver, and when Olivia looked back at them she could see they were turning. They'd be on top of her and Manny again in an instant.

Olivia set her jaw. Fine. She'd be *beached* in an instant.

"Hold on," she shouted to Manny.

The boat hit the beach with a thunderous, shaking crash. Olivia, tossed back on her butt, heard gravel suck into the manifold of the engine and said a quick prayer for the brave little boat. It had done itself proud.

She shot to her feet as soon as she stopped skidding backward, and with the skirt of her orange dress hiked to her hips, ran for the stern, Manny hot on her heels. She jumped on top of the cushions of the bench seat and, without a moment's hesitation, leaped into the shallow surf.

She fell to her knees but struggled up again at once. She didn't bother to look for Manuel. If he wasn't with her, then she'd have to go it alone.

But he was with her, muttering about lunatic asylums and straight jackets as they plowed up the beach. Behind them, Cervantes was screaming at his driver to beach the expensive craft. Olivia knew he'd never do it. Once a man had piloted a boat as gorgeous and responsive as that one, he'd never hurt her. Men were much more careful with boats than they were with women, Olivia mused.

"Why aren't they firing at us?" Olivia yelled over her shoulder at Manuel.

"I don't know. Just run, *maniaca*," Manuel shouted back.

I'm not a maniac, Olivia thought desperately. *I only want to stay alive so I can make that Rafael Camayo pay for breaking my heart.*

They reached the dunes just as Olivia heard splashing behind her. So Cervantes wanted her enough to swim for her, did he? Maybe the sharks would get him before he reached the beach.

No such luck. She could hear him shouting for someone to search the fishing boat for Rafe and Bobby, then shrieking at her to stop. She took another dune at a dead run. She'd never stop running. She'd never let the bastard get her. He'd have to shoot her first.

A single shot rang out. Olivia braced for the impact in the back of her head, but it never came. And she took another ten strides before she realized Manuel was no longer running at her side.

Oh, no. *No.* She glanced back over her shoulder in time to see Cervantes emerge from the surf a hundred yards back, lowering his weapon to his side. Manuel lay facedown in the dune, the sand beneath him soaking up his blood.

Ay Dios. Ay Dios.

She'd never in any nightmare expected to see something

like this. She'd known there were people in the world who would so casually take the lives of others, but she'd never imagined she would see it firsthand.

She stumbled, wild-eyed and terrorized, but righted herself. She was going to die, she was going to die, just like Manuel. *Oh, Manuel. I'm so sorry, Manuel.*

Another shot was fired, another warning given, but Olivia kept running. The voices were fainter. She didn't know if it was because of the drone like a million bees in her head, or because she was outrunning them.

It didn't matter. She only knew that she had to keep running. Olivia never knew where the resolve came from. She was strong and agile, had been all her life. She just hadn't known she was so damn tough. Funny how a terrified woman with a broken heart could run so hard.

She fled into the dunes.

Chapter 13

The sun was almost directly overhead by the time Rafe saw the two matching, safari-green Land Cruisers traverse the winding road that led to the beach.

"Finally," he breathed.

"Let the games begin," Bobby murmured at his side.

Rafe scrutinized the dunes behind them. "Wonder where our backup is?"

"You don't think they'll be in position?"

"We don't even know if they all made it back from La Paz. I wish we had the damn phone, or a radio or something."

"So do we follow the plan, or wait to see if we have backup?"

"We follow the plan. If they don't show…" His voice trailed off.

"We're up against Cervantes and his goons on our own," Bobby finished. "Not to mention the boys in the boat, there."

"We'll wait as long as we can. Maybe they'll pull out

before Cervantes leaves. If not, I'm sure they'll take off at the first sign of trouble. They're just the delivery boys."

Bobby watched the incoming vehicles. "So long as we land the big fish, the guppies can swim all the way back to the mainland."

Rafe scowled at his partner. "You have a way with words."

"I know."

"A bad way."

Bobby chuckled. "Olivia thinks I'm a riot."

Rafe grunted noncommittally and allowed his gaze to wander back to the beach. Casually. No sense letting Bobby know he was only half in the game. That his other half, the best part of who he was, was still in that little bunk with Olivia, holding her for the last time.

He rolled his lips over his teeth, disgusted with himself. That the mere mention of her name would make him hurt was unacceptable. He had another sixty years on this earth to live without Olivia; he couldn't let his stomach drop to his feet and his chest swell painfully every time he heard her name. Or thought of her. Or came within a hundred miles of the scent of the ocean.

And now, particularly, was not a good time to be wondering where she was, praying fervently that if nothing else right happened today, she was safely away. That she'd remember him, just a little, after she married some brilliant and rich and educated son of a bitch who didn't deserve her and couldn't possibly love her until he was sick with it.

"They're coming in," Bobby muttered. "You want to pay some attention, here, *vato?*"

Rafe rolled to his side, yanked his gun out of his waistband and checked the load. "I'm paying attention," he muttered.

Bobby followed Rafe's lead and palmed his gun. "Good. Because I don't want to go down there like Zorro and find out you're still back on that boat with Olivia."

"Don't worry about me," Rafe said testily. "I don't see Cervantes yet. I wish I had the binoculars. Dammit. The bastard better show up."

"He's there. He's just getting out of the second cruiser."

Rafe's mouth went dry. "Oh, *hell.*"

"What?"

"Look at his pants."

"Oh, hell," Bobby echoed. "He's been in the water."

"She better have gotten off the boat before he found it," Rafe said fiercely.

"I'm sure she did," Bobby said. "But if she didn't, Rafe, you can't do a damn thing about it."

Rafe's teeth were clenched so hard he thought he might pop a molar. "I can shoot him where he stands," he hissed, his lips barely moving.

"Yeah, you can do that. And then, if he's got her, if he's holding her somewhere, you'll never know, will you," Bobby asked quietly. "Jeez, Rafe, pull yourself together. She got off the boat. It's past eleven o'clock, and he's just now showing up with his pants wet. If she radioed out at eight o'clock like you told her to, she'd have been long gone by the time he found the boat. *If* he found it." Bobby narrowed his eyes, followed Cervantes's approach to the beach. "Maybe he's just so scared of us, *primo,* that he's pissed himself."

Rafe didn't answer. He was working desperately at keeping himself together, at not finding out for himself how many plugs he could put in Cervantes before he killed him. He had to focus on the matter at hand. If he killed Cervantes now, and Cervantes had gotten to Olivia this morning, Rafe might never find her. Dead or alive.

He felt a strange buzzing in his head at that terrible thought, and his tongue thickened against his clenched teeth. Funny, he'd never noticed before how many physical manifestations there were to a man's fear. Maybe he'd never really been afraid before.

Olivia couldn't be dead. He'd been willing, just barely, to give her up to her old life. But he'd be damned if he'd give her up to death.

Olivia was alive, but only by the narrowest margin of luck and the superior speed and stamina of youth.

She took in another shuddering breath. Every few minutes the scene would replay in her mind, of Cervantes standing in the surf, of Manuel's blood saturating the sand, of the moment when she realized she was alone and running from a madman.

Thank heaven the madman had finally given up an hour or so ago and gone back—to his zippy little boat, Olivia presumed. Apparently there were things more pressing than following one woman through the desert. Like a drug shipment to protect.

Cervantes probably thought she'd die out here, anyway. But he underestimated her, she knew. Dr. Olivia Galpas had overcome every obstacle ever set in front of her. She'd broken through the race and gender barriers in her profession and had been published and promoted and applauded. There was no way in hell she was going to let Ernesto Cervantes mow someone down in cold blood and get away with it. She'd be screaming his name from the rooftops until he was put behind bars.

First, she had to get out of this desert.

The sun was becoming unforgivably hot on the back of her neck and the arroyos and creek beds she crossed gave up not a drop of water. She'd sucked on a stem of barrel cactus carefully snapped from a large specimen, but it was a poor substitute for a nice glass of iced tea, which, since about an hour earlier, had become the focus of all her desires.

Meanwhile, her anger at Rafe grew, as his words ran in circles through her head.

So, he doesn't love me, she thought, the frustration giving her renewed energy to trudge over another hill. *Not that he's not sexually attracted to me. I was just there. To put it bluntly. Not that we'd ever run into each other.*

As she pushed on through the hot sand, anger wrestled with the ache in her heart. How could she fall for a drug agent? Maybe he was no better for her than a common thief. He probably would be gone all the time, making friends with criminals, and would most likely end up getting killed in the line of duty.

She thought of her family, how they expected her to marry a white-collar professional. A Latino doctor or lawyer or something, but not a drug agent.

So, fine. Let Rafe walk out, she told herself. Who needs him? She could feel tears welling up from her chest, then spilling down her cheeks.

"Not me!" she shouted as loudly as her dry throat would allow.

She slogged doggedly on toward Aldea Viejo, keeping well clear of the coastline. Olivia had no idea on which beach the drug exchange was to take place, and she was taking no chances.

It didn't matter, anyway, Olivia decided, as long as it wasn't in the middle of town. She intended to make her way to Aldea Viejo and slip into the village unnoticed. That would be much easier to do if the two men she'd been involved with during the past month weren't shooting at each other in the streets.

Olivia squared her shoulders, lifted her chin, pursed her lips resolutely. She'd learned a lot from Rafael in the past few days. She was now an expert in covert activity. She'd be just fine.

Her lips trembled just a little. Oh, Lord, it was an idiotic plan. Even sunstruck and frightened and miserable with heartache as she was, she could see how impossible it would be to get in and out of Aldea Viejo without someone who worked for Cervantes seeing her and alerting the ever-present, khaki-uniformed thugs.

But she had no choice.

Aldea Viejo was the only town around for miles. She knew she had to take her chances there. Because the only other option was to take her chances here, in this arid wasteland. She would do just fine if someone would plop an ocean down in front of her, but the desert baffled her.

Aldea Viejo was also where she'd left all her money, her identification and her plane ticket home. The little motel where she'd dressed for Ernesto's party—was it just last Friday?—would surely have held her belongings for her. Once she had money, a decent pair of shoes on her feet, and at least one clean pair of underwear, nothing could stop her from finding a way to make Cervantes pay for Manuel's death.

She skidded down another wash, wondering crossly where all the water was that had formed the thousands of gullies she'd forded since escaping Cervantes. She was concentrating on keeping at least some of the dirt out of her shoe, so she didn't see the man until she was almost on top of him.

She shrieked abruptly in surprise. He loomed in front of her like a mirage in the shimmering glare of the noon sun. One moment he wasn't there, the next he was. In his khaki uniform and with his big, shiny gun.

Olivia almost dropped to her knees and wept.

"Dr. Galpas. I've been waiting for you."

Cervantes must have radioed his people to be on the lookout for her. She should have known: she'd seen him shoot Manuel; he'd never leave her alone.

Olivia stood stock-still, weighing her options, realizing she didn't actually have any. The man hadn't raised his weapon to her, but Olivia knew he wouldn't hesitate to do so if she gave him any trouble.

"I'm sorry to have been so long," she said calmly. She pointed to her feet. "The wrong shoes, you understand."

He apparently did not, the big dummy. He stared at her feet a moment, then grunted. "Come along. *Señor* Cervantes wants to talk to you."

* * *

"Okay, that's it. Let's go."

Rafe and Bobby had been lying on their bellies for nearly an hour, watching Cervantes's men off-load the cargo from the boat. Cervantes surveyed the whole process from the beach, arms crossed, the arrogant overlord. Rafe would have arrested him for the smug expression on his face alone, if he could have. Cervantes was so certain his presence and the display of muscle and the midday exchange would keep away the little maggots that had been stealing from him that he didn't even bother to swivel his head every once in a while to see who might be coming out of the dunes.

Well, Rafe and Bobby were coming out of the dunes. And Cervantes's twenty-year reign as drug king of Aldea Viejo was over.

So focused was Rafe that he missed the flash of sun reflecting off the windshield of the third Land Cruiser as it made its way down the beach road. Bobby saw it, however, and hooked an arm around Rafe's ankles as he rose, dragging him back to the sand.

"What?"

Bobby pointed. "More company."

Rafe swore viciously. "We have no choice but to go in, anyway," he said, impatient and frustrated. "They're nearly finished unloading. This is too good to pass up."

"I don't think so," Bobby said grimly. "Look—"

The cruiser stopped next to Cervantes. The driver got out and opened the back door and dragged something—someone?—from the back seat.

Rafe's insides froze solid despite the rising heat of the day.

Olivia.

Bobby began a low, foul litany against Manny first, then against the man who yanked Olivia from the vehicle, then changed focus and swore steadily under his breath at Cervantes, who was admiring the restraints that held Olivia's wrists together.

Rafe didn't even hear him.

He watched, stupefied, as Cervantes said something to her. Olivia said something back, and was backhanded for her trouble. Rafe's vision blurred. He didn't notice that the delivery boat roared off toward the open sea, just as he'd supposed it would, at the first sign of trouble.

He did not panic or weaken, as he had back in that little bunk, telling Olivia goodbye. He rose from the sand like a giant, feeling as strong as ten men.

No drug-dealing son of a bitch was going to hurt Olivia Galpas and live to tell the tale.

"What the hell are you doing?" Bobby asked.

"I'm going to get her."

Bobby tackled Rafe again, sitting on his chest when his cousin began to struggle mightily. "Calm down, you idiot. You're going to get her killed. *Calm down.*"

Rafe flipped Bobby off him as though his partner weighed no more than a pup, and started back down the dune. Bobby hit him behind the knees this time and took him down. Rafe hung on, cursing at his partner.

"Do you have a plan? Any way to get to her without getting shot, then get her off the beach alive? Rafe!"

In the distance, Rafe saw Cervantes slap Olivia again, saw her teeter on her feet.

"I'm going to break every bone in his hand," Rafe said ominously. "And then I'm going to break every other bone in his body. That's my plan, *primo.*"

"Well, it's not much of a plan," Bobby said. "Why don't you spend a minute or two thinking up a better one."

On the beach, Olivia stood her ground before Cervantes, after having been hauled roughly out of the back of the Land Cruiser. The mirage man had strapped her hands behind her back before he'd shoved her in there, and then had set the child safety locks so that even if she wriggled free, she wouldn't be able to get out of the car. He was, apparently, not as dumb as he looked.

Ah, and there was Ernesto. The pig. She stumbled when her captor pushed her lightly between the shoulder blades and she ended up toe-to-toe with the man who had chased her across half of Baja California.

"Olivia," he said cordially.

She set her mutinous jaw and glared at him. He looked hideous. All the handsome veneer was obliterated by a lumpy jaw, two black eyes and a veiny brick in the center of his face that passed for a broken nose. *Good work, Rafael,* Olivia thought.

Cervantes raised his remaining perfect feature, one shapely eyebrow. Olivia wondered nastily if he plucked it.

"Cat got your tongue?"

"You killed that man in cold blood."

"Ah, no. I did not. I merely shot an escaping fugitive, after warning him to stop. I am the sheriff of this district, Olivia, and I had reason to believe this man was a drug runner. I saw him in the company of two known narcotics smugglers only two days ago, on the same boat." He smiled, clucked his tongue. "As I did you, Olivia. You should be more careful of the company you keep."

Olivia shook her head derisively, summoned up her best Rafael sneer. "Like you?"

Cervantes cocked his head, gave Olivia a regretful look. "Ah, but you had your chance, *querida.*"

"I would rather keep company with the scorpions. You're a monster."

He backhanded her casually. Olivia saw stars, tasted blood. "I'm a businessman," he said pleasantly enough. "You have caused me no end of embarrassment, Olivia. You ruined my party, and I had to make explanations to everyone."

Her eyes flashed. "I'd like to kick in your capped teeth, Cervantes."

He hit her again. She almost went down with that one,

but steadied herself defiantly. She wouldn't give him the satisfaction of seeing her drop to her knees.

"I don't have time to trade insults with you, Olivia." He motioned the men behind him forward with the barrel of his gun. "Put her back in the car. We'll have to take her back to the house with us."

"Why? Are you worried that if you stay any longer, Rafael will come and steal your poison out from under your nose, as he has for months now?"

Cervantes laughed, but his face flushed darkly and Olivia could see his nonchalance was forced. "So, he told you about that, did he?"

"That you are a drug smuggler and a killer? Yes." Olivia smiled slowly, narrowed her eyes. "He told me many things," she said. "He is my lover."

Cervantes's red face turned purple. He spat a filthy name at her, a name her brothers would have beaten him for speaking, but Olivia only laughed.

"All the time you were courting me with those long, boring speeches about wine and art, I was with him," she lied, taunting him. "Since the very beginning."

"You put yourself in peril, woman," Cervantes bit out.

"No, Ernesto, you have put me in peril. You and your lies and your fraudulent life." She gave him a disgusted once-over. "You pretend to be a man of family and education, but you are nothing but a common, low criminal, as your father was before you."

She was pulling the tail of the shark, she knew, but she couldn't bring herself to care. She knew perfectly well that he was going to kill her, and she was not about to go down like a mewling miss.

The shark only grew calmer, the more she yanked, however. He was looking at her, considering her now. Olivia felt a trickle of dread slip down her spine.

"Lovers?" He pulled his pistol from the holster at his hip, cocked it.

Olivia held her breath.

Cervantes smiled. "Lovers?"

His gun hand twitched. Olivia knew he wanted to kill her.

But he wasn't going to. Not just yet. Because of her brash words, she was to be used as bait to lure Rafael into a trap, she realized with a sudden sick emptiness in the pit of her stomach.

Well, she assured herself, whatever Cervantes's plan was, it wouldn't work. She almost looked forward to seeing his battered face when he realized she was no better at being bait than she was at being the ideal wife-to-be of the local sheriff.

Rafael would never compromise himself or his operation for her. She was simply a woman he'd had sex with—and, judging from his amazing skill in that particular area, one of many. But Cervantes was the man who'd killed Rafe's brother, the man he'd dedicated his entire life to bringing to justice.

Olivia knew Rafael wouldn't choose to save her at the risk of losing Cervantes. Never. Never.

Cervantes put his hand in her tangled hair, yanked her around so that her back was pressed against his chest.

"Come out, *cabrón*," he shouted in a enticing, mocking voice that sent goose bumps down Olivia's arms.

Olivia smiled bitterly, triumphantly. "It won't work."

Cervantes yanked brutally on her hair. "We'll see." He ground the barrel of the pistol to her temple and yelled again, "Are you out there, *cabrón?*"

There was a long silence, broken only by the sound of the surf. Olivia focused on that. She was glad, actually, that the sound of the ocean would be the last she ever heard.

"I'll kill her where she stands," Cervantes yelled.

Olivia closed her eyes. Odd that at the last moment of her life, it would be Rafael's face she would see—not her mother's or her father's, faces she'd known a lifetime. His face. And it was smiling. How very odd.

"I'm here."

Olivia's eyes snapped open. She stared at Rafe as he walked down the dune, his hands in the air. A sob wrenched from her throat. She hadn't wept when she thought she was going to die, but the sight of Rafael walking across the dunes made her cry out in agony.

Oh, she didn't want to die. She was terribly afraid and she didn't want to die. But more than that, she didn't want Rafe to die.

"Don't," she screamed in English.

Cervantes yanked her hair again until her chin pointed to the sky. "Shut up," he said in her ear. He watched Rafe slip on his heels down a sand hill. "Stop where you are. Lift up your shirt."

Rafe stood, yanked his shirt up around his chest. Olivia saw that his bruises had turned a sickly yellow color over the past two days.

"Turn around."

Rafe pivoted slowly, letting Cervantes see that he carried no weapon.

"Let her go, Cervantes," he said ominously. "You want me, you got me."

"Don't do it," she said, again in English. "He's going to kill me, anyway. I saw him kill Manuel. Don't, Rafael."

"He won't kill you," Rafe said, his eyes focused intently on Cervantes. "I have something he wants, Olivia. And he won't get it unless he lets you go."

"What do you have that I want, *cabrón?* Except your blood on my hands."

Rafe reached them. He looked neither right nor left. All his attention was on Cervantes. If his backup was there, wonderful. If they weren't, he and Bobby would pull this off themselves.

All that mattered in the world was saving Olivia.

"I have a badge."

Cervantes stood stock-still for a good thirty seconds. Olivia could no longer even feel his chest move at her back. Finally, he began breathing again in a great exhalation that breezed past Olivia's ear.

"You have a badge," he stated flatly.

"I'm DEA."

"An American? An American has been stealing from me?" Cervantes shook his head. "You will pay for this, *cabrón.*"

"I want to deal."

Cervantes lifted a corner of his mouth sardonically. "Deal?"

"I get the woman, you get into one of these shiny green sports utility vehicles you're so proud of and drive away. We go home, you go home."

Cervantes laughed. "That is no deal, *cabrón.* I could kill you both right now, and I get to go home, anyway."

"Not for long." The movement of men behind Cervantes caught Rafe's eye, but he had no way of knowing whose men they were, his or Cervantes's. "You kill an American agent and a prominent scientist from an important university, there'll be no place in the world you can hide. Baja will be crawling with cops from both sides of the border before you even make it past your own welcome mat."

Cervantes considered. "I give you Olivia, you leave Baja. But for how long?"

Rafe kept his voice steady, his eyes pinned on his enemy. But in his peripheral vision, he saw someone take out the pig who'd driven in with Olivia. He willed Cervantes's attention away from the silent activity going on behind him. "Forever."

"Rafael," Olivia began, but Cervantes snatched her hair in his fist and snapped her head back.

Rafe forced his hands not to close into fists and concentrated on keeping his breathing even. Just a little longer, he told himself, and he would pound this dirtbag into bloody bits. In the meantime, all he had to do was stay

calm and keep from looking into Olivia's terrified, liquid
eyes.

Olivia could feel as well as hear the diabolical little
chuckle that came from Cervantes. "But you are a thief,
Rafael. You may be DEA, but if it looks like a thief and
steals like a thief, it's a thief. Is that not how your American expression goes?"

"Something like that."

"How can I trust you will keep your word?"

Rafe moved his shoulders. "You will just have to take
a chance. You have no choice."

Cervantes smirked at him. "I have no choice?"

"Not if you want to continue this little empire you've
got going here, Ernesto."

"Would you like to know what I think, *cabrón?* I think
this woman can accidentally drown on a lovely Tuesday
afternoon such as this one, and I think you can be shot
through the head and left in the desert so the coyotes chew
your bones. And I think no one will question Ernesto Cervantes because Ernesto Cervantes has more power in Baja
than your DEA and the *federales* put together."

Rafe grinned. "I don't think so."

Cervantes shrugged elegantly and smiled. "Ah, but you
are not very smart, Rafael—"

"I'm smarter than he is," Bobby cut in, pressing his
gun to the back of Cervantes's head. "And I don't think
so, either."

Cervantes's eyes bugged a little. "Are you both crazy?
I have men surrounding this beach in every direction."

"That's funny," Bobby said. "So do we. I wonder if
some of them aren't the same men?"

Cervantes looked frantically around, keeping his gun
barrel positioned carefully at Olivia's temple.

Olivia hadn't taken her eyes off Rafael since he'd come
from his hiding place in the dunes. He wouldn't look at
her. She knew why, of course. She'd almost cost him Cervantes.

Rafe stood ready for anything. Cervantes kept his gun on Olivia, Bobby kept his on Cervantes. There was no move to be made until Cervantes decided whether he wanted to kill Olivia more than he wanted to stay alive himself.

"Let her go," Rafe said.

Cervantes's eyes were wild as he looked to the sand hills for assistance. *"Andale!"* he screamed. "Let's go!"

No one answered.

"It's just you, Cervantes. Give up the woman."

Olivia could feel Cervantes's chest heaving against her back. His hand was rock steady on the gun, but she knew from the breath rushing past her ear that he was beginning to panic.

He shouted again for help, then looked at Rafe. His eyes bored into the man.

"I'll kill her," he shrieked. He was turning in circles, looking up and down the beach. Bobby followed him around in the dizzying spin. Olivia closed her eyes and let Cervantes drag her around in the sand. She knew any move she made could be her last.

No, that wasn't true. She'd seen Rafael's eyes. He would never let Cervantes shoot her.

Never, never.

"Drop the gun, *cabrón!"* Bobby shouted. "Drop the gun, drop the gun!"

"Let her go!" Rafe yelled at the same time. "Let her go!"

Their shouts made Cervantes more frantic. He pointed the pistol first at Rafe, then back at Olivia. "I'll kill you both," he screeched pitifully, all pretense of grace and courage wiped from his face and his manner. Mucus ran from his horrible broken nose, and his bruised eyes were feral spots of black in his twisting head.

The gun swung around on Rafe once more. "I'll kill you both."

Olivia would swear for the rest of her life that she never

saw Rafe exchange a single glance with Bobby. Yet somehow, at the instant when Cervantes pointed the pistol at
Rafe, Bobby kneed Cervantes in the back and struck Olivia
hard between her shoulder blades, shoving her facefirst
into the sand. And Rafe lunged forward.

Olivia squeezed her eyes shut and began to scream to
drown out the sound of the shot that killed Rafael. She
screamed loud and long, as would befit a woman who'd
caused the death of the man she loved.

"Olivia!"

Rafe was on his knees beside her, removing her restraints with quick, anxious movements. "Olivia!"

She stopped screaming but didn't take her face out of
the warm, damp sand. Her shoulders shook with reaction
and her arms fell limply to her sides. "No," she moaned.
"No."

"Olivia," Rafe said sharply again. "Are you hurt? Did
he hurt you? Olivia!"

She turned her head and opened her eyes slowly, blinking sand away.

There had been no gunshot. No sound at all from Cervantes. He was on his belly, unarmed and unmanned, and
Bobby leaned over him, his knee at the back of Cervantes's neck and his gun at the back of his head. Olivia
looked up at Rafael with frightened and questioning eyes.

"Did he hurt *you?*"

Rafe shook his head, gently dusted sand off her cheek
with the back of his hand. He could see Cervantes's
knuckle prints on the side of her face. "No," he said, his
voice trembling ever so slightly.

She scrambled awkwardly to her knees and collapsed
onto him, trembling in shock and terror. "Oh, Rafael. Oh,
God."

Rafe stroked her back. "Shh. I know. Be quiet, *mi'ja.*
You're all right now."

"He killed Manny. He killed Manny," she mumbled

frantically, her lips numb with strain, her voice quivery with reaction.

"Okay, *princesa,* okay."

"You can arrest him, now. You can make him pay for everything, Rafael."

"Yes, I can make him pay." He dragged her to her feet. "Get in the Land Cruiser, Olivia. Right now."

"Why? It's over. Isn't it over?"

"It's over," he reassured her, though his own hands were still shaking. He'd come so close to losing her. He'd almost botched the whole thing. He'd almost let the bastard shoot her. "I want you to get in the front seat, put your head between your knees, and stay down until Bobby or I come get you."

"Why?"

"We need to make sure our *federales* have all their men, okay? Get in the truck."

"Rafael."

"What, *mi'ja?*"

"You lied to me on the boat."

"Yes, I did."

"You love me."

Rafe couldn't have denied it to save either of their lives. "Yes, Olivia. I do."

Chapter 14

Rafe put Olivia in the front of the closest Land Cruiser and shut the door. Then he walked to Bobby and Cervantes.

He suspected the Mexican *federales* were safely in control of their targets—Bobby would never have been able to sneak up on Cervantes and things would have been much noisier, and much bloodier, if they hadn't been—but Rafe didn't want to take a single additional chance with Olivia. Letting her stay in her little tent on the beach three weeks ago had been chance enough. Kissing her in Cervantes's bedroom, dragging her through the desert, leaving her on the fishing boat with Manny—all were chances he should never have taken with Olivia's life. He was almost as furious with himself as he was with Cervantes.

Bobby was wearing his fiercest frown, as Rafe approached the pair on the sand. "Did you see the marks on her face?"

Rafe nodded grimly. "Get him on his feet."

Bobby yanked Cervantes up by his collar. Rafe took a

step forward, using the momentum of his stride to put extra power behind the backhand.

Cervantes staggered and would have fallen but for Bobby holding a handful of khaki at the back of his shirt.

"You chased her," Rafe ground out. He swung again, using his left hand this time. He wanted the bruises to match the ones on Olivia. "And you hurt her."

He stepped close enough that his nose was nearly touching the sweating, bleeding snout of his lifelong enemy. He looked deeply into the eyes of the man who'd killed his brother so many years ago.

"I should kill you where you stand for those things, Cervantes." Rafe smiled thinly. "But I made a pact many years ago, to make sure you suffered before you died, you miserable, murdering son of a bitch. And I will do everything in my power as a United States drug agent to ensure that happens.

"You are going to spend the rest of your life in a Mexican prison, *amigo*. For the possession of illegal narcotics with intent to transport across international borders and for the murder of Manuel Gomez Arrieta, an officer of the La Paz City Police of Baja California, Mexico."

Rafe took Cervantes's face in his hand. He dug his thumb and index finger into the hollows of the formerly handsome man's elegantly high cheekbones. "And if you ever do find yourself on the outside again, I will have you extradited, tried and lethally injected for the murder of my brother, George Camayo." He felt the print of teeth on the pad of his thumb, and blood began to trickle from Cervantes's distorted mouth.

One of the *federales* came out of the dunes, shoving a handcuffed, khaki-clad man in front of him. Another reappeared from behind the cruiser that had brought Olivia in, with his own handcuffed prisoner. One by one, a dozen more *federales* came in from the dunes, each with one of Cervantes's men. Rafe didn't recognize most of them.

He leaned over and snagged Olivia's wrist restraints

from the sand. He handed them to Bobby, who roughly secured their captive.

Rafe turned to the first Mexican officer who made it to the beach. "I'll be escorting the prisoners to La Paz."

"Sí, señor."

"I want Dr. Galpas to be able to leave the country. Call your people and arrange a plane out of Loreto."

"Sí, señor."

Rafe looked around. "Round up anyone still on the beach, and call in your men to secure the house in Aldea Viejo and seize the computer system and any records." He gave Cervantes a withering glance. "You're one of the riffraff now, Ernesto. Just like the rest of us."

He left his enemy bleeding, and walked back to Olivia. She was seated sideways on the front seat of the cruiser. Her little feet, in those damn impractical sandals, were perched on the bottom of the door frame.

"I'm escorting Cervantes in to La Paz," he told her briskly.

"I want to see for myself that he's safely in a cell before I file a report. Bobby will take you to Loreto. There's a plane waiting for you there."

Olivia watched Rafael carefully. His face was weary, she thought, but expressionless. She could see grains of sand clinging to his thickening beard and to the shallow frown lines around his eyes. She wanted to blow them off with pursed lips, and then kiss him until that look of death eased from his hard and handsome face.

"All right."

Rafe ran a hand roughly over his chin, avoiding her eyes. Cervantes was even now being driven away in the back of one of his own Land Cruisers, but Rafe felt the worst of the terrible day was yet to come. He still had to say goodbye, again, to Olivia.

"You'll have to come back to Mexico to testify, of course. About Manny."

Olivia battled back the pain in her chest when she

thought of Manny. She knew perfectly well that Cervantes would have killed them both whether she'd beached the boat and taken off or not, but she still felt sick at the thought that she'd been in any way responsible for his death.

"I know," she said. "I will be happy to."

"But that won't be for a while. Considering everything, the Mexican government isn't going to give you any trouble about leaving for the States right away. I'll call as soon as I get back to Aldea Viejo, make sure the feds have cut through the red tape."

"Okay."

She was being awfully calm. "Are you all right?" he asked, searching her face for the first time.

Olivia smiled weakly. "Don't I look all right?" Her horrible orange dress was in shreds, her face was bruised in every place it was not sunburned, scratched or sand scoured. Her hair was one wicked tangle from the roots to the ends.

Rafe thought, as he always had, that she was the most beautiful woman in the world.

"You look fine. You might want to get Bobby to buy you something to wear home, though."

Olivia looked down. "Yes, this will all be impossible enough to explain without showing up looking like a war refugee."

He wanted to kiss her goodbye, tell her…what? Nothing. He'd said everything that morning. "All right, then," he said awkwardly.

She lifted her head, slaying him with a single look from those dark eyes. "Rafael?"

"I've got to get going," he said impatiently. *Before I lose it altogether.*

"I know you do."

He leaned forward, kissed her lightly on her poor cheek. "Goodbye, Olivia."

She twisted her fist into his shirtfront. "Don't say good-bye to me like that, Rafael."

"I have to."

"Why?" she demanded. She'd been through hell over the past several days, but nothing had hurt her as this did. She was willing to throw her considerable Galpas pride down a rat hole, if only she could know why he was doing this.

"This is not the time to discuss it."

"Rafael, you just saved my life. You walked up to a man who would have liked nothing more than to put a bullet in your brain, just to save my life. I have been chased halfway across Baja today—in these damn sandals, I might add—and held at gunpoint. You've told me you were just using me for sex, then admitted, under duress, that you lied about that."

She took a deep breath. "I am leaving for Loreto and a plane back to San Diego. I don't know where you live, I don't know your phone number, I don't know anything about your life there. I have this hollow feeling in my stomach that tells me if we don't talk about this now, I may never see you again. And if I have to go the rest of my life never seeing you again, Rafael, I think it may do me in in a way far more painful and slow than anything Ernesto Cervantes could have dreamed up."

"Don't say that."

"Then tell me why you're saying goodbye to me as if you'll never see me again."

"I won't see you again, Olivia."

Olivia felt a sting at the back of her eyes. It didn't help at all that Rafael looked even more likely to burst into tears than she did.

"Why?" she asked softly. "Are you married? Are you terminally ill? Are you a priest?"

Rafe chuckled damply. She could make him laugh even when his life was being ripped out from under him. "I'm not any of those things. Definitely not a priest."

She shook him by the shirt she still had clutched in her hand. "I'm not any of those things, either."

He met her eyes, tamped down his pride and worked up his courage. "No. You're a scientist."

Olivia knew this was important, but could not begin to fathom why. "So?"

"Where were you born, Olivia?"

"Where? In San Diego."

"I mean, where?"

"You mean, what hospital?" She shook her head. "Coronado, I think."

That figured. "I was born at home, in my parents' bed. The last of nine children."

She narrowed her eyes. "We all have big families, Rafael. It was our parents' generation."

"I didn't have my own pair of shoes, or a shirt, or even underwear that hadn't been worn by somebody else—until I was thirteen."

"Rafael."

"I slept with my brothers in a bed my mother dragged home from the dump."

"Okay."

"I worked in the avocado groves, Olivia, with the rats. I've slept in places you wouldn't let your dog lie down in. I've eaten things that crawl across the ground to fill my empty belly. My parents came to this country by swimming the canals. They're wetbacks, Olivia. Have you ever heard that expression? They don't speak English even after thirty years in the United States. Half my brothers and sisters come to dinner with dirt under their fingernails. All my friends are either cops or homeboys. I am the youngest son of illegal immigrants, and I've lived the life that entails."

Olivia shook her head in warning. "I will never forgive you if you say this, Rafael. Please be very careful."

"You and I met under intense circumstances. They taught us about this kind of relationship in the Academy."

They'd never told him how he would feel, however. Or he'd never have joined up at all. "We have nothing in common. You are a Galpas from San Diego. I'm a barefoot nobody from Lakeside."

Olivia slowly uncurled her fist from his shirt, let it drop into her lap. "And I'm too good for you," she said, aghast.

Rafe smiled sadly. "You're too good for anyone, Olivia," he said.

"I could hate you for saying this to me."

Rafe swallowed thickly. "You'd hate me even more after you realized I didn't know anything about the art world or which fork is for fish. Or how to make more than a drug agent's salary to support my wife and children."

"Which fork is for fish?" She bit down hard on her bottom lip. "God, I do hate you for this," she whispered.

"I know. But it'll be easier for both of us to end this now."

"Well, by all means make this easy on me, Rafael. After all, I am a *princesa*. Shallow and weak and greedy."

"No."

Olivia nodded her head. "Oh, yes. That's what you mean. You Neanderthal."

"I don't mean that!"

She shoved him as hard as she could away from the vehicle. "Get away from me."

"Olivia. You have to understand. It's romantic to think we can live happily ever after. But women like you live happily ever after with men who have condos in La Jolla, not with greasers from the *barrio*."

"That's what you are? A greaser from the *barrio*?" She swung her arms to indicate the beach, empty now except for Bobby and two of the Mexican federal agents, who were arranging transport of the cocaine to La Paz as evidence. "You did all this? You planned this operation for twenty years and despite every monkey wrench thrown into the works, pulled it off and saved my life at the same time?"

"That's my job," he said tightly. "I never said I didn't know how to work."

She jumped from the seat of the cruiser and stalked him. "Well, oceanography is my job. If I had to get a PhD after my name in order to do my job, and those three little initials make you feel like less than the man I know you are, them's the breaks. Too bad for me." She poked him in the chest. "Too bad for you.

"You're a snob," she continued furiously. "You will stand there and break my heart and your own rather than face a world that scares you. You stomp on scorpions without a blink, you rescue women and shoot at bad guys and do all kinds of things that make me want to throw up— but you're afraid of me. You're a coward, Rafael Camayo, and I was wrong about being in love with you."

He grabbed her wrists, pulled her up short. "Olivia," he snapped. "Stop it." If she said it out loud, if she said she loved him, he couldn't bear it.

"I was wrong," she said, her voice catching on the lie. She was suddenly grateful for the dehydration she was suffering. This was going to be much more believable if she didn't start weeping all over him. She met his dark eyes with her own. "Because I could never love a coward."

He didn't eat, he didn't sleep, he could barely work.

Bobby looked him over as they rode across the border from El Centro into Mexicali.

"You do understand you're going to kill yourself acting like such a *tonto,*" he said sharply.

Rafe grunted absently. "Look at that map again. Where the hell are we supposed to meet this informant guy?"

"*Tonto,*" Bobby said disgustedly, and yanked out a map from under the passenger seat.

"I'm not a fool," Rafe muttered.

"Really? You act like you're perpetually chewing on broken glass and you've lost ten pounds you can't afford to lose. For God's sake, it's been almost a month since you packed her off with me to Loreto, looking like she could barely keep from curling into a little ball and throwing herself out the window.''

"Will you stop saying stuff like that!''

"Will you stop acting like such a *tonto?*''

"Call me that again, *primo*,'' Rafe said through his teeth, "and you'll be sorry.''

"I'm already sorry. I'm sorry I'm even related to you.''

"What the hell is that supposed to mean?''

"It means, if we were just partners, I could go home at the end of the day and forget your pitiful face and your miserable disposition. But as it is, I have your sisters calling me every other night, asking me if I know what the hell's wrong with you. And your mother called my mother last week to see if she knew why you've been skipping Sunday dinners at the house.''

"Why would your mother know?'' Rafe muttered. He felt a little guilty. He'd known they'd all been worried about him; he'd just been too miserable—and pitiful, evidently—to care.

"Because of me. They both are under the impression I tell her everything.''

"You do tell her everything,'' Rafe said crossly. "You told her about that time we helped those McNulty sisters ditch St. Elizabeth's Catholic High School and went down to the racetrack—''

"We were sixteen!'' Bobby objected.

"Still. You tell your mother everything.''

"Listen, *vato*, let's not get off the subject.''

"Which is?''

"When you're going to go find Olivia and beg forgiveness.''

Rafe moved his shoulders. "She's better off without me.'' He'd never be able to admit that to anyone but Bobby. Bobby knew her. Knew how wonderful she was.

Bobby heaved a heavy sigh. *"Tonto.''*

"I'm going to beat the hell out of you right after we talk to this informant. Remind me later, will you?"

Bobby ignored the threat. "Better off without you, even though you guys are crazy about each other? Even though you had some sort of love-at-first-sight, fairy-tale thing going on?"

"Fairy tale? What the hell kinds of fairy tales do you read? Besides, it was four days, Bobby."

"I was there, Rafe. Four days doesn't have anything to do with it." He sucked on his teeth. "And even if it did, it's been a month since, and you're still not over her."

"I'm getting over her."

"Yeah? Well, if this is you getting over her, I'm going to have to request a new partner and find a new family."

Rafe shrugged.

Bobby waited a minute. "What did you say to her when you dumped her, again?"

"I didn't dump her," Rafe muttered tersely. "We came to a mutual agreement."

"Oh, because she was crying a lot for a woman who came to a mutual agreement."

"Stop saying that."

Bobby sniffed and looked out his window. A master of timing, he waited another minute before he pulled out the big guns. "You know," he said, looking forlornly out the passenger window at the passing *barrio,* "I hear your state of mind can really affect the baby if you're pregnant."

There was long, terrible silence from the driver's side. "What?"

"I'm not saying she is pregnant. I hope she's not, if it's true about the state-of-mind thing."

"She's not."

Bobby shrugged. "I hope not." He indicated the street where Rafe needed to turn. "Of course, you used protection."

He hadn't, mostly because it had come as a delirious

sort of shock every time she'd let him touch her. "She's not pregnant," Rafe said tightly.

Bobby shook his head. "Yeah, you're probably right." He waited a beat. "And even if she is, her family has plenty of money. They'll be able to take care of a baby."

Rafe's jaw worked furiously as he stared, unseeing, out the front windshield.

"She'll probably name it after you. That would be nice." Bobby turned his head away from Rafe, for safety. And grinned. "Rafael Galpas."

"Camayo."

"Sorry?"

Rafe swung the car into the next side street he passed. He knew he was being manipulated. He was grateful for it. He'd spent twenty-six long nights trying to think of an excuse to see her before the trial in Mexico in June.

"Camayo," he said, his jaw so tight he could barely open his mouth to speak. He headed back to the border. "Rafael Camayo."

The house was everything he'd feared it would be. Huge, elegant, with views of the Pacific and of the treetops of Balboa Park. It was also, he noted in horror, staffed with a gardener outside and a housekeeper in uniform who answered the front door.

He was nauseated with fear, ringing that bell and facing that maid. But it was better than facing a lifetime without Olivia. He knew that now without a doubt. He'd been arrogant to think he was stronger than his love for her.

"I'd like to speak to Olivia Galpas," he said politely, in English. He supposed they all spoke English at home. If he'd had a hat, it would have been in his hands. As it was, his knees were quaking. "Is she home?"

"May I tell her who is calling?" the maid asked in Spanish.

"Rafael Camayo."

"Please come in," she said, waving him across the threshold. "Would you like a glass of iced tea?"

He'd never had a glass of iced tea in his life. "No, thank you," he said.

The maid smiled at him and disappeared through a door at his left. A big door. With marble-topped tables at either side and huge bird-of-paradise fronds in giant crystal vases on top.

Good God, he'd have to get promoted to captain to be able to afford even one of those vases. He took a deep breath. Fine. He'd be a good captain. He was a natural leader and the men looked up to him. He could be a captain.

The maid came back. "I'm sorry. Dr. Galpas is indisposed."

Rafe turned white. "Is she sick?" He'd heard how many women had trouble with morning sickness. His own sisters never had a hint of it, but then Olivia was probably much more delicate. He'd forgotten, in his panic, the days she'd spent on the lam through the unforgiving Baja desert.

The maid twisted her hands nervously. "No. I mean, yes, she's a little bit sick."

"Olivia!" he shouted in the direction of the stairs.

"Señor!" the housekeeper scolded him, scandalized.

His first breach of etiquette, Rafe thought. Screaming down the mansion was probably a huge one. He didn't care. "Olivia!"

"Señor, stop yelling!"

He started up the stairs at a jog. He'd open every door in the house until he found her, and judging from the monstrous size of the place it might take him a while.

He was halfway to the first landing when he was met by three handsome young men coming down. Olivia's brothers, he surmised by their aristocratic noses, their dark eyes, their casual but expensive clothes. The gods. Rafe sized them up. He thought there was an outlet store in

Chula Vista where he could buy clothes like that on his salary. If that's what she wanted, that's what he'd wear.

"Olivia!"

The brothers pounded down the stairs. "Get out," one of them said bravely. "She doesn't want to see you."

Rafe estimated it would take him about twenty seconds to beat the crap out of all three of these whelps. But he didn't think Olivia or her parents would appreciate him whumping on the Galpas princes, so he howled instead. "Olivia!"

"Shut up," another brother ordered him.

"Your brothers are going to beat me up," he shouted. "Olivia! Help me!"

He was grinning up at her when she came racing to the top of the stairs. She took one look at Rafael's smiling face and glared down at him. "You're an *idiot!*"

Rafe laughed. "Are you pregnant, Olivia?"

Her eyes went the size of saucers. "No!" she said, mortified. Her brothers were looking from her to Rafe with undisguised curiosity. "Now get out of here."

"Do you want to be?"

"Oh, my Lord. Is that all you came here for? To see if I was—" She glanced testily at her brothers. "To see if I was *that?*"

"It was the only excuse I thought you'd buy," he admitted. "I've done a lot of thinking about what you might buy."

"Well, you were wrong. Now go away." She turned and went back down the hall.

"Olivia!" he bawled, his head thrown back.

She reappeared, looking frantic. "What?"

"Look how brave I'm being."

"What?" she asked incredulously.

He looked up at her. She was so beautiful, he thought, dazzled. She'd obviously come from work, because she had a lab coat on over a pair of slacks and a sedate silk blouse. He'd have to ask her to pay for her own work clothes after they got married, he thought, frowning slightly. He didn't think he could afford a work wardrobe like that, even on a captain's salary.

It seemed so simple now. He loved her, adored her. Could not live without her. Why he'd ever thought anything else mattered was beyond him.

"I'm not a coward, Olivia," he said, more quietly. He stared at her over the wide shoulders of her younger brothers.

Olivia put a trembling hand to her mouth. "Don't do this, Rafael. I'm just now getting over you."

"Well, I'm not even close to getting over you," he said. "And I'm very courageously facing your three stout-hearted brothers here, and your housekeeper and this freaking mansion on the hill to tell you that."

Olivia laughed in spite of herself. "I see that."

"And do you want to know why I'm not getting over you?"

"Yes."

"Because I love you, Olivia Galpas. I love you so much. I can't stop loving you even long enough to think straight."

Olivia put both her hands to her mouth. She laughed behind them.

"I love you, too," she said, sounding slightly surprised at herself.

The smile that bloomed on his sharp and handsome face started all the way down at his toes. "Still? Or are you just now getting around to it?"

"Still," she said, laughing, crying. She came down the stairs, pushed past her astonished brothers as though they weren't even there. She threw herself into his arms. "From the start, I think."

He hugged her so tightly, she thought her ribs might crack. "Because I'm brave?"

"No," she mumbled against his chest. His wide, wonderful chest. "Because you're a naturally happy person."

He threw back his head and laughed. "Olivia." He took her shoulders and leaned away from her so he could look into her face. He smiled gently, wiping the tears from her face with his thumbs. "Did I make you cry, *mi'ja?*"

"Yes," she admitted. "Did I make you cry?"

"Yes." He kissed her firmly. "I don't want to do that again, Olivia. It's unmanly."

"Okay," she said, smiling. "Do you want to get married, then?"

He felt relief hit him like a bat to the head. Now he wouldn't have to ask her, risk her looking at him in confusion and dismay, which is how he'd imagined it for twenty-six and one half days in a row. "Yes. We'll have to live in my apartment in Lemon Grove until we can afford something better."

She wanted to tell him they could afford anything they wanted, but decided that would be an argument better postponed until after their fifth or sixth wedding anniversary.

"All right," she conceded. "And we'll have a big Mexican wedding which my father will pay for, and you won't fight with me over the cost of my dress."

He swallowed nervously. "I won't even *ask* you the cost of your dress."

She kissed him, deliriously in love. "How long do you want to wait until we start a family?"

Rafe glanced up at her brothers. "About five minutes," he whispered in her ear.

She hugged him hard, giggling foolishly. "You make me laugh, Rafael Camayo."

He closed his eyes, the better to let the feeling of her seep into his lonely body. "You make me laugh, too, *princesa.*" He kissed the top of her shiny hair. "And that's much harder to do."

* * * * *

Award Winner

MAGGIE SHAYNE

continues her exciting series

★★★★★★★★★★★★★★★★★★★★★★★★★★
THE TE✗AS BRAND
★★★★★★★★★★★★★★★★★★★★★★★★★★

with

THE HOMECOMING

On sale June 2001

After witnessing a brutal crime, Jasmine Jones left
town with nothing but her seven-year-old son and
the building blocks of a whole new identity. She
hadn't meant to deceive the close-knit Texas Brands,
claiming to be their long-lost relative, Jenny Lee.
But it was her only chance at survival. Jasmine's
secret was safe until Luke Brand—a man it was all
too easy to open up to—started getting *very* close.

Available at your favorite retail outlet.

Silhouette®

Where love comes alive™

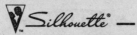

Look in the back pages of
all June Silhouette series books to find an
exciting new contest with fabulous prizes!
Available exclusively through Silhouette.

Don't miss it!

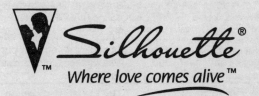

Where love comes alive™

*P.S. Watch for details on how you can meet
your favorite Silhouette author.*

Meet 50 loving dads in

babies
& BACHELORS USA

Take 4 FREE BOOKS,
Plus get a FREE GIFT!

Babies & Bachelors USA is a heartwarming new collection of reissued novels featuring 50 sexy heroes from every state who experience the ups and downs of fatherhood and find time for love all the same. All of the books, hand-picked by our editors, are outstanding romances by some of the world's bestselling authors, including Stella Bagwell, Kristine Rolofson, Judith Arnold and Marie Ferrarella!

Don't delay, order today! Call customer service at
1-800-873-8635.
Or
Clip this page and mail to The Reader Service:

In U.S.A.
P.O. Box 9049
Buffalo, NY
14269-9049

In CANADA
P.O. Box 616
Fort Erie, Ontario
L2A 5X3

YES! Please send me four FREE BOOKS and FREE GIFT along with the next four novels on a 14-day free home preview. If I like the books and decide to keep them, I'll pay just $15.96* U.S. or $18.00* CAN., and there's no charge for shipping and handling. Otherwise, I'll keep the 4 FREE BOOKS and FREE GIFT and return the rest. If I decide to continue, I'll receive six books each month—two of which are always free—until I've received the entire collection. In other words, if I collect all 50 volumes, I will have paid for 32 and received 18 absolutely free!

267 HCK 4537
467 HCK 4538

Name	(Please Print)		
Address			Apt. #
City		State/Prov.	Zip/Postal Code

* Terms and prices subject to change without notice.
  Sales Tax applicable in N.Y. Canadian residents will be charged applicable provincial taxes
  and GST. All orders are subject to approval.

DIRBAB02

© 2000 Harlequin Enterprises Limited

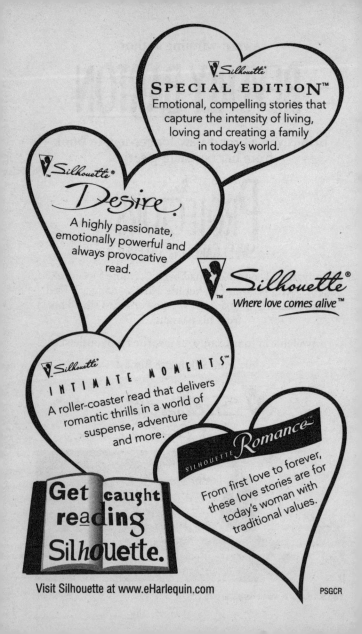